# The
# BIRTHPARENTS

## Frank Santo

# The
# BIRTHPARENTS

## Frank Santo

**Tortoise Books**
Chicago

*For Andrea*

How can a man who is warm understand a man who is cold?
— Solzhenitsyn

# 1.

**I am walking around an apple orchard** on a crisp fall morning in the far north of New Hampshire. The grass beneath my boots is dried and golden-green, the coffee in my cup is steaming, and red and orange trees rise up like little fires on the hillsides all around. My two-and-a-half-year-old daughter Liliana scampers up and down the neat rows of Honeycrisps and Galas. "Dada, Dada, I found another one!" she calls each time she finds an apple low enough on the branch for her to pick. And as she runs back toward me holding up her latest find, snot dripping down her reddened face, her messy black hair frizzing out beneath her too-tight pink hoodie, I think to myself: this, my friend, is heaven.

"Eat it!" my daughter yells when she arrives knee-side.

"I'm not sure I'm in the mood for apples right now, honey." I realize this is an odd stance to take, given that I'm the one who insisted on driving two hours for the sole purpose of picking apples. But lately I've been worried she's been getting bossy.

"Daddy, you eat it, okaaaay?"

"What do you say when you want someone to do something?"

"Please!" She's more emphatic than polite. "Eat it now. Please! Okaay?"

Still, my point's been made. She gives me her playful, gap-toothed grin while I take the apple from her little hand. It's a McIntosh, red fading into green. The skin snaps as I bite into it. But as the juice seeps from my teeth onto my tongue, something catches in my throat. My heart dents up my ribcage. I'm tasting an apple I ate ten years ago, on an apple orchard much like this one, except five hundred miles south, in some sleepy town in Westchester, New York, just a few miles up the highway from the Bronx. The sun ducks behind a veil of clouds. It's not dark yet, but the moon's already risen, an ashy, glowing sliver. Rain comes down in fits and starts—a light rain, gentle, somewhere between a mist and sprinkle. I'm twenty-six years old, and I'm supervising a family visit between Margarita Sand and her two children, Harley and Jojo. It's one of the last times I will ever see them all together—though, of course, we don't know that yet.

"So what—we just pick 'em? That's it?" Margarita asks me boredly, tapping at an apple as we all walk down the row, her gold, sparkly fingernails poking out beneath her gigantic sweatshirt—her husband's maybe, or another boyfriend's.

"Well, yeah." I don't know what she was expecting. She looks just like I remember her—the black stars tattooed at her temple, her sallow olive complexion and hazel eyes too large for their sockets, that frazzled, twitchy energy powering her every movement, like at any moment she might break into a sprint. The only thing I can't see is the color of her hair: is it still red, or are we in Rita's short-lived blue period?

Harley, her eleven year old—sweet, moody, doomed Harley—her wrists still wrapped because, as her therapist at

Mount Pleasant had wryly told me, "she's decided to try cutting"—picks a rotten apple off of the ground and hucks it sidearm up the hillside, eliciting concerned stares from a nearby family who already suspects, due to my presence, that something about this situation is awry. With her other arm she pushes Jojo, her baby brother, in the stroller I'd borrowed from his foster mother. He lies flat on his back, fast asleep, mouth agape, one hand over his eyes.

I pull an apple from a hanging branch and take a bite. "Oh, wow!" I say, really overselling it because I'm beginning to get self-conscious about the apparent lameness of the trip I've planned. "Rita, you gotta try this. They're so much fresher than at the store."

"Oh I will, for sure!" she says, eyes wide with exaggerated earnestness to make it clear her interest in this activity is entirely sarcastic.

Harley, to my surprise, turns and laughs, which is the reaction her Mom was going for. "Yo, Lee," she says. "Apple picking *sucks.*"

My daughter runs back towards me. She trips and falls and gets back up, brushing dirt and dead grass off her jacket with her hands. I shake my mind free of the Sands. All that was so long ago.

"Another apple for me, honey?" I say.

"No!" Lily happily places a bruised Granny Smith into my hand. "Don't eat this one, okay?"

"Why not?"

For a moment, my daughter is flummoxed by my impudence. A darkness comes into her features. She really has to learn some patience. Her mother lets her get away with murder.

"Don't eat it!" she warns.

"What if I want to though?" I say, teasing.

"Noooo! This apple is for Arnold!"

My smile dashes off.

"Who is Arnold?"

My daughter senses an energy within me shifting. For a moment, she seems to weigh the consequences of elaborating. Then, instead, she says:

"That apple is for Arnold. Don't *eat* it! Please! Okay?"

Satisfied she's made her orders clear, she marches back off down the row, kicking fallen apples with her dirty light-up sneakers. I tell myself to calm down. Arnold could be anybody—a stuffed animal, a new boy at daycare, an imaginary friend. My ex wouldn't bring new men around my daughter—not without talking to me first. We agreed on that, at least. But, then again, even if she did—well, what can I do? Scream? Yell? Show up with my stepdad's antique hunting rifle and try and scare the guy away? In the long run, it won't make a difference, will it? It's all out of my control. I turn down the row and see Liliana lifting her face up to the sunlight and spinning around in circles. God, it's such a helpless feeling. To love your kid this much.

I wonder if Rita knows that feeling. I think she does. But that was always our whole problem, wasn't it? I never knew how she felt.

The rain is picking up now, falling in reams across the gently shaking trees. All three of the Sands are huddled beneath a stepladder, making fun of me for getting wet, even though their makeshift cover isn't really working either. I slip across a patch of mud but catch my footing before I fall. My jacket doesn't have a hood, so I have to pull it up and hunch. Apple-picking, on the whole, has been a disaster. But as the rain breaks for a moment and we all jog toward the rusted metal gate that marks the exit of the orchard, I feel good about the day. It's been nice to get out of the Bronx. Plus, Margarita and Harley's shared annoyance with me has become a point of common ground, which the two of them could always use some more of. "Did you see? This dude ate like six fucking apples!" Harley says when we get back to the rental car. "Hey Lee," Rita jumps in; her light eyes get lighter when she knows she's being funny: "I know they don't pay caseworkers so good, but if you're really going hungry, just ask me for some money!" I laugh along with them, partly because I can never think of comebacks quickly. But also because in my heart of hearts—despite all that's happened between us, despite the pain I represent to them, I want to feel like we're all friends. That I'm part of this too. That we share the same cause. *"Ha ha,"* I say. "Very funny, guys. *Ha* ha. *Ha* ha."

Arnold's apple is a core now. I throw it off into the distance in case Lily calls me back in for questioning. No body: no crime. I turn down the row of Fujis and realize I've lost sight of my daughter. Did she run off? Oh god, oh no. I am the worst father in America. I can't be trusted with my child. Men like me should have to wear a special badge or something, I'm so fucking stupid. Oh, wait, is that…?

There she is, hiding underneath the low branches of an apple tree, flat on her stomach, grinning at me through the leaves. She gets more mischievous when she's tired. Seeing that she's caught, she shrieks with laughter.

"Come on, honey," I say. "I told your mom I'd have you home by four." On the path that runs alongside the orchard, there's a pickup truck ricketing slowly back and forth, giving children hayrides. But I think it's time to go.

"Nooooo," she says, voice verging, abruptly, toward despair: "I don't want to go there."

This sudden change in tone raises an alarm. The chill I feel now is the same one I'd get in foster homes when I'd have to ask a kid about some recent incident, then see the light in their eyes duck behind their pupil, hear that terror shaking in their breath. I would try to keep my expression steady, my eyes full of empathy and understanding, while my heart beat so hard that I could taste it.

"Because of Arnold?" I say.

"Okay."

I crouch down to her level.

"You don't want to go home because of Arnold?"

"Arnold wants to eat my apple, Daddy. Okay?"

"Honey, you have to tell me. Does Mommy have a new friend? Is his name Arnold? Was Arnold mean to you?"

My daughter looks up at me—those big brown eyes, full of fear and need, welling with emotions she can't understand. I pull her toward me and hold her. She begins to cry.

"I don't want to go home, Dada. I want to stay with you."

That settles it. What more do I need to hear?

I lift her onto my hip. She rests her forehead on my shoulder and wipes her nose on my neck as we walk back to the car. I feel just like I used to: desperate. Blind. Standing at the mouth of something I can't see into—shouting pointlessly into the coming dark. There's nothing in the world I wouldn't do for her. It's just that ever since my wife handed me the papers—I don't know what to do.

When we get back to the rental car, the Sands are already buckled in. Margarita is in the passenger seat, texting with her husband or a boyfriend even though she'd sworn her phone was out of minutes. Harley's asleep in the back, headphones on, blasting French Montana. Jojo is on his sister's lap, giving me a stern glare in the rearview.

Liliana's banging her head against the window, screaming. "Daddy, daddy! No, Daddy! Please? I don't want to go home. Please! Okay?"

I know what I have to do. If only I could be the type of man to do it. The type of man I would have been, if only I had known.

Outside, the sky strobes: morning to night to night to morning. Rain and sunlight alternate. My brain is a rotten apple. Insides brown. Wriggling worms. Bitter, brown juices dripping down black lips, pierced by blackened yellow teeth. Margarita sits beside me in the passenger seat, sneakers off, purple socks up on the dashboard. Her pink-glossed lips curled into a wry but absent smile—she could be thinking anything. Her hazel eyes are rimmed red with sleeplessness. The stars tattooed on her temples. The foxlike angles of her cheekbones. What can we do, Rita? If you only you had told me, I could have been of some use. But even now, Rita gives no answer. I want to grab her by the shoulders. I want to slam my head in the car door. I want to drive so far that the future will never find us. So far that our fate just never comes. But Rita just pulls the hood up of her sweatshirt over her hair of red or blue, crosses one arm over the other. Forget it, Lee, she says, and disappears. I close my eyes, and when I open them, there's just a paper sack of apples on the passenger seat. My heartbeat slows. The sun is shining. In the parking space beside us, a father in a purple fleece opens up the hatchback of his Subaru and loads two pumpkins into the trunk. In the back, Liliana kicks the car seat with her dirty light-up sneakers. I put the keys in the ignition. All that was so long ago. I have to get her to her mom's by four.

# 2.

**The first time I met Margarita,** she seemed like any other birthparent. I came down into the lobby of the Children's Future foster care agency, on 172nd Street in the Bronx, to find her shouting at the receptionist through the bulletproof glass, bony shoulder blades jutting out beneath a purple tank top. Her hair was candy red and darkened at the roots, tied back in two thick, stiff braids. Upstairs, when I'd reviewed the casefile, I'd discovered something interesting: the two of us were the exact same age. But given the circumstances of our first meeting, I figured she might be somewhat less than charmed by the coincidence.

"Lee Todd," I said. After 3 PM, the lobby was pure chaos: skinny teenagers pacing the floor with headphones in their ears and earrings through their eyebrows, wearing black jeans and camo hoodies, rapping aloud in little bursts; ten or fifteen birthparents hanging out by the windows, glaring at their feet and muttering about injustice. I raised my voice a little as I held out my hand. "It's nice to meet you, Ms. Sand."

Margarita left me hanging on the handshake. The black stars tattooed from her temple to her cheekbone looked like a broken party mask. Her hazel eyes seemed to play along with a joke I wasn't making, as though she'd heard some gossip about me—like my disaster with LaDawn after the Christmas party—that rendered my authority absurd.

"You the one who's been leaving all those messages on my phone?" she said over the din.

Something crashed against my knee. I looked down to see a toddler staring back up at me, eyes full of accusation.

"Excuse me," I told Margarita, then lifted him onto my hip. "Whose is this?" I asked the lineup of foster mothers sitting along the edges of the lobby. Caseworkers passed through like ghosts at a party. "Rodriguez?" one said. "Rodriguez? Is there a Rodriguez here to see me? Rod-riiii-guuez..." My voice got lost on its way across the room.

A foster mother—Conley, I think—hobbled through the fray. She took the crying toddler from my arms and kissed the tears off his cheeks. I turned back toward Margarita and the receptionist, a commanding woman named Shantal.

"Yoo-hoo, Pea-Pod," said Shantal, utilizing a workplace nickname which I'd told myself was loving. "This little girl's been getting fresh. Tell her if she can't give me an I.D and sign the sign-in book, she doesn't get to see her kids today."

Margarita laughed. At once playful and aggressive—her accent thick as asphalt. She said the N-word constantly, as though being part Puerto Rican gave her license to. Well, maybe it did. What do I know?

"You're breaking my heart, Shanti," she said. "You really don't remember me?"

Shantal squinted at the game of solitaire on her computer. In most interactions, her main concern was to make clear to the other person that she didn't think that they were special. Margarita looked a little hurt.

"You told me once that when I grow up I should be an actress, 'cuz I got so dramatic."

Shantal clicked her mouse. Where should she put the six of clubs?

"We got a lotta kids that come through here," she said without looking up.

"You really don't remember? Must have been like fifteen years ago. You and me both was half our size." Margarita opened her eyes wide and very slightly turned her head askance, as though astonished by her own wit.

Shantal finally looked up, with a glower. A child of divorce, I've always prided myself on my ability to defuse a coming conflict; I jumped in to interject.

"If you could just sign the book real quick, we can go upstairs and get you situated. Harley and Jojo will be here to visit in an hour or so. So we'll have some time to get to know each other."

Margarita raised an eyebrow. There were three slashes through it at even intervals.

"Excuse you?" she said, with a crooked, Popeye smile. Suddenly, I felt self-conscious. This was a special talent she had: to be the one with tattoos on her temple and hair the color of a clown's wig, and still be able to make me feel like *I* was being weird. I supposed though, that I was a little off my game today, given the rock fight going on behind my forehead. I'd been drinking heavily for months, ever since I'd found those texts on my fiancée's phone.

"Sign the book or leave my lobby, Ms.," said Shantal. And then to me: "Get it together, Pea-Pod. Damn."

I let out a long, dramatic sigh that sounded like *Hhhhhhffffff*. This was a habit I'd picked up over my years as a caseworker. Before Children's Future, I don't know if I had ever once sighed. I was not naturally a sigher. Now, I sounded like a preteen girl whose parents had taken her iPad at the dinner table.

"What if we could skip the sign-in this time, Shantal?" I said. "Maybe we could do it after the visit?"

"Oh sure, Lee. Cause you're the only caseworker in this place. You're the special little white boy we let break all the rules."

Margarita was delighted by our conflict. She pressed her palms together.

"How about this, Todd? You tell this heifer I'm not signing her little book unless she ask me fucking nicely. I saw her fat ass once a week for half my childhood. It's not my fault she don't remember."

I sighed so hard I started coughing.

"What if I signed the book on her behalf?" I asked Shantal.

"Come on now, Lee. That's not how it..."

"And buy you lunch the rest of the week?"

Something in the way my voice had cracked at last drew Shantal's sympathy. Her frown grew more maternal. "You're lucky you're cute Pea-Pod," she said. Beneath that East Tremont attitude, she always was a softie. To this day, she still 'likes' every photo of my daughter that I post on Facebook.

"Welcome back to Children's Future, little 'Rita Sand," she added, as I signed Margarita's name. "Didn't recognize you beneath...all that."

I led my new client across the lobby towards the elevator, ducking to avoid a whizzing Jenga block aimed at my head by some other unwatched child. The doors closed with a ping. Alone now, together, we both stared at the buttons on the panel, lighting up with every floor. Margarita shifted weight between her sneakers. I sighed like my favorite song was playing, and not one boy had asked me to dance.

"Sorry about that back there," she said finally, twisting the end of a braid between her fingers. "I get a little crazy when I'm nervous."

I told her she had nothing to be nervous about. And that's how it all started: with a lie.

◆

From the day I took her children, I gave Margarita fifteen months to prove to me that she should have them back. Fifteen months to prove that she was qualified to parent. Fifteen months to change her life. Of course, when I say 'I'—it's not like this was my idea. This was my job as a caseworker, to tell her how the System worked. While the two of us reclined in opposing beanbag chairs in Visiting Room 9, I talked about the ins and outs of Children's Future. The walls of the room were cotton pink and baby blue, the carpet emblazoned with the cherubic face of Thomas the Tank Engine and littered with the limbs and torsos of GI Joes and Barbie dolls. Margarita flipped idly through a dogeared copy of *Oh! The Places You'll Go* which she'd taken from a mostly empty bookcase in the corner. The whole room smelled of soup. If, at the end of that fifteen months, I explained, she had not completed a long host of mandatory 'recommended' services, it would be my job to testify in Bronx Family Court, on behalf of Children's Future, that she was not fit to mother. The Court would terminate her parental rights, and legally 'free' the children. "But I'm sure it won't come to that," I muttered, avoiding eye contact as I said it, because, of course, it almost always did.

I should have put more effort into this conversation. I should have empathized. I should have cared. If I were still a decent caseworker, I would have told Margarita that I'd be there with her every step of the way—that, while it was my job to testify, it was also my job to guide her through the System. To encourage her. To advocate on her behalf, should she present as the best option for the children. And in my first few years at Children's Future that's what I would have told her. When I was twenty-two, I'd been bursting with empathy for everyone, regardless of their circumstance. But by the time that I met Rita, I had been a caseworker for years already, which is to say I'd burned out long ago. My nerves were cooked. My soul was toast. I'd developed an eye twitch that made me look as though I had a human heart hidden somewhere in the floorboards beneath my beanbag chair. Intellectually I still believed that every birthparent in the Bronx deserved compassion and sensitivity, no matter why they'd lost their children. But after years in the System, I couldn't feel a thing.

"Would you mind telling me why you think that all this happened?" I asked Margarita, after my spiel about the fifteen months. This was the question that began every case. Fifteen months from now, I'd have to prove to the judge that she showed no insight into the behaviors that had led her children into care. I touched my pen to my notepad, prepared to add another lie to my collection.

Margarita placed her purse beside a dried milk stain on the floor and sat with her legs crossed. She made little circles with her sneaker.

"I guess I just don't love them enough," she said.

I swallowed a burp, tasting last night's gin. I hadn't come prepared for honesty.

"Well, I'm sure you love them."

Margarita exchanged a dark glance with her fingernails.

"I was sure too, Todd. I mean, I gave them what I had. But it's like it cost a dollar, and all I had was fifty cents."

I frowned into my notebook. This wasn't how this conversation was supposed to go. Birthparents were supposed to tell me how, contrary to all the evidence in my casefile, they were actually great parents. That they had been unfairly targeted by the Administration of Children's Services, that their CPS worker had held a grudge since high school, that the judge looked like a pedophile. They were supposed to give the same old lines, to which I'd give my own: of course, of course, I understand, I'd say—I see it all the time. Of course you love Jahanya, Ms. Nixon, that's why you tried to sell her to a trucker in the parking lot of Howard Johnson's. Or, yes, surely you want nothing less than the best for Ivan, Mr. Santiago, that's why you had to strip him naked and rub ghost peppers on his penis. You love little Daniel to the moon, Ms. Halloran, why else would you have gone to North Carolina with your boyfriend and left your toddler with a box of Gushers?

It's not that they were lying when they told me they loved their children. We just didn't agree. So, in the bleary logic of my hangover, when Margarita told me how she felt, or didn't feel, about Harley and Jojo, it didn't make me think she was a monster. Instead I thought: at least she and I agree what love is not. We can distinguish it from whatever she's been doing. Maybe, with a little push, I could get her to surrender, and these kids would be adopted quickly. That's the way the System thinks.

"One more thing I have to add," I said, "and I only say this to let you know—not out of some assumption…"

Margarita crossed her arms. You'd think I'd have more compunctions about what I was about to say. And I had, the first few hundred times I'd said it.

"If you happen to have a baby while your children remain in care…well, I'm sorry, but I'll have to take that too."

◆

As badly as this conversation went—as many times as Margarita's eyes rolled like hazel planets through a galaxy of black stars and blue mascara, I knew the worst part was still coming. Because usually, most birthparents already knew all of the information that I'd given to this point. Either they'd grown up in foster care themselves, or were friends with other birthparents, or they themselves had already lost a couple children, so they knew about the fifteen months. They knew that Children's Future existed not to help reunify their families, but really, to turn their babies into orphans. None of that was personal. No, it wasn't until their children came to the agency for that first supervised visit that they felt the white-hot shame of their position, the singe of a stranger's judgment, of being found inadequate as a parent, as a human being—hell, as an organism—by this sleepy-eyed twenty-something white idiot in wrinkled khakis. The first time they went to hug their children and felt my watery gaze upon them: that's when they understood that 'Lee Todd' was something I just called myself. To them, my name was Death.

But Margarita didn't seem to take this whole thing all that seriously. Or at least she wouldn't give me that much credit. When I told her that, from this point forward, I'd be supervising all of her interactions with her children, she shared a glance with her fingernails and paused to take this information in. After a moment, she sat up straight in the beanbag chair. She looked Death in the face and shrugged.

"So what's your deal, Todd? How'd you end up in the Bronx? You here to save the world? Or do you just *like* taking little babies from their mothers?"

My eyelid twitched like a smashed insect. I knew that whatever motivation a middle-class white kid from New Hampshire might claim for working child welfare in the Bronx was bound to come off patronizing to someone actually from there. Still, I probably should have given her *some* kind of recognizably human answer. *I wanted to be helpful,* I could have said. *I am interested in people and their problems. Actually, I first moved to New York to be a musician but took this job as a backup plan in case, at some point in the future, I might consider law school.* As I avoided Margarita's prying gaze, I considered briefly, giving her some combination of these answers, which had all once contained trace elements of truth. But the problem was, after all these years at Children's Future, any earnest answer to her question would have been equally nonsensical. Like asking a dead body why it feels the need to rot.

"Let's not worry about why *I'm* here," I said.

This answer achieved the effect that I was hoping for. I was spared from further questioning.

Margarita's kids arrived a little while later. She jumped up from the beanbag chair when she saw them. Jojo—short for Ty junior, after the father in the casefile—was a stern-faced toddler with braids ending in little beads and severe speech delays, a common symptom of neglect. When he saw his mother, he shrieked in glee and spat up on his little polo; he took in rapid breaths as though Margarita were air and he'd just been pulled up from the ocean. He grabbed her hair in his fists. He tried to bite her shoulder. Harley hovered by the doorway. She was eleven and looked just like her mother, but with darker eyes, a slightly crooked chin, and a bull-ring piercing through her septum. "Hey, Ma," she said, in a husky whisper, her eyes sweeping the floor.

Margarita hugged them, and if she really didn't love them, maybe Shantal should have been a talent scout instead of a receptionist. Margarita's portrayal of a lovesick mother even almost moved me, and I was barely half alive. She pulled them both on top of her, held them close and breathed them in, felt the warmth of their heads against her face. She couldn't get them close enough. They were her babies, she said over and over, no matter what nobody tells you, laughing through her tears.

After a time, Harley pulled herself away from the embrace, drying her eyes, fixing her hair. She shot me a look of embarrassment I pretended not to notice and moved toward the couch opposite her mother. For my part, I had moved from the couch and wedged myself into the tiny chair at the miniature Fisher Price table to peruse the internet for sports news on my phone.

Margarita reached into the pocket of her jeans and pulled out a piece of notebook paper, folded into a square. "Listen, baby," she said. "You're mad as hell and I deserve it. But I wrote this for you—maybe you could read it later, when you get back to..."

Someone sighed loudly enough to interrupt. Was that me? Jesus.

"I'm sorry, Ms. Sand." I said. "But I'll have to take a look at that."

Margarita blinked in my direction. She had forgotten I was here.

"Excuse you?"

When I'd first started, I never would have enforced these kinds of rules. However, a few months prior to this, Mr. Santiago had written a letter to his son Ivan about how the little guy was an ungrateful little faggot and it made Daddy's sickness worse every time his son showed up to visits not wearing the new sneakers Daddy bought him. Next thing I knew, the little guy had set fire to his foster mother's bedspread, and I suddenly didn't feel like such a champion of compassion.

"It's against the rules," I said.

Margarita put the letter back into her pocket. "Oh, it's against the rules?"

I nodded.

"Did you hear that Harley?" she said. "Todd here says it's against the rules."

The key to riding out these tense moments is to act like you don't notice them. I smiled emptily, like we had all come together and decided, without a shred of sarcasm or disharmony: it was against the rules.

"You know what, fuck it," said Margarita. "It just says that I'm sorry that I let you down, baby. But I'm not giving up, so don't give up on me, alright? Cuz I used to visit my Mom in this same dirty little room. So if anyone knows how you're feeling, its me."

Harley leaned against the arm of the opposite couch with her feet pulled up beneath her knees on the cushion, angling herself as far away from her mother as the small room would allow. For a long time, no one said anything. The sounds of the agency filtered through the silence: the clacking of high heels in the hallway, caseworkers chasing after fleeing children, the crackling of a walkie-talkie on the belt of a police officer who'd come to arrest one of the teenagers hiding in the trauma unit.

"Cool," said Harley, and took out her phone.

◆

The children had been in foster care for a week or so already by then.

The night it all went down, Anita Flores had called me around midnight with directions to pick up them up from the ICU at St. Bonaventure and bring them to their placement. I'd been home drinking with my new roommates, three grad students I'd found on Craiglist, and was a little high to boot, so it wasn't until after 1 AM that I got an Uber to take me from Morningside Heights up to the Bronx. As we approached the foster home, a pack of teenagers smoking cigarettes on the stairs kicked the door open. "Hey little mama," one said to Harley, in a deep voice for effect, and they fell into boyish titters. She carried Jojo on her shoulder. I hauled the car seat and their luggage up the stairs.

Their foster mother—Graciela Gigante, or Titi, as she preferred—was an elderly Dominican with warm eyes and careworn skin and absolutely outrageous eyebrows. With their heightened angles and feathered edges, she looked like she had an eagle taking off from between her eyes, spreading out its wings. A few months back, when I'd first met her, my first thought was: she's insane. Only an insane person would think that that's how eyebrows are supposed to look. But as it turned out, eyebrows are an unreliable indicator of someone's character. Prior to Harley and Jojo, she'd been the foster mother for another of my cases—Cortez Wallace—before we'd had to ship him up to Mount Pleasant for selling all her jewelry. "You tell him that he can keep the money if he promises to visit me on Christmas," she'd told me when I came back for his things, her laugh full of rasp and sorrow.

Unlike many foster homes, Titi's apartment was not a shrine to Jesus, though she had some Mary figurines on top of the refrigerator. Instead, she decorated her pre-war three-bedroom mostly with different types of bird-themed affects. A lamp in the shape and color of two smooching parakeets glowed neon pink in the entryway. Plush owls and toucans reclined on the cushion of a recliner in the TV room. High-resolution photos of soaring ospreys and diving red-tailed hawks that she'd taken herself on a trip to Yellowstone with her since-deceased husband, plus some artistic shots of the crows that stalk Crotona Park, were framed in gold about the place. The only thing her aviary was missing was an actual, living bird. Later she would tell me that she couldn't bear to keep one caged.

When we came in that night, the old woman greeted us wearing a Tweety Bird apron and oven mitts with scorch marks on the thumbs. A strawberry shortcake was waiting in the oven, though Harley said she wasn't hungry. Jojo was already asleep on his sister's shoulder, unaware that his life had changed forever.

Titi offered me some coffee before I left: "Because you look a little...tired, Bubba." I said I'd take some whiskey if she had it, which was the kind of off-key joke I'd only make if I'd been drinking. Kindly as she was, I don't think I ever saw old Titi laugh.

"She seems alright," Harley told me a few nights later, as we sat in her bedroom with the door open. It was the same narrow, cluttered bedroom in which Cortez Wallace used to read me his latest lyrics from his notebook. He'd had a collage of Penthouse cutouts taped to the wall beside the bed. I'd often found it difficult to lecture him on the importance of studying for math class while his eyes kept drifting towards a poster of a woman wearing only sunglasses and sitting spread-eagle, with one hand across her knee, the other beckoning him towards her with a finger. Now, the walls were empty. Titi and Jojo were in the kitchen tending to a flan. Pots clanged. Soft *bachata* music and Jojo's delighted shrieking filtered through the opened door. Harley sucked her teeth. "I mean, like, she's a nice lady. It's just the..."

"Eyebrows?" I said, looking up from my checklist.

"Huh?"

"Nothing. Forget that."

Harley returned her attention to a bowl of instant mac and cheese on her lap. There was another bowl on the bedstand and three more on the desk.

"It's just that Titi's, like, a hundred. She knows a lot about like...animals, I guess. But I don't have anyone to talk to about, like...you know...

"You can always talk to me," I said, without looking up from my notebook.

"About girl stuff, Mr. Lee?"

At this point, I considered myself a pro at handling brutal conversations. I had interviewed at least fifteen recently molested children; I'd informed upwards of fifty parents to their faces that they would never see their kids again; I had brought a toddler to visit his triple-murderer of a birthfather awaiting trial at the Federal MCC complex downtown and had him look me dead in the eye and ask: What's New Hampshire like this time of year? Don't your Mom get cold up there, all alone?

So now, in this narrow, cluttered bedroom, facing this scared and lonely little girl, I prepared myself for battle. The trick is to recede completely within yourself. It's not you behind your eyes.

"The thing about your body," I said. "Is—"

Harley looked like she might melt into her bowl of macaroni if I said another word. I interrupted myself with a cough into my hand. Taking mercy on the two of us, I let the thought die right there.

"I just wish I could talk to her still," she said. "She'd make it, like, funny. Like a joke between us we could laugh at."

Many of my colleagues, in this situation, would have hugged the little girl. They would have provided the affection she was craving. But at this point, I didn't know how much longer I'd be around for. Maybe I'd move home to New Hampshire. Or Florida. Or shatter into a million pieces and be eaten by a pack of pigeons. Who knew? It felt shortsighted, even selfish, to form a bond with kids in need. Wouldn't that just make me another adult to disappoint her? And anyway, most of my colleagues had the advantage of being female. Who wants to get hugged by a man?

"Do you want me to get Titi for you?" I said, instead, as compassionately as one can pass the buck.

Harley curled on the bed and pulled her knees into her chest. Her eyes traced the ghosts of Cortez's lovers on the wall.

"No, Mr. Lee," she said. "No thanks."

◆

In Visiting Room 9, Harley showed none of this vulnerability. As her mother scoured her face for some sign that her apology had been accepted, Harley swiped Instagram on her phone. Titi had gotten her the latest iPhone as a welcome gift.

Margarita dried her tears with her forearm. The hazel in her eyes took on an emerald tint against her reddened eyelids. She drummed her hands on her thighs. Then she turned to baby Jojo. He'd been fiddling with her golden hoops.

"How you doing, little man? You hate your mother too?"

Jojo had an old man's soul behind his eyes. At two years old, he'd seen enough already. He looked at his mother like she was some new dance trend he disapproved of.

"Oh!" she said. "I almost forgot! Look what I brought you, baby." She reached into her purse and retrieved a plastic sippy cup, adorned with half-peeled stickers of cartoon giraffes and elephants, and filled to the brim with bright red juice. "Your favorite cuppy-cup." Then she turned to me: "That OK with you, boss man?"

My shoulders slumped. I imagined myself pirouetting out the window. Or swallowing my phone.

"There's no food or drink allowed in family visits," I told her with a sigh.

My position was untenable. Margarita had only wanted to perform that most basic of maternal functions: to nurture, to feed, to remind her children she could still provide them sustenance and comfort, and here I was, sticking up for rules instead of reason. But I swear to God, there was good reason for this policy as well. About nine months previous, one of my clients, Ms. Cheeks, had seasoned some tater tots with ipecac and served them to her three children at a family visit in an attempt to make them sick enough so she could blame their illness on the foster mother. My boss, Anita Flores, had made me scrub the vomit up myself.

Margarita threw up her hands. "What, Todd? Really?" she said. "You afraid he's gonna make a mess?"

Her eyes rolled around the filthy room, across the splotches of milk caked into the carpet, the smattering of blackish mold in the shape of two eyes and a mouth looking down from the ceiling. The red soup stains on the wall behind my head dripped down like a stab wound.

"Those are the rules, Ms. Sand," I said.

Margarita glared holy murder. She slapped the sippy-cup like a billy club into her palm. Jojo began to whimper. Then, again, to cry. Margarita took her baby in her arms and sheathed the bottle in her purse.

"So how you been?" she said, turning back to Harley, hands shaking slightly as she calmed herself.

Harley picked up a disembodied Barbie's head off the floor, stroked its blonde hair between her fingers. "I don't know."

Margarita slacked her jaw. "I don't know," she said, in a caveman's monotone. She might have meant this to be funny, but it came off hostile when her daughter didn't laugh. Harley flicked the Barbie's head back to the pile of toy corpses on the carpet. It rolled across the carpet.

"You see the new princesses movie?" Margarita tried again, her voice rising a little. I think she meant *Frozen*.

"I don't know."

"How do you not know if you've seen a movie?"

"I don't even know what movie you're talking about."

For his part, Jojo had rebounded from his disappointment. He climbed across his mother's lap, striving towards her purse. Margarita slapped his hand away, and the boy resumed his crying, louder now. I noted the slap in my notebook, but this time could not find the energy or bravery required to 'redirect the parent' again out loud.

"You're both dressed so nice," she said. "Like, shining."

"I make sure he's clean," said Harley. "The water in the shower don't burn us up like at your place."

Jojo threw himself onto the carpet, face covered in saliva, kicking and bawling. Margarita looked from her daughter, to her son, to me. I swallowed hard, pretended not to feel her gaze, to instead be intently focused on writing something important in my notebook: *Am I going to get stabbed?* I wrote.

"How's school?"

"It's alright," said Harley. "There's this guy I'm talking to, his eyes are like this light brown, like sweet light, and I know he want to be with me but my friend Kiko say he like this other girl too and—"

"What's the foster mother like?"

Harley shared her mother's detest for interruption. She sucked her teeth.

"She don't burn the chicken nuggets at least."

Jojo's cries raised another decibel. Desperate, lonely, abandoned crying. The kind of cries that know no answer's coming. The cries of the condemned. Margarita's eyes pulled at my face, clawing back my skin, peeling it off my skull in strips with every baby's scream. I underlined my latest query. _Am I going to get stabbed?_

"You know they pay her, right?" said Margarita, turning back to her daughter. "She might act nice. But just remember, the only people that really love you is—"

"Shut the fuck up, Ma," Harley muttered.

As soon as she said it, her eyes widened, in disbelief of her own boldness, as though the gun she'd thought was empty had just gone off in her hands.

"What'd you say to me?" said Margarita.

Jojo's anguish had spun into a frenzy. He was screaming all the pain in human history. He rolled around the carpet, aimless and crazed, and at last, in my direction. I pulled him onto my lap and tried my best to soothe him. His face turned purple as he screamed and screamed and screamed. By the time I felt her staring at me, it was too late to put him down.

Margarita rose like a tidal wave on the horizon. She came towards me, growing, heightening. The waters sucked the shore into the distance. The depths rose to a mighty wall.

"You gonna let me feed my child, motherfucker?" she was on me now, brandishing the bottle by her side. "Or you just like to hear a baby scream?"

"It's the rule, Ms. Sand, the rule, it's...there's nothing I can—"

But I didn't get the chance to complete my explanation. Instead, I sat there, knees pinned beneath the tiny table, stunned and dripping wet. For Margarita had unscrewed the lid to the sippy cup and dumped it on my head.

# 3.

**I don't know why I reacted the way I did.** There was nothing so unusual about this particular incident. In fact, this was the fourth time in a year I'd been physically attacked by a parent on my caseload, and none of the previous incidents had inspired the slightest bit of self-reflection.

And yet, as Margarita bounced the empty sippy cup off my forehead, her eyes daring me to dole out some new consequence, as Jojo screamed and Harley doubled over laughing on the couch, I felt an odd sensation. It wasn't anger, or embarrassment, or the familiar comfort of despair. Instead, I felt—well, not cured, exactly, but corrected. Set straight. Slapped back to my senses. It's always a relief to get what you deserve.

Because this was not who I was meant to be, was it? This gray-faced human notebook. This glib lump of scorched dirt and self-pity sighing families into submission. No wonder my fiancée left me! Who *wouldn't* want to dump juice on my head? Years ago, when I'd first started at Children's Future, I'd felt like I'd been plugged into a power source. I wasn't just any other white kid anymore, sitting in my mother's salmon-colored couch in her salmon-colored living room, eating Triscuits with peanut butter and tweeting about inequality. No, I was in it. I was *here*. Every time I counseled some kid in Riverside Towers, or coaxed some birthmother to a breakthrough, or even just walked down Webster Avenue and listened to the shouts and conversations and music blaring from the stereos of cars parked along the playgrounds, I felt a sense of communion with humanity that I'd been chasing my whole life. They were part of me and I was part of them and together we were everybody. But that feeling, strong as I may have felt it in the beginning, wasn't strong enough to last. These days, I didn't want to be part of anything with anybody. Frankly, that sounded kind of gross. You might think bearing witness to injustice and poverty, and unchecked mental illness, and the myriad savageries wrought upon society's most vulnerable would have kept my sense of purpose burning. Instead, I'd receded further and further from it. Into the dark. The cold. The wilderness of apathy. No, after all these years at Children's Future, I didn't give a shit about the Bronx—it was just the setting for my casefiles. And every time Shantal pressed the button beneath the reception desk that opened up the double doors, in walked another birthparent.

Now though, as the juice dripped down my hair, onto my face and neck and seeped into my button-down, I felt a stirring in my soul. I knew I deserved it—every drop of it. But now I'd been washed clean. I tried to stand up from the tiny Fisher Price table, stumbling to the floor because both of my legs had fallen asleep. I looked up through stinging eyes at my assailant. She took two steps backward, her eyes brimming with anger and regret, her fists clenched at her waist, as though in case I charged. If only I could get to know this person, I thought. This red-haired, star-faced...what was her name again? Margarita? If only I could understand her. Then I'd be myself again.

This burst of empathy or narcissism—to this day, I'm not sure which—lasted only a few hours. Because as I was about to leave that day, my boss, Anita Flores, called me into her office and informed me that I'd be transferred off the case.

"We can't have parents pouring juice on people, Todd," she said. "It just doesn't make much sense."

If I'd burned out after a few years at Children's Future, Anita Flores was Pompeii. In her twenty years as Deputy Director, she'd seen every horror you could think of, inspected every shape of bruise, burn, and skin infection, survived two stabbings in the parking lot, and the near-publication of a scathing exposé of Children's Future's alleged racial biases in *The New York Times*, which had only been spiked at press time because we'd all denied our quotes. Of the thousands of foster children that had passed through her dominion, only three had died as result of her decisions, though ninety-six were missing. These were figures she'd downplayed to the reporter but referenced frequently at Happy Hour, full of pride and mourning and at least five amaretto sours. Beautiful in her youth, if the family photos on her desk were any indication, she was still handsome in her fifties: frail but stylish, with lush gray hair and early-stage Parkinson's disease which made her hands tremble and her voice sound thin and nervous, despite the unwavering certainty behind her eyes. A pink scar that she'd incurred in childhood hung like a string of beads across her throat, though she covered it with scarves or pearls, depending on the occasion. She could be harsh, at times; sarcastic, almost always. But the reason we all feared her—clients and staff alike—was because, above all, we all knew she was fair.

But today I wasn't interested in fairness. As she explained to me the many obvious reasons why I could no longer keep the case, I wasn't really listening. Since the morning, I'd felt like I'd escaped from prison. I was fleeing through a darkened woods. Anita's warbly, measured tone was the sound of bloodhounds in the distance.

"I just think it'd send the wrong message to transfer it," I said, catching my flicking eyelid between two fingers.

Anita sipped daintily from a mug of tea emblazoned with a map of the Bahamas. Crayon drawings of families with red teeth and animals with children's faces lined the office walls. Her office was small and dark, lit only by a single porthole window partially covered by a bookcase and a row of lit candles flickering atop her desk. *It is easier to build strong children than repair a broken man* read a Frederick Douglass aphorism which she'd printed out and taped to her computer the day before the reporter from the *Times* stopped by. She kept the lights low and wore purplish transition lenses to cut down on her migraines. To this day, she remains the only person I have ever met who could pull those lenses off.

"What message is that?"

"That we don't care. Or worse, that our caring is conditional. Aren't we trying to make them better parents, after all? Shouldn't I show her how to stick around when things get dicey?"

The phone on Anita's desk rang. She lifted it and hung it up.

"You know her daughter almost died, right?" she said.

"I read that case report, and it didn't seem that clear to me that..."

"Your girl was just lying on the floor, watching TV, playing with the baby, la-dee-da."

"She's not my girl..."

"Come on, kid. I know you've been having a hard time lately, with the engagement thing. But don't get stupid on me now."

I blinked.

"A hard time? Who said that? LaDawn?"

"I don't think *hard* is the word she would use, no."

My face turned as red as if she'd slapped me. To this day, I still think about my botched tryst with LaDawn, the tall, pretty caseworker with her lilting laugh and mellow eyes and blue bra that I got tears all over that night after the Christmas party. For months prior to that, LaDawn and I had shared the Cruz case, since one of the older kids had HIV, and during that time I'd developed an admiration for the caring, kind manner in which she talked to everybody—even Mr. Cruz, who was legitimately a serial rapist; the way her faint lisp softened her heavy New York accent; how she'd once leaned her head on my shoulder and cried all the way back to the agency from the hospital, the night the older Cruz kid's T-cells plunged. "It's my ex-fiancée," I'd slurred that disastrous night in her apartment, frantic, drunk, wearing that stupid, floppy Santa Hat that made this whole scene feel macabre. "I just love her so much, still..." The worst part was—that wasn't even true. I was just desperate for some excuse that would explain the abrupt and jarring hesitance that had come over me as soon as I'd begun to struggle with the condom wrapper, and heartbreak was the best I could come up with. LaDawn told me that she understood, but I could tell she didn't buy it.

"You know, Todd," Anita continued. "Marriage ain't all it's cracked up to be. My son's father hosts a Men's Rights Workshop in Yonkers. You might have dodged a bullet."

"It's really not about that."

"Then what? You're just being stupid for no reason?"

How could I explain what I was feeling to a person like Anita? It didn't even make sense to me.

"Look, I know this might sound crazy," I said instead. "I know she's probably like the rest of them. But after what happened with Ms. Washington... I'd just like to remember what it feels like to have a little faith."

Faith—the word made Anita chortle. To a child welfare worker, faith just means delusion. She sat back and nodded diagnostically.

"So that's what this is about. Listen, kid. Ms. Washington wasn't your fault."

Ms. Washington was four-foot-nine and moony-eyed and prone to burning little Curtis with the pasta water every time her boyfriend left. A few weeks before I'd recommended to the judge that she never see her son again, I'd received a call from her therapist at Odyssey House. "If she doesn't have her baby Curtis," she'd said. "I don't think you've left her much to live for." Not too long later, they'd found her bloated body bobbing in the Hudson.

"I know it's not my fault," I said. "It's just—"

"No, you don't know," said Anita, her dark eyes getting darker. "That therapist should be shot, in my opinion, putting that bullshit on a caseworker. You know I called her boss, right? I said, you put that girl on the street or I'll make damn sure your little rinky-dink rehab never gets another damn referral."

"She was right though, wasn't she? Even at the time I knew she was."

"Who cares? It wasn't your decision. It was me who made you do it. And do you think I've lost an ounce of sleep? That little boy is better off without her. The *world* is better off without her. You should have seen this woman's funeral, Lee. If I'd stayed another minute I think one of the pallbearers would have tried to sell me fentanyl."

Anita chuckled cattily at the memory. Like any warrior, she took a certain pride in every scalp. At least that's how she wanted us to see her. Still, every so often, she'd slip up and allow a glimpse of something sentimental.

"You went to her funeral?"

Anita scowled.

"The point is, guilt is stupid. It's destructive. Every bad call I've ever made was out of guilt. And faith is even dumber. Margarita Sand is a severe neglect case. Domestic violence, borderline personality, bipolar, every substance that she can get her claws on...this junkie skips the first two visits, then assaults you in front of her children—and you come in here singing George Michael?"

The bloodhounds had caught my scent again. The dogs will always find you. At the edge of the woods, I came to a ravine. Shouts sounded through the looming wilderness as flashlights lit the forest floor. The brays and howls were getting closer. Soon they'd tear me limb from limb.

"If you move me off this case, I quit," I said.

Anita sipped from her mug, peering through the rising steam. Each time a caseworker left—which was about once a month back in those opioid days—every case on their caseload would descend to chaos for however long it took to hire and train a replacement. In the meantime, all those duties fell on her. "Come on, Lee..." she muttered darkly.

The phone rang again. This time she answered it. Outside, a light rain began to tap against the window. Down on Southern Boulevard, a woman pulled up a furry hood and corralled her children by the shoulders as they ran for cover, laughing. A man in army camo fell out the door to the billiards hall across the street and started shouting at the darkened sky. In the visiting room that abutted Anita's office, someone threw a chair against the wall. Anita sighed and told the foster mother on the other line, "If you're so overwhelmed, I'll just remove them all, how's that?"

After she'd hung up, she directed her attention back to me. The crayon monsters on the wall gnashed their teeth and whinnied. The scar on her throat writhed as she took a sip of tea and swallowed.

"After all we've been through together, you'd just throw it all away?" she said.

All these years, I'd never once defied her—other than one moment of weakness with the reporter from the *Times*, which came to nothing anyway. Anita was my Khan. My Caesar. If

Children's Future were an army rather than a foster care agency, she could have conquered Russia.

"I just need one mother to believe in," I said, so softly I could barely hear it.

I realized how naïve I sounded. I didn't know Margarita or her children. There was no logical reason to give her another chance. But as I looked back to Anita, expecting her to banish me from the Bronx back to the salmon-colored living room from which I'd spawned, I saw instead that she had closed her eyes. Her scowl had softened. She savored my naivete. That's good naivete—full bodied, fruit-forward. What year is that naivete?

"We'll have to suspend her visitation," she said at last. "Tack on ten weeks of anger management."

"Of course."

"I'm talking a full stay-away motion. These birthparents talk—if we go easy on her, it'll be chaos in these hallways. You're going to testify that she assaulted you. And you're going to call the little girl's therapist and get a statement about how traumatizing it was for her to witness violence in the family visit."

"Sure. No problem. No problem at all."

Practically, this would make my mission impossible—suspension of visitation was a death knell for any family's chances at reunification. A few hours earlier, this edict would have caused me to collapse into a pile of breathless sighing. I might have sighed myself to death. Now though, for the first time in forever, I was ecstatic. I was hopeful. I was high on either empathy or narcissism, but was in any event ready, at last, to plug back into the great electric current of humanity, to help someone who needed it, to live a story I'd be proud to tell someday, instead of just another of my two thousand depressing anecdotes that made my friends wonder if I might be turning racist, and caused my fiancée to run off with a law student named Craig.

I stood to leave. "Thank you, Anita. I can't tell you how much—"

She interrupted me with a lift of her palsied finger. She hated to be thanked.

"Listen, kid. Can I give you some advice?"

"Sure."

What she said next, I didn't think too much about, in the moment.

"You can't feel another person's pain," she said.

I stopped in the threshold. Out in the hallway, a toddler fled a visiting room, hooting and shrieking. LaDawn came chasing after him, tripping on her heels when she saw me in the door. I looked back to Anita. Her smirk made me think she might be joking—or mocking me somehow.

"What do you mean?" I said.

Anita turned back to her computer. The candle-flames danced. The red-fanged crayon monsters slavered and moaned.

"I wasted half my life trying, Todd. And in the end, all I ever got was echoes."

That's not what I was after, was it? To this day, I'm still not sure. But lately I'll be up at night, in my barely furnished condo, staring at photos of my family on my ex-wife's Instagram. My cheap IKEA bed will ache and crick. The pines will hiss their names. And I'll think to myself—these must be the echoes Anita Flores warned me about. But for me, they're more like ghosts.

# 4.

**True to her word, Anita Flores** filed to suspend Margarita's visits the next morning. But a legal quirk of the System allowed my freshly resurrected sense of purpose to remain on life-support a little longer. Yes, in a few weeks, I would have to sit before a Bronx Family Court judge and explain, with a straight face, that a woman dumping a small amount of fruit juice on my head amounted to a clear threat to her children's well-being. And yes, of course, as soon as my ass touched the witness chair, any chance that Rita might ever trust me would scuttle down the boulevard like a rat exposed to sunlight. But between now and then, at least until the judge said otherwise, Children's Future would still be legally obligated to continue supervising family visits. Maybe, I thought, I could use these visits to somehow build some reservoir of trust to draw from later? I had to show her, somehow, that despite all appearances, I was not just some twitchy-eyed white ghoul sent by the System to destroy her family. No. Quite the opposite. I was a ghoul who'd like to help.

The problem was I wasn't sure I had the skill to pull it off. Over the years, I'd grown so comfortable with being hated by the birthparents that it felt unnatural now, even disingenuous, somehow, to try and win her trust.

The next time I saw Rita at the agency, I extended my hand and asked if we could start over. We were in Visiting Room 9 again, sitting on our opposing beanbag chairs. Her hair was tied up in two small twists above each temple like an alien's antennae. Jojo reclined on Harley's lap, pawing at her phone as she Facetimed with a group of friends from school. For a moment, Rita stared down at my hand. What can I do, I wondered, if she's too proud to take the peace I'm offering? But then she sighed, nodded, took my hand and shook it. "Alright then," she said. "We're cool."

That was as far as the conversation went. As the clock ticked above the doorway, I tried to bring up the pending motion with her once or twice, but each time I'd lose my nerve, trailing off irrelevantly the moment that she met my gaze. I guess I couldn't stand to tarnish that feeling of understanding we'd just shared, however fleeting, however compulsory: I couldn't lose the sudden hope of me and Rita being cool. As long as she didn't *know* I was her enemy, a delusional voice within me reasoned, maybe I didn't have to be? Maybe, I'll just *never* tell her about the coming court date. Yeah. *Yeah.* I'll act just as shocked and dismayed as her: Wait, we have to go to *court?* Huh? *Why?*

Obviously, this wouldn't work. Still, at Rita's next two visits I just sat there for two hours on the beanbag chair, reading blogs about the Patriots on my phone, teething on my pen cap. Evidently her lawyer hadn't told her about the motion either, because she kept showing up to the agency like she was visiting her kids at summer camp, like foster care was a quiet lake in New Hampshire and they'd be home in a few weeks.

"Don't worry, baby," she told Harley one Tuesday evening, as I escorted them towards the lobby after the visit: "I got this. You know I got this, right?" And I just stood there, watching this, smiling blankly at the elevator. There was no way to break the news without also breaking this woman's spirit. It was impossible. No caseworker on earth could do it—except for maybe one.

That night, after all the visits had cleared out for the day and the janitors had started sweeping, I stopped by LaDawn's cubicle on my way out. She sat at her computer, headphones in, typing up a case report. She was always the last of us to leave.

"How are you doing?" I said, tapping my fingers along the rim of her cubicle.

LaDawn took out her headphones, swinging the cord around her finger, her mellow eyes tired and watery behind her gold-wire glasses. "Huh?" she said.

"I said 'How are you doing?'"

"Oh. I'm good."

"How's Cruz? I saw Mom on Freeman Street the other day and—"

"Lee, I'm kinda busy. I've got court in the morning."

"Right. Hey, could I ask for your advice on something?"

Already, I could tell I was pushing it. While her head nodded, her eyes said, *is this guy fucking kidding?* Still, she was the best caseworker at Children's Future. I really did need her help.

"I have this new case. I really want to help this mother. But we got off on the wrong foot. Now Anita wants me to suspend her visitation, and I think I'm gonna have to tell her at a home visit, but I'm nervous that—"

"Nervous?" said LaDawn.

"Yeah, I just feel like—"

"You really want my advice?"

"Please. All your parents love you. Even when you tell the truth."

LaDawn sat back and crossed the arms of her pink, fuzzy sweater. On her desk was a jar of Jolly Ranchers that she handed out to all her kids.

"I think you place too much importance on how *you* feel."

"Yeah, I get that. It's just that I—"

"I mean, you're talking about *nervous*—but look at you. Who cares if *you're* nervous? You know what I mean? This isn't your life. You're not even really *you*. Look at it from the mom's perspective—she's in this. She's got no way out. You're about to cut this woman's heart out, and you're worried about how *you* feel?"

This was blunter than I'd expected. She was much more delicate with her clients. Still, I thanked her for her honesty, rapping my hand on the top of her cubicle. I suggested maybe we could get lunch sometime, like we used to do...

LaDawn uncrossed her arms, smiled warmly again and said, "Let's do it," though we both knew we never would.

"Listen," I said, before I turned to leave. "About the Christmas party. I know things are weird between us now, and that's all my fault, I know. But like I told you, with my fiancée leaving me, I've just been..."

LaDawn looked back to her computer. She put one headphone back in her ear.

"You don't have to explain yourself. But can you do me one favor?"

"Sure."

"Don't ask me how I'm doing if you don't really care."

◆

Margarita's building was grand and crumbling, in that old New York way: a prewar walk-up with pigeon spikes over the entrance and a tile mosaic of a Mediterranean fishing port in the lobby—a holdover I guess, from the time before most of the Italians had fled the Bronx. Her apartment was on the fourth floor, at the end of a cracked-plaster hallway, with a black sticker across the peephole that read *I feed my dog with Jehovah's Witnesses.* I knocked on the door and called her name for a good five minutes before I finally heard some rustling.

I was supposed to make home visits to the birthparents once per month, though this was impossible in practice. Most lived on the street, or in cars, or prison, or the apartments of friends or johns whose addresses they'd refuse to give me. We were encouraged to bring along a 'buddy', for safety purposes, and maybe I should have, given what I had to tell her—but the only two caseworkers from my unit who were available that day were Angelo, who would've called me a *maricon* for asking, or LaDawn. So here I was, alone.

"Is the dog locked up?" I asked when Margarita finally came to the door. She stood in the threshold, her hair a cardinal's nest of red and black. It was around 4 PM, but she was in her PJs. They had SpongeBob SquarePants on them.

"What dog?"

I hesitated a moment in the doorway. Caseworkers are like vampires—we can't come in unless invited. "Take your shoes off," she said. That was close enough.

In my years at Children's Future, I'd walked into some gnarly scenes: emaciated pit bulls howling in padlocked bathrooms, bloody underwear stuffed into coffee mugs on kitchen tables, bottles shattered on the entry stairs, vials in the sink, that guy on Ms. Halloran's couch who I'm pretty sure was dead. So when I came into Margarita's apartment, shoes in hand, I was prepared for all manners of unpleasantness. What I hadn't anticipated was that it might be pretty tidy. The kitchen was clean, other than a few dotted fly strips hanging from the ceiling and a smattering of decapitated sugar packets on the table. Alphabet magnets spelled B E H A P P Y on the refrigerator. The living room smelled pleasantly of cigarettes and cinnamon, with a large TV paused on the same reality show about people addicted to plastic surgery that my sister and I used to binge on Christmas breaks from college. The walls were burnt orange, and hung with framed photos of mostly Harley and Jojo, and none of Margarita. This lack of self-portraits was unusual enough for me to note it in my notebook. The lion's share of the birthparents on my caseload were irredeemable narcissists.

The children's bedroom was messier: "They can clean up when I get them home," Margarita explained, gesturing at half-drunk soda-cans, bags of Fritos, a dresser covered in smudgy glasses and instant mac and cheese, a single unmade bed. There were movie posters on the walls, glow-in-the-dark stars glued to the ceiling, an anime-style drawing of some kind of warrior-princess with a cat's face drawn directly onto the wall in marker. "That's where I found her," Margarita said, standing behind me in the threshold, pointing to the floor. "Rolling around in vomit—wearing the hell out of my favorite dress and shoes."

"Uh huh," I said. I didn't want to get into that with her now. The more I knew, the more reservations I might have about helping her. And what good would those do?

"You gotta see my room too?" Margarita nodded towards a closed door off the living room. I told her that it wasn't necessary, though of course I was supposed to. Ever since the time Ms. Mills had tried to lick my earlobe, I'd stopped inspecting birthmother's bedrooms.

At last I sat down at a table in the kitchen for the conversation I'd been dreading. I'd been running through my speech the whole walk over from the agency. *It will just be temporary setback. A month. Two months tops. Hey, if it were up to me, believe me, I wouldn't have to tell the judge a thing...*

Margarita brought me a cup of coffee that I hadn't asked for, loaded with an absolutely preposterous amount of sugar.

"Just so you know," she said. "I'm recording this on my phone." She propped her phone against a stack of magazines on the table. "Got to keep the System honest."

This was not allowed, but I told her it was fine. In fact, as I'd later learn, she'd record most of our conversations this way—but this wasn't the time to make an issue. I couldn't afford to start things on the wrong foot. With clients past, I would have just plowed through the conversation, hacked her bloody with my scythe. But now I felt oddly nervous. The Grim Reaper had grown a conscience, I guess. He could share a cup of coffee first.

"You've got a nice place here," I said.

Margarita took another sugar packet from the table. Her long nails made her fingers useless: she tore it open with her teeth. "That a surprise?"

"No, its just...I'm a slob, myself. Drives my fiancée crazy."

Why did I just lie, I wondered? Would Death lie about his failed engagement? No, that's something Lee would do—which meant I was myself now. Me, just me. Without my hood. Without protection. Margarita's gaze became suspicious.

"I bet you go to some pretty nasty places, huh?" she said. "Dealing with people who don't love their babies."

"I wouldn't say that they don't love—"

"Why not? Plenty people around here don't care. My girl Taz's got three kids she leaves at home half the time with fuckin' Pop Tarts for their dinner. I let them come by here and play with the turtles, just so I can keep an eye on them. But it's *my* kids you want your hands on, huh?"

In the corner, an old radiator started clacking. The noise was calm but insistent, the clacks evenly timed. Seconds later, an exposed pipe over the refrigerator sprayed mist against the wall.

"Did you say...turtles?"

Margarita sighed. She lit a cigarette with a lighter from the pocket of her PJs. Smoke rose in swizzling ribbons. Steam hissed out of the pipes. I took out my Children's Future birth home visit checklist and started running down the standard questions:

"How long have you lived at this residence?"

"Couple years," she said. "It's my ex-husband's aunt's Section 8, but she moved in with her girlfriend and the landlord don't mind, so long as he gets his."

"And what's rent?"

"Rent is what you pay a landlord, Todd."

"No, I mean...what do you pay each month?"

She brushed a rogue strand of red behind her ear. "It's different things..."

"What do you mean?"

Margarita raised her eyebrow. She hadn't meant to tip me off, but I knew enough now. Two other women on my caseload, Ms. Nixon and Ms. Halloran, were tenants of similarly repugnant men.

"Well, we all do what we have to do to get by," I said, as though I too sometimes had to sleep with my landlord.

"I don't *have* to do anything."

In the lull that followed, I chewed my pen until the plastic split. I knew this pause was coming off judgmental, but I couldn't think of what to say. No, I was simply freezing. Searching deep within myself and coming up with nothing: just like with LaDawn.

In the corner, the clacking grew impatient: louder, louder. I guess the radiator was as uncomfortable with this silence as I was. I sipped my coffee, crunching granules of unmixed sugar between my molars.

"And how are the visits going with the kids?" I said.

"You tell me, Todd."

"I know it can't be easy with me in there watching."

"When I'm with them, I don't even see you, bro. Outside of that one time, ha."

She gave me her crooked smile—half apology, half smirk. I could tell I'd gained some credit with her by not mentioning the juice incident in any of the visits since it had happened. Which brought me to the task at hand.

"Listen," I began. I couldn't put it off any longer. This was my *job,* my duty. How had LaDawn put it—it didn't matter how *I* felt. "I know, deep down, you love your children," I began, "even though you said you didn't. But the thing is, my—"

Margarita's shifted one leg beneath the other in the chair. "Wait—hold up. *I* said that?"

"Well, yeah." I clasped one hand in the other. "That first day, you told me that—"

"Fuck outta here. I would never say that."

"Ok—well. Nevermind then. It's not important."

"It's not important if I love my children?"

"It's not important what you said or didn't say."

"Show me in your little book where I said that."

I blinked.

"Do you really want me to?"

"Show me where I said that, motherfucker. You gonna make me ask again?"

Margarita pointed her cigarette between my eyes. A wisp of steam rose from my coffee. Seeing no alternative, I sifted through my notebook, landed on a stiff page encrusted with drops of sticky red. There, I found the sentence underlined. I read it back aloud.

"'It's like it cost a dollar and all I had was fifty cents.'"

Margarita stared at me a good ten seconds, then closed her eyes and turned away. She rubbed the stars tattooed along her cheekbone, as though so that they might come off.

"I thought it was pretty brave actually," I said. "For you to tell me that."

It had been a long time since I'd tried to say something so sincere. Maybe that's why it rang so falsely. Margarita looked at me like I'd just started drooling on her table.

"You think its brave for somebody not to love their children?"

The radiator couldn't stand the tension. It interrupted with an outburst of nervous clicks and clacks. Steam shot in all directions from the ceiling pipe. A piece of sodden wallpaper keeled over from the wall. It was about a hundred degrees in there.

"I just meant that there's no right or wrong way to love somebody."

"Of course there is."

"I want to help you, Ms. Sand."

"What the fuck kind of caseworker are you, anyway? Come into people's homes, steal their kids and call them brave? Man, why don't you get the fuck up out of my—"

Margarita's eyes suddenly went wide. She stopped herself mid-outburst.

I stared, puzzled. "What?"

"SHHH. You hear that?" She held up a finger. We sat in silence for a moment, listening together. *Click. Clack. Bonk bonk bonk. BONK BONK BONK.*

"You should really get that radiator looked at..."

"Oh fuck," Margarita mouthed. She sprang from the table and reached the door in an instant, snapped the door chain back into place before the person on the other side could get their keys into the keyhole.

"Hey...what?" a man's voice grumbled, on the other side.

The door jolted inward but caught against the chain. Margarita leaned into the ajar space and spit at the intruder.

"What the fuck, Rita?" the voice was angry now. Margarita threw herself against the door and tried to get the bolt in place. But she couldn't get it shut.

"I'm calling the cops," she yelled. "You hear that? You want to get your ass beat again?"

"Come ON with that," the man grunted, with another burst of force against the door.

"Hello, 911? My ex is violating an Order of Protection. He's standing at my house looking wild, saying he gonna choke the life outta me again and..."

"I know you're not really calling."

"Five minutes, you say? OK, yes, thank you very much. Bye."

"You didn't give an address, Rita! Don't make me break this door down."

At last, I gained my bearings.

"Is there a problem?" I asked her, in my most courageous tone.

The door went slack. Margarita shot me a look like I was the dumbest motherfucker in America. A calm came into the man's voice.

"You got somebody in there?"

In my direction, Margarita held her hand to her throat and vigorously slashed it. She would have cut her head clean off if her fingers had been a blade.

"What?" she said. "No, crazy. It was the TV."

She mimed a remote control with her hands. Of course, I should not have played along. I should have ignored Margarita's frantic hand motions and informed the man on the other side of the door that I was her caseworker—his too, in fact, assuming that he was who I suspected. But the violence at the door unnerved me. All I knew was I didn't want it to come in. Instead, I went from the table to the couch, stepping lightly in my socks, found the remote between the cushions, and pressed play. On the screen, a tan, ivory-toothed doctor resumed counseling a woman who was unhappy with her cheekbones. I turned up the volume. Margarita gave me a thumbs-up.

"HEY DAVEY, THAT YOU?" the man yelled. "I swear to God, Rita—"

"There's nobody in here. I'm just watching my show."

"You think I'm fucking stupid?"

Margarita and I locked eyes. Why doesn't she just let him in? I wondered. What am I doing? Crazed or not, this man will plainly see I am not Davey. I tried my best to indicate this question using hand gestures, but she waved me off.

"I ain't heard from you in three months and now you think that you can show up like you live here?" she said.

"You told me not to come back."

"But here you are, though."

"I just want to see my kids."

"Harley's at school, dumbass. Jojo's at Ms. Janice's house," she said. For a moment, I was confused. Then she gave an explanatory wince in my direction. Now, her position made more sense.

"How they doing?" said the man.

"Fuck you, Ty."

Ty—that was his name: the shadow who stalked the margins of her casefile. Who had eleven felonies for intent to distribute, two gun charges, four for A+B. Who'd sent her to the hospital last Thanksgiving. Who'd been cut out of some of the family photos above the TV, judging by their jagged edges. I must have called the phone number listed for him in the file fifteen times—here was the ghost, in the flesh.

He threw himself against the door again. His force was wild. "My own fucking cousin, Rita?" He screamed. "You was always easy! Always sick! Always need a man to make you feel like something special!" The door bulged. The flimsy chain would not withstand much more. "Any man, huh, Rita? Well, if Davey *was* a man he'd come out and face me! You hear that, D? You hear that?!?!"

I couldn't think of a way out. What were our options? Tell this enraged felon that the voice he'd heard belonged not to a man who'd been sleeping with his wife but one who had absconded with his children? Would that really calm him down? The door barked like a Doberman on the chain. "Come ON!" he said. "Come ON, RITA!"

I felt like I might faint.

Margarita, for her part, had more experience with violence. She turned toward me then, her posture straight, a calm, commanding presence. Her eyes looked almost golden when she had a good idea.

"Hide," she mouthed.

I don't know what it says about my character that I've always been so good at hiding. It might be my most innate skill. Many a time, playing hide-and-go-seek with my sister and cousins amongst the nooks and corners of our house, I'd stow away someplace ingenious—like the washing machine, or that one trunk in the attic that Dad never came back for—and stay there for an hour, until I realized they'd given up the game to play Nintendo in the basement. Which is to say, I'd won.

Now, I scanned the Sands' apartment: Under the bed? No, too obvious. The linen closet in the hallway? Of course he'd look there. Same went for the cabinet beneath the sink. What about behind the curtains? The shower? No. Fuck. She'd blocked the fire-escape with an armoire. FUCK.

Desperate now, I tiptoed into Margarita's bedroom, and then at last, inspiration struck. On the far side of the bed there was a wicker hamper filled with clothes. I looked to Margarita, who winced and nodded, and a moment later, I was crouching down within it, legs crossed, head ducked, buried deep beneath her laundry. Margarita stuffed another bedspread over the top and sealed me within the vinegarish scent of stale sweat, strawberry perfume and cigarettes.

She left the bedroom door open, to discourage his suspicions. I peered out through the wicker, eyes burning from sweat and dust.

Margarita opened the door and ushered Ty into the apartment. He was light-skinned and wiry—smaller than his rage had made him seem—with bad skin, deep-set eyes, and long hair pulled back in a frizzy ponytail. He wore a pink and black polo shirt, with a jaunty gold wristwatch and heavy boots. He moved from room to room, his anger cooling to frustration, then impatience, like he was looking for his keys instead of some naked lover.

As he came into the bedroom, I almost gasped aloud—for I remembered all at once, like a punch in the stomach, that I'd left my oxfords on the shoe rack.

"You sure you don't want to check the closets, crazy?" said Margarita, sauntering behind him, calm as a serial killer. "Maybe I got him hiding in the bathtub, Ty! Oh, I know! He's in the hamper!"

She seemed to be enjoying this. I almost stood up then. Instead, I held my breath and watched as they came into the neat and overwhelmingly purple bedroom. The blinds were drawn; the only light in the room came from a glowing terrarium on her dresser which, I supposed, contained the turtles. Margarita's fingers fiddled idly with the drawstring of her sweatpants: "You really think I'd have somebody over, wearing SpongeBob on my PJs?"

Ty stared her up and down. Had he taken two steps closer toward the bed, he might have heard the hamper wheezing like a broken ribcage. Instead, with a heavy, almost sheepish sigh, he seemed to concede there was no lover. It was the TV that he'd heard. "The place is a fucking mess, Rita," he said, tapping his fingers against the terrarium on the dresser. "What are Harley's turtles doing in our room?"

"I'm the only one who feeds them anyway. Speaking of...if you're all done terrorizing me, I've got to get dinner started."

Margarita went back into the kitchen. She ran the water in the sink. The gas stove clicked and flumed. It was approximately the temperature of hell inside the hamper. My sister and my cousin would have been two rounds into Mario Kart by now. Ty turned back to the terrarium, exhausted now that he thought the drama over. He pressed his forehead to the glass.

"How you been, my dudes?" he asked the turtles. He stood there a good few minutes: brow furrowed, shoulders slumped, as though the turtles were giving him a full report. "She's not feeding you enough, is she?" he said at last, tapping flakes of food into the water from a plastic bottle. Then he left all three of us alone.

In the living room, he sat down on the couch, his elbows on his knees and his head in his hands. The television cast his face in blueish silver. Margarita came up behind him, slowly, carefully, gripping a heavy saucepan with both hands at the hilt. The water in it fizzed and spit.

"What are you gonna do with that, chicken wing?" he said, without looking up.

"Don't move."

"I won't say I don't deserve it."

Margarita took another step across the hardwood. The water sloshed in the pan, spilling over the sides and hissing as it hit the floor.

"You know how many times I called you? What I had to tell the kids?"

"Always with the drama, Rita."

Margarita held the pan steady, took another step towards him. Ty sat back on the couch looking back at her with faint amusement, like this were a joke he'd heard before. Rita threw the water against the wall. Steam shot out in grasping plumes towards the two of them. It was the punchline Ty had been expecting.

"I guess this means you weren't really making dinner?"

Rita seemed to cool off with the steam, relieved, I think, to not be taken seriously. If Ty had for a moment thought she'd do it, she might have really had to.

Grumbling about her sanity, Ty went into the kitchen. Cupboards whinged and shut. Rita scurried out of frame. When she reappeared, a second later, she was carrying my shoes. "You're lucky I been doing therapy," she called idly, opening up a window and throwing them out onto the street. "The old me would have cooked your head like ramen noodles."

A moment later, Ty came back into the living room with a bowl of cereal.

"Listen. The thing with Davey..."

"You really want to bring that up?"

"No. No. I haven't been myself, is what I mean."

"Oh yeah? Cause I was kinda thinking that you haven't changed a bit."

"Please. Don't act like I don't know about your little boy- and girlfriends. I might be crazy, but I'm not crazy."

"Can you watch it with the cereal, bro? Have you ever held a fucking spoon before? You're spilling milk on my couch."

"Your couch? That you bought with all your money, right? That you had to spend all day putting together while *your* wife got her nails done?"

What followed was a funny kind of argument. It de-escalated more with every grievance. There was a gravity between them, drawing them closer as their anger grew. Before long, they were sitting just a few inches from each other—each running down a list of betrayals and infidelities while their hands brushed each other's kneecap. He kept calling her his chicken wing. She said he was trash, and put her elbow on his shoulder.

Finally, Ty reached into his back pocket and pulled out what looked like a blank CD.

"Don't tell me that you made another mixtape…"

"Ha. Fuck you. No. Check this out: *Frozen*. My boy came in with the new DVDs. It's still in theaters. Harley loves that Disney shit. You remember how she used to make us watch *Mulan* over and over?"

"Mmm-hmm."

"What? You don't think she'll like it?"

Margarita took the disc.

"I don't know what she likes anymore. She's so damn moody lately. I guess she got too much from me."

"You're a good Mom, Rita."

"No. I'm really not."

Margarita said this with such a rawness, such tremolo in her voice, that for a moment I worried that she might be working her nerve up to tell the truth.

"This shit with ACS…" said Ty. "You got your little great depressions, and I got my ins and outs. But we been through worse than this before, right? If they were going to take them, they'd be gone already..."

So, I thought, he wasn't completely in the cold. The Administration of Children's Services investigation had gone on for six months before the night they finally took them. Ty had still been living in the dark part of the casefile, in parts obscure to foster care caseworkers who have to piece the story together from the half-completed notes of other agencies, in the shadowy nether-time before things go from bad to worse.

"You're kidding, right?" said Margarita.

"What?"

"You know what I been through since you left?"

"I know, I know."

"Oh, you know? That's how smart you are. You can be gone three months, off on the moon or Mars or with some nasty bitch in Jersey—and you come back and now you know."

Surely she was about to tell him. I could hear it in her voice. That nihilism. That whatever. Would I have the guts to come storming out of the hamper, I wondered, if her husband started swinging? Admittedly, the fact that I was hiding in a battered woman's hamper did not suggest courageousness.

Margarita's voice took on that calm tone again.

"You know what? It doesn't matter. Because ACS dropped the case last week. So turns out, we don't need a thing from you."

She said it with such certitude, such conviction, that for a moment, even I believed her. Ty jumped to his feet, ecstatic and confused, an atheist whose prayers had just been answered.

"Really?" he said. "They just...dropped it?"

Rita snapped her fingers: just like that.

"I told you you could do it, didn't I? I told you! I knew it! Thank God! God! I always knew! My girl! My girl! Ha ha!"

Margarita shrugged. "I don't give a fuck how you feel about it."

"Well, I don't give a fuck that *you* don't give a fuck, do I? Because I knew you had it in you. Cuz when shit gets real, we get realer, baby. I knew it. I knew it! That's my goddamn Rita. That's the girl I fuckin' love!"

"You just left, Ty. You put it all on me."

"I'm gonna make it up to you. To Harley and little man too. Shit, I feel like a loaded gun, baby. Everything. Like that. Like *that*. Hey—why don't we all go out to dinner? Fuck the Bronx. I'm talking someplace *nice*!"

"Fuck you, Ty."

"I love you so much, chicken wing."

Ty hugged her by the shoulders, kissed her cheeks and temples. She went stiff in his arms. For my part, I felt like I was dreaming. I must have imagined this same scene a hundred different times—every time I read through a new case on my desk: That happy moment where the System spares the family. The version of the story in which we never meet at all.

Triumph—however make-believe—made Margarita indignant. Suddenly, she was all eyerolls and hair-flicks. If she were chewing gum, she would have smacked it.

"I don't think you should be here when the kids get home," she said, pushing off her husband. "You know how it messes with Harley when you come and go. I've been having enough trouble with her already. Last thing we need is for her act out again...get us a whole new investigation."

"Yeah, but..." Ty blinked. "...just for a little while? We could all watch *Frozen*? Or I could just take little man around the block in the stroller?"

"You can't just see them when you feel like it. Don't be selfish, for once, alright?"

Ty continued protesting, but not that strongly. The news was what he'd come for. He'd do anything she asked. "Fine," he said, finally. "I get it. It's cool. Can you tell the kids I love them though? What if I came back in a few days?"

"I can't stop you, can I? Knock first though, in case I'm in here twisted up with Davey."

Ty laughed—ha ha. She followed him toward the door. Before he left, he lingered a moment in the threshold.

"Listen," he said, he reached into his pocket and pulled out a money clip. He counted off a stack of bills. "I got myself a little promotion. Coming up a little, I guess. Stay off the street, alright?"

Margarita seemed unimpressed by the giant wad of cash. She took the money in her hands and started counting, her fingers quick and dexterous and accustomed to the task.

"Really though," he said. "That's for them. Food, rent, clothes. For them, Rita. Alright?"

"What's that supposed to mean?"

"Nothing, nothing. I just—"

"I don't need a thing from you, Ty," she said. But this was only for the record. She put the money in her pocket of her PJs and slammed the door in his face.

When she came back into the apartment, the heat was kicking on. The radiator's bones rattled. She lit a cigarette and sat down at the table. When I was sure the coast was clear, I came out of the bedroom, slick with sweat, a little haughty to compensate for my embarrassment, dripping socks and leggings.

"Yo, there he is," she said. "Where you been, Davey?"

I had an urge to tell her then. To reassert some level of professional distance into this afternoon. *The agency will be filing to suspend your visitation, Ms. Sand. Because you poured juice on my head.*

But when I looked at her, I saw that this was not the time for bad news. And I didn't spend all afternoon crouching like a goddamn armadillo in her laundry just for her to hate me anyway. I asked if she was all right. If there was anything that I could do.

The glint in her eyes slipped beneath the surface. Smoke from her cigarette rose like its departing soul.

"You wanted to talk about love, right? Maybe you can tell me why I only love the things that hurt."

# 5.

**The savage calm in Ty's voice when he'd thought I was her lover,** the aborted baptism with boiling holy water, the lies their truce was built on—none of this should have inspired confidence in the strength of their relationship. Still, after I'd emerged from the cocoon of Margarita's hamper and stomped back to the subway, my feet jammed into a pair of Ty's old Timberlands, I couldn't quite condemn them either—at least not completely. Sure, I thought, their love seemed unstable to me— but what did *I* know about love? What special knowledge did I have? Not only had my own engagement fallen through, but it hadn't even been a *real* engagement.

Yes, I had technically asked Estelle to marry me—but even at the time, it had felt like more of a last-ditch effort than a long-term plan. We'd been out with friends one night at some hipster club in Bushwick, and as she and a group of them took their drinks out onto the dance floor, I saw her fingers hook with her friend Craig's hand for just a second, so quickly that it might have been an accident, or just some playful thing. I watched this happen from the bar, and in that moment, with the way she looked in her black jeans, the flick of her hair as the DJ put on "Hotline Bling", and the mirror-ball hanging from the ceiling spinning like a thousand silver eyes, flashing at me periodically, twirling, winking, inquiring what it was that kept me standing on the sidelines sipping on a Red Bull vodka—in that soggy, desperate moment I'd thought: if I lose her now, I'll disappear.

"I know things haven't been so great between us lately…" was how I began my speech that night when we came home to the apartment that her father mostly paid for, my knee touching down on the linoleum in our cluttered galley kitchen. I tried to make my most romantic, steadfast expression while my eye twitched like a mad scientist's assistant's. She did say yes—but even in the moment, it didn't bring the satisfaction I'd imagined. For months, years even, I'd had this unmoored, weightless feeling, and I guess I'd hoped marrying Estelle would make life feel more solid. Of course, the added weight only made us both feel more unbalanced. In fact, Estelle started sleeping over at Craig's less than three months after I'd proposed—and if I'm honest, when she'd told me, tearful and apologetic, my first emotion was relief. I'd never even gotten around to buying her a ring. All told, I'd probably called her 'my fiancée' more times *since* she'd ended things than I had when we were actually engaged.

So I guess it was through the prism of my own experience, plus a heap of unwashed clothes, that I observed Rita and Ty's relationship. Since moving out from Estelle's, I'd been living in a cramped and musky two-bedroom apartment in Morningside Heights that I shared with three Columbia grad students I'd found on Craiglist. We'd all gotten along fine at first—until one night, at one of their weekly activist book-groups on the couches in the living room, a young Jamaican woman getting her PhD in Neo-Colonial Studies diagnosed me with a white savior complex after hearing about my work at

Children's Future. Trying to seem fashionably world-weary and self-deprecating, but having drunk far too much red wine to walk that line, I'd retorted: How could that be true if, in all my years in the Bronx,  I've never saved a single person? Shortly afterward, the woman packed her purse and left.

From then on I'd been persona non grata with the grad students—cancelled from their social circle, so to speak, though they still needed me to make rent. At night, I slept on a leaky, sighing air mattress in an L-shaped bedroom that I shared with a sociology student named Kyle, partitioned by a shoddy, rightward slouching Target bookcase that I'd had since college, lined with Kyle's novelty ashtrays and draped with an American flag that he'd defaced with an anarchist's symbol written in purple Sharpie. Personally, I'd seen enough unchecked human cruelty at Children's Future to find the idea of anarchism sort of childish, but what could I say? It was not my flag. It was not my room. It wasn't even really my life—or at least, I couldn't accept it as such. How could I? Here I was, closer to thirty than twenty, and back to living like a college freshman. My bedside table was a stack of wrinkled paperbacks, crowned usually by the plastic whiskey nips I'd drunk alone the night before. I had a guitar I hadn't played in six months in a case against the wall, and a rickety 18-inch TV mounted atop a plastic dresser—the drawers of which would slide open if I loaded them with even one too many socks, bringing the whole thing crashing down. My window looked into brick alley between our building and the Peruvian chicken restaurant next door, which always smelled delicious, like rosemary and canola oil, but where I could not afford to eat. Of course, on a Children's Future salary, this was the case with almost every restaurant in New York. At the end of each month, I'd have like forty-two dollars in my bank account, and would have to live on eggs and tortillas until my next paycheck hit the bank.

But although I sometimes thought that how badly I was doing somehow proved my commitment to doing Good, that I must *really* care, the truth was—even *that* was self-deception. Because there's an entire world of difference between being broke and being poor. Yes, I was out of money—but I knew I could move back home to New Hampshire at any moment if I really wanted. Or at the very least, I could call my Mom and Ken and beg for cash. So this martyr thing I was doing? Even *I* didn't really buy it. So my loneliness, my longing, hell, even my nightly hunger pangs—did I even really feel them? Or was I still just chasing echoes? I don't know.

What I do know is this: the night after I returned home from Margarita's hamper, I lay back on my perpetually deflating mattress, serenaded by the sounds of a make-believe anarchist watching *The Office* on his laptop through the cheap bookcase partition. I closed my eyes and saw the tender look that Ty and Rita had shared as he'd stood in the threshold of their apartment, full of bitterness and disappointment and loyalty and affection. The glint of admiration in his eyes, even as she'd cursed him out. The mournful way she'd run her hand through her hair after she'd slammed the door in his face and sat back down at the table. I didn't know what it was I was looking at: but it had to be  *some*thing, didn't it? I wanted so badly to believe it was real.

Was this optimism or delusion? Either way, it lasted only a few weeks. Because one week before Thanksgiving, Margarita showed up to a family visit with one eye caved in.

"You wanted me to get here early?" she said slurring slightly, wincing as she sat across from me in the booth of a McDonald's around the corner from the agency. Her parka made her look like a lion in disguise as a tiger, or maybe the other way around, with a mane-like furry hood pulled over her head to hide her face, and black-and-orange stripes going up and down her arms. I could hardly hear her over some nearby high schoolers who'd packed into the booths that lined the windows, flirting and over-laughing and playing music from their phones.

We didn't normally meet in public, but all of the visiting rooms were booked by other cases—the agency was slammed in those days, with oxycontin, heroin, and fentanyl charging like horsemen of the endtimes through the Bronx. Plus, I figured, holding her visits at McDonald's would keep her off Anita's radar.

"There's something we have to talk about..." I began, as Rita settled in the booth. But before I could give the news, she lowered the hood of her parka. That's when I saw the gash that ran along her cheekbone. Her eye looked like an onion skin, purplish and swollen halfway shut. "What the hell happened?"

Margarita shrugged. "I caught an elbow playing basketball at the park."

"...Basketball?"

"It's this game where you bounce a big orange ball around..."

"This isn't funny, Rita."

"I was trying to dunk it."

Rita was about five feet tall and flatfooted. Once, during a family visit, she and Jojo played catch with a Koosh ball and it was a toss-up who was more coordinated. I felt almost insulted by the lack of effort she'd put into this lie. "You...what?"

"You know. Dunk that shit. Right into the basketball basket."

"It's just called the basket, Rita."

Any pretense of convincing me was already out the window. Now, she was amusing herself. The one eye she could open glimmered playfully beneath its swollen lid.

"What do you know? Y'all probably play with a snowball in New Hampshire. Here in the Boogie, that's what we call it. The ball hole. The basketball basket. The hoop-de-hoop. We got our own slang."

"It was him, wasn't it?"

"Who?"

"Did he find out about the kids?"

"I don't know who you're talking about."

"Let me take you to a shelter. Away from him. You'll be safe there."

"Hold up. You want to make me homeless?"

Before I could respond, a soft-spoken teenaged McDonald's employee interrupted. He hovered uncertainly by the end of our table. "My manager says we can't let you guys sit here again all afternoon if you're not gonna buy anything."

Margarita stared at the kid, unblinking, for a good thirty seconds. The noise of the rowdy teenagers rose to a chorus, echoing off the walls and booths and windows of the restaurant.

The boy shrugged and walked away. Margarita stared him all the way back behind the counter.

"Look," I said. "I can refer him to a batterer's program. He won't know that you told me—I'll say that I had concerns about prior incidents in the casefile."

"Can we talk about something else?" she said. "I'm so tired, man."

"I know you weren't playing basketball. I have to hear you say it."

"Sherlock Todd over here."

"I need you to be honest—"

"It wasn't Ty, alright!" Margarita slapped the table with her open palm. "Goddamn are you annoying!"

I suppose I must have wanted to believe her. Or I just didn't want to be annoying. "So who then? Davey?"

"Please. Davey's a little bitch. I'd beat *his* ass."

"Then who?"

"Are you really gonna make me say it?"

"If you don't tell me, I have no choice but to assume..."

Margarita's eyes begged me not to push it any further. But it was my job. I had to know.

Finally, she broke. "I worked last night. You happy?"

For months, Margarita and I had an unspoken agreement: when we discussed her source of income, she'd make up jobs for herself at random, and I'd pretend I believed her. That I hadn't read the casefile. One week, she'd claim to have a job cleaning cages at the Bronx Zoo ('I just really love those little lemurs'); another time, she was interviewing to join a bus driver's training program, despite the fact she didn't have a driver's license ('you get that through the program, I think'); for a while she'd claimed to be a florist's assistant ('tulips and shit, cutting off the stems'). By making her admit this, I'd committed the kind of subtle violation you can't retract, much less apologize for, without doing further damage. All you can do is carry on in gentler tones.

"But he gave you all that money…"

"Yeah, well, maybe money don't buy class."

Rita tried to smirk but winced. She touched a hand to the scabs and blisters sprinkled through the stars. It had happened at the end of the night, she told me. Some trucker on his way out of the city who didn't want to pay. It was harder now, with the internet and everything—all the pimps were out of business, so it was just her against the world out there.

"What are you going to tell him?"

"Ty?"

"Isn't he going to want to know how what happened to your eye?"

Rita considered this a moment, then gave a long, soft sigh that triggered something in me. I thought of my own mom sitting at the kitchen table, before she met my stepdad, consoling herself with white wine from the fridge after another bad date at the 99.

"I haven't seen him lately—"

"I thought he told you he'd back?"

"You could hear all that from the hamper? I don't listen to a word he says."

I still had a feeling I was being lied to. But it's not such an easy thing to interrogate a battered woman while she's bleeding from her face. What would a normal person say in such a situation? What did I used to say to Mom?

"You're better off without him."

"Mmm-hmm."

"You deserve better, Rita. You deserve to be treated with all the respect that you...deserve."

She squinted at me wryly with her good eye. One too many deserves there. I'd hoped she hadn't noticed.

"Listen, bro. I appreciate what you've been doing for me. And I know you think this is all some sad-ass movie. But let me tell you, I've had more love in my life than you could ever dream of. And my husband? He's got his little tantrums, yeah—but the two of us has walked through hell together and come right out the other side."

I remembered Anita Flores's warning: you can't feel another person's pain. Still, as I met Rita's gaze across the table, I felt something pass from her to me. Some energy. Some feeling. Whether it was pain, or love, or just an echo, I didn't know. It didn't matter. At this point, I'd take anything.

"So tell me, then," I said.

◆

The story Margarita told me that afternoon inside the McDonald's on the corner of 172$^{nd}$ Street and Boston Road has stuck with me ever since. Long after I moved home to New Hampshire and tried to move on with my life, it would still spring from the darkness out of nowhere. I'll be bringing the trash barrels to end of the cul-de-sac, or standing in the corner, nursing a drink at an office Christmas party, and suddenly, as though in revolt against banality, I'll see Margarita and Ty, both fifteen years old, meeting each other in the line for pizza in the cafeteria of the Mount Pleasant Residential Treatment Center. They'd both been sent there after nightmare stints in foster care—after Children's Future had deemed them both too difficult for regular foster homes. I think of how they fell in love so quickly, so desperately, like only kids can do. Of her sneaking out of her dorm room to meet him outside in the courtyard. Of Ty, waiting for Rita where he always did at the picnic table by the trashcans, flicking his lighter in the dark. And Rita wearing one of his sweatshirts to conceal her growing baby bump. The sky above is a starless, nuclear purple, glowing from the distant city lights. The jingling sound of crickets in the distance rises up, then fades into the background, a sound two kids shipped upstate from the Bronx might have found unnerving—but in my head, it's music.

And now, when my own failings feel insurmountable, when my ex-wife shows up to my condo fifteen minutes before the time we'd agreed on, and my daughter just hops up from the couch where we've been watching *Muppet Babies* and runs into her mother's arms like I'm not even there, like I'm just some stranger who watches *Muppet Babies* with her—I try to put myself in Ty's mindset that night in the courtyard, when he first heard the news. He's sitting on the picnic table while she's below him on the bench, ripping up leaves and pine needles as she tells him, for the first time, that she's pregnant. And that she's been that way since a month before they met.

The story of the baby's father is awful. The kind of story you hear a lot as a caseworker. But you don't actually get numb to that kind of thing with more exposure—you might think you do, but really you're just another story closer to coming apart. When she told it to me that day in the McDonald's, I wanted to crawl into my backpack and zip the zipper shut.

But this night, when Rita tells Ty, that isn't his reaction. He doesn't shudder or look down, or really even blink. As Margarita draws spirals with her sneaker in the dirt of the treatment center courtyard; as she says I understand if you don't love me anymore, if you think I'm sick, I'm nasty; as the crickets scream and the moon leers down on the two of them like a foster father through a keyhole, Ty looks within himself for something that all young men spend our adolescence imagining that we're capable of, so long as we never have to prove it.

"When she grows up," he says, kissing her gently on the forehead, "we'll just tell her I'm her daddy."

◆

That was all she could tell me that day. Or maybe that was all that I could stand to hear. Later, once we'd betrayed each other so many times that we'd begun to build up a kind of trust, she'd fill in more details. She'd tell me how, a few weeks later, they fled the facility together. How they took a Greyhound from Penn Station to Pennsylvania and gave birth to Harley there, because the System doesn't chase across state lines. How one day months later, after they'd come back to the Boogie to scratch out a life together, Ty rolled up on her former foster dad's game of dominoes and put two bullets in his Kangol hat, and another in his balls.

Today, though, when her story came to its conclusion, Margarita took two Advils from her purse and swallowed them without any water.

"So don't tell me that Ty don't really love me, or any other social worker bullshit. He might do his thing sometimes. He might treat me a little careless. But if I called him today and gave the make and model of the guy who did this to me, the cops would find the motherfucker's body out in Jersey. Because the thing about Ty is, when I need him, like I really, really need him? He comes through every time."

I didn't know what to say. All that came to mind was, well, social worker bullshit. Later, I mumbled something about how she must be hungry, then left her in the booth and joined the line growing at the register. As I looked around the booths of rowdy teenagers, I saw a dozen Ty and Margaritas. Was that true love in the eyes of the boy with the baseball hat over his eyes, with his hand inside the jean pocket of his girlfriend, laughing at some joke being passed around the booth? What about the one girl with long braids and the other with her head shaved, making eyes and throwing fries at each other across the booth—what would they do for love? What acts of sacrifice or heroism would *their* story require? When the chips were down, would they come through?

One of the girls caught my glance and motioned to her friends. I looked back down at my shoes. At once, I felt acutely aware of being the only white guy in this McDonald's. "There's a problem, brodie?" one of the kids called. The others laughed. I pretended that I hadn't heard. What the fuck was I doing anyway, staring at teenagers? Did I even have a right to care? Anyway, what kind of a creep wanders through McDonald's, rooting for the romances of random strangers? I looked back at Margarita, bruised and purpled, making duck-lips at her phone and uploading selfies onto Instagram. What she'd told me was so intimate, so close—I felt like I had stolen it. I shouldn't have it, I thought. It's not for me.

I came back to the booth bearing a Big Mac and a milkshake. Some part of me hoped it would end up on my head.

"The agency has filed to suspend your visitation with the children," I finally said. "I'm sorry, but there's nothing I can do."

# 6.

**Ah, there they were: my old familiar ways.** Giving bad news, imposing hardship on the hard-up, tightening the System's vise around a woman's head and squeezing out tears blackened by mascara. For months, I'd done all I could to change who I'd become, or at least to change the way Rita saw me. But that reporter from *The New York Times* was right, at least in part— my job was not to reunite struggling families, but to ensure they stayed separate. To guide them straight to Hell. No, I wasn't any kind of savior, white or otherwise: I was a ferry captain on the River Styx.

"Let me ask you something," the reporter had asked when we'd met for coffee at the 161<sup>st</sup> Street diner across from the family courthouse: "Do you feel like the System works?" She was middle-aged and freckled and wore a teal scrunchy on her wrist. The guts of her tuna salad sandwich dripped in clumps onto the plate. Her name was something like Elizabeth Quimby. I'd just walked in from a successful termination trial across the street, in which I'd testified to Judge Screen that, in the opinion of my agency, Ms. Charles' own unchecked diabetes prevented her from being able to effectively parent her two diabetic children.

"It depends," I'd said.

"On what?"

"On what you think the System's for, I guess."

The reporter wiped a dab of mayonnaise that had been hiding in the corner of her lips. She wrote this answer down, smirking.

"And what do you think about the racial aspect?" she said. "Considering that Children's Future terminates the rights of minority birthparents at a higher clip than any foster care agency in the country?"

I knew she had a point. Of course she did. In all my time at Children's Future, every single one of my birthparents was either Black or Hispanic. Still, I told Quimby that I couldn't comment. Because I couldn't. What could I say?

I can't say for sure how much our racial differences impacted Margarita's case. Would she have preferred to hear the news about her suspended visitation from a Black man? Would a woman of color have cut her heart out with more empathy? Who am I to say?

For our part, Margarita and I discussed race outright only once. It was towards the end of our time together, on one of our long drives back to the agency from Westchester, as our fate began to lick its lips. We'd been listening to Hot 97 on a throwback Thursday, and "Kiss" by Prince came on. Instinctively, I turned up the volume. Rita's eyes were behind dark sunglasses, but I could still feel them rolling through the lenses. "Come on, Lee," she said.

"What?"

"*You* like this song?"

"Why can't *I* like this song? My mother used to play this all the time."

"I don't believe you, that's why."

"You think I'm pretending to like Prince?"

"Yeah, kinda."

For a moment, I was legitimately offended. I'll grant that maybe white boys shouldn't be foster care caseworkers in the Bronx. But I'll be damned if we can't love Prince.

Rita pursed her lips and waggled her slashed eyebrows to let me know she was teasing.

"I'll have you know," I said. "I used to be in a band in college. We played this song all the time. We'd have the whole party going."

"Now I *know* you're lying. 'Cuz if I was at that party with a bunch of Lee Todds playing Prince, I'd jump out the fucking window. Admit it, Lee. You've never heard this song before in your life. You just heard it and thought: 'Oh, I bet *Rita* loves this shit!'"

"That's pretty racist, Rita! I've got plenty of rhythm. Don't stereotype me."

Rita laughed, but there was a shortness to it, a bite—a little hint of warning. I hadn't quite crossed the line, but something in her laugh pointed out I was close. In the rental car speakers, Prince's falsetto went absolutely feral while describing the different types of girls that turn him on.

"You know," she said, turning down the music, "sometimes I wonder how all this might go different, if I was some white girl from New Hampshire."

"What do you mean?"

Softly, in the background, Prince's guitar bent the note until it called out for more. I bit my lip and twisted my head.

Rita lowered her sunglasses, peered at me over the bedazzled rims, her lips not quite smiling. "Like if we met at a party or something."

I couldn't tell what she was getting at. I never could. Was she sincere, or just working me, as usual? And for what? "Uh huh," I said, obtusely.

Rita pulled the ends of her blue hair across her throat, raising her eyebrow at her reflection in the side-mirror. "Nevermind." She turned up the radio. "You can listen to your song."

Prince was screaming now, shrieking, emoting. The guitar line was practically gyrating. The drums kicked up a riot. As 95 slid into Fordham Heights, the background vocals brought the chorus home: *Ain't no particular sign I'm more compatible with...* Rita adjusted her sunglasses. The wind whipped through the car window and sent her hair into a frenzy. *I just want your extra time and your...* Prince made staccato smooching noises.

*...kiss.*

◆

So I can't claim to have much insight into how my clients felt about my race. Still, the day I told her I'd suspended her visitation, I'm pretty sure Rita didn't care whether I was white, black, brown, or purple because, as she put it: "All you cocksuckers are the same." And for my part, had Margarita been a white girl from New Hampshire—some girl from my high school named Katie or Lauren, a ruddy-cheeked Irish-Catholic wearing Ugg boots and a North Face—I would have felt a whole lot less guilty about making her cry in a McDonald's.

Once Rita stormed out of the booth, I sat there alone, sipping on my strawberry milkshake and watching as she walked directly through a fistfight between two teenagers in the parking lot, screaming "MOVE!" as they parted for her to pass. I wondered if this was how executioners felt, peering out through the eyes of their hood as the body made its final twitches. Guilty, yes, and callous, but also maybe, in an irrelevant and disconnected way, a little proud? After all, hadn't I done my job correctly? Good job, Lee. You did it. Go you.

I felt a mitten on my shoulder.

Titi Gigante loomed over me, her eyebrows cocked and angry; Harley stood behind her, holding Jojo on her hip. "What?" Titi asked. "Little girl left already? Come on, Bubba, you couldn't have called to let me know?"

Once we'd all sat down, I explained that there would be a hearing in a few weeks to determine whether or not they would be allowed to see their mother. I'd expected a tearful scene to follow, but Jojo was already fast asleep on his sister's shoulder—and Harley seemed relieved.

"I'm just glad nobody's gonna see me chilling with my mother and my caseworker in McDonald's," she said. "'Cuz that shit is *mad* embarrassing."

"It's OK to feel hurt," I said: monotone, robotic. It is important to validate feelings—I am FeelingsBot 2000. "I'm sure this news is very hurtful."

Harley sucked her teeth. "My lawyer told me all that like two weeks ago. I thought *you* didn't know. Can we go home now, Titi?"

I should have taken her aside and asked more pointed questions. I should have shown her I cared. But the trouble was, it had been so long since I'd made any effort to make an emotional connection with a child on my caseload that I'd forgotten how to do it. And as we all walked out of the McDonald's, and Titi ushered the Sands into the same Uber that had brought them, I realized I didn't know these kids at all. Did they even *want* to go home with their mother? Maybe, instead, they should end up with Ty—who was a criminal, yes, but at least he could provide for them, and was loving in his careless way, according to his wife. Would they have rather been adopted by Titi Gigante? Or what about some other placement entirely, in some other home on the Children's Future roster? How about Ms. Almonte, the secret millionaire in Throgg's Neck, who though a little cold and OCD, would send them both to private school and put their board checks into trust funds? Or maybe I should send them to live with Ty's birthmother in New Jersey, with her savage cough and cartoons playing in the background every time she called to ask for a visit that I was not legally allowed to arrange, given the grisly details of her own case. At least they'd be with family. Point is: I didn't know. How could I have? The few times I'd asked Harley about her feelings, she'd looked at me like I'd just led her to a prison cell and then asked: 'How's the view?' So I had no way of knowing.

Well, actually, that's not true. Titi Gigante did have one way of finding out:

"My nephew, he's real good with computers. He put this app out on her phone so I can read all her texts without her seeing," she'd told me one afternoon at my monthly foster home visit. "Next time he's here, we'll give him your phone so he can add you to the list."

Maybe I should have done it. With the push of a button, I could have downloaded Titi's nephew's spyware—a buggy little app called ParentInfo 2.0—and learned all I would ever need to know about Harley's private life: how she felt about foster care, what she hoped for from her mother, her goals, her dreams, her fears, etc. I could have really helped her if I'd been willing to bend the rules. At the time, I suppose I thought I was being ethical. Or maybe I just liked having the excuse of being ignorant, as in: If I didn't know, what could I have done?

Whatever the reason, I told Titi thanks, but it would be wrong for me to betray the girl's trust.

The old woman chortled warmly. "Hate to break it to you, Bubba. I don't think you got much to betray."

"I meant more like—in theory."

Titi's owlish eyebrows roosted. "You can keep your theories. I like to know what's going on."

◆

A couple weeks before Margarita's court date, I met with Harley and her guidance counselor in a cluttered, narrow office in PS 95 to discuss the girl's recent behavioral issues. The guidance counselor wore a brown shirt and bread-colored tie that made me think of hot dogs. Harley fiddled with the buttons on her uniform. Though her visits were soon going to be suspended, Margarita was still allowed—in fact, mandated—to attend school- and health-related meetings for her children. But today, she didn't show.

While the guidance counselor read off a list of Harley's crimes—stealing jewelry from the teacher's desk, throwing milk cartons in the cafeteria, one vague report of 'horseplay' with a boy beneath the gym bleachers that (to the great relief of all) I asked no follow-up questions about, and more—she twisted a button off her uniform's lapel and flicked it towards a metal trash bin by the desk. It missed her target and hit me in the ear.

As the button skittered across the floor, I made an exaggeratedly pained face in her direction, to show I could take a joke.

Harley sank into her chair.

"It didn't really hurt," I explained later, as Harley and I walked across a gravel parking lot behind the school to the bright purple Acura SUV I'd borrowed from Anita Flores. "The button thing."

"Thank God," said Harley, but though she tried to emulate her mother's sarcasm, she wasn't fully committed to it. There was a hesitance to her hostility. As a result, it sort of seemed to me as though, deep down, she was relieved.

"And look," I said. "I want you to know your mother did want to be there today. I think she was confused about when the suspension..."

"You said what?" Harley had already put her headphones in.

I turned the key in the ignition. She pressed her forehead to the passenger side window and sang quietly along to songs I didn't recognize.

When we came into the foster home, Titi was in the kitchen, sautéing garlic and onions in a shallow pan. Jojo sat at a highchair at the table, gnawing on the wooden base of a pink flamingo figurine. Whenever the little boy saw me, he'd start furiously bicycle-kicking, a wordless baby's warning to keep my distance.

I took the figurine out of his mouth right before he went to swallow it; he wailed in terror.

"How did the meeting go?" said Titi, scraping the pan with a wooden spatula.

Harley planted a kiss on the old woman's cheek. "I got straight A's, Titi," she said. "They're giving me a medal." Titi slapped her backside with the spatula.

(Just last week, I'd tried to tell the old woman to take Harley's grades more seriously. "Believe me," Titi had told me: "School is the last thing on this little girl's mind right now, Bubba. But I guess you wouldn't know...")

When I followed Harley into her room, she leapt ahead to slam shut the drawer in which she kept her teacher's stolen jewelry. Underwear and jeans and sweatshirts lay in heaps on the floor, on the chair, hanging from a bedside lamp. A city of bowls and dishes and water glasses was under construction atop a wooden children's desk: a boomtown for the roaches too. Her bed was covered in a layer of shoes and homework. To most caseworkers, the mess might have raised red flags on their checklists. But I've always felt a kinship with other messy people. It's us against the world.

"I know things have been stressful, lately..." I began, brushing socks off of the desk chair, sitting down. "With the court date coming and all. Not knowing how long it might be until you see your mom again..."

Harley sat on the bed with her shoes still on. Every time she shifted her weight, a piece of paper beneath her crinkled. She seemed to consider what I'd said for a moment. Then she took off her shoes and tossed them on the floor with a flourish, like she was casting jewels into the sea.

"But even if the judge does rule against her," I continued, "all she'll have to do is complete a few classes and then—"

"Can I see your backpack?" Harley interrupted. Before I realized what was happening, she had it in on her lap. She took a marker from the bedstand and touched it to the outside pocket. "I'm really good at drawing. Can I draw you something?"

How much was a new backpack? Not more than the value of Harley possibly hating me a little less, I reasoned. Her asking to deface my property was the closest thing to a tender moment we had ever shared. And the bag was on its last legs anyway— with a fraying handle, broken zipper, and the perpetual smell of pesto from some spilled lunch long ago. Maybe I could call my Mom and get a new one for my birthday.

"How about a...tiger?" I said.

Somehow this was the wrong answer. "A tiger?"

"What's wrong with a tiger?"

"I don't draw tigers."

"Fine."

"What about Wonder Woman? I draw her. My Dad taught me all the superheroes."

I recalled Margarita once telling me that Ty used to draw anime on the hallway walls at Mount Pleasant. Looking pleased, Harley touched the marker to my backpack and started sketching. To me, this felt like progress.

"So, you like superheroes?" I said. "Did you see the new Avengers? Pretty crazy."

Harley looked at me as though I were so stupid that it actually concerned her. Like she was earnestly worried, for my sake, that I'd be able to function in society. "I just draw superheroes, Lee. I don't like them."

"Yeah, me neither," I said, a little quickly. "So lame..."

This wasn't going well. I was losing my momentum. Do kids still say lame? Should I have said 'whack' or 'cheeks?' Do kids still call things 'gay'? I looked around the room for signs of interests that we might have in common: Being messy? Other than the Drake poster on the wall behind her bed, and some stuffed animals inherited from previous tenants, the only mentionable affect in the room was National Geographic poster of a yellow-billed loon grazing in a marshland, but I was pretty sure that that was Titi's. Should I pretend to like Drake?

Finally, Harley looked up from her drawing. "You ever think that this is what she wanted to happen?"

"What do you mean?"

"Margarita's only putting up a fight because she knows she's gonna lose."

I leaned back on her desk and knocked my elbow against a glass of water, which spilled over into a bowl of mac and cheese and created an orange lake.

"Is this why you're acting out in school?" I said.

"Mr. Lapkin's a little bitch."

"He seemed nice enough to me."

"Now that we're gone, she's acting like it's the worst thing that ever happened to her. But, deep down, she just loves to kick and scream. You know, before they came and took us, she left me and Jojo alone in the house for like three days? Then she just came back in one morning like it was nothing. Like 'Oh, hi guys—how you been?'"

As Harley spoke, I opened up the notebook on my lap. This was a mistake—a rookie move, really.

She looked at me as though I'd pulled a gun. "You have to write everything down, Mr. Lee?"

"It's my job to tell the judge what you want to happen."

"Do you have to, though?"

"I'll tell them whatever you want me to."

Her marker scratched to a stop. "If you tell them I don't want to go home, I'll kill myself."

In the long silence that followed, Harley returned her attention to the masterpiece she was drawing on my backpack. A twirl of the wrist. A wince at some errant stroke. I knew I had to choose my next words carefully—but I couldn't think of any to choose from. My mind was a black river: my thoughts were bodies bobbing. Given how frequently I heard this kind of thing from the kids on my caseload, I wouldn't normally take a threat of suicide all that seriously. But now, all I could hear was Ms.

Washington's drunk-ass therapist in my ear: You know they found her *dead,* right?

"So...you do...want to go home then?" I said.

Harley put the cap back on her marker. "I don't want to be involved at all."

She tossed my backpack at me. On the outside pocket, Wonder Woman stuck her fist up to the sky, her legs bursting from tall boots, veins straining in taut muscles, wind-blown hair, and absolutely humongous boobs.

"I can do it better, usually." Harley shrugged humbly.

I holstered my notebook within my pornographic backpack. Later, when I had to go to Family Court to testify on Santiago, I'd have to leave it with the guards outside the courtroom so as to not to offend the judge.

"It's so...detailed." I said.

"That's how my dad taught me."

"I'm impressed. You've got a lot of talent."

"That's what Titi says too."

"You and her get along, don't you?"

"She's cool. I like the way she do potatoes. We watch *Law and Order* every night. Sometimes, Jojo and I stick pieces of paper up her nose while she snores her ass off on the couch. She don't wake up for nothing. Is it true though, what my mom said?"

"What did she say?"

"That foster mothers are only in it for the money?"

"Of course not," I said, although of course it was sometimes true. Really, it depended on the foster mother—and the kid.

"She doesn't love me though."

"What makes you say that?"

"Why should she?"

"Why shouldn't she?"

"Because some nights, when she's sleeping, I think about shaving off her eyebrows. Just whish-swish-whish."

Harley gauged my face for a reaction. I wasn't sure if she was kidding. I laughed, as though this might persuade her that she was.

Through the open door, I heard Titi's nephew come back in from his errands. Keys collapsing in a jingling heap onto the entryway credenza—I've always loved that sound. It sounds like comfort. Like the end of loneliness. Finally, somebody's home.

Jojo's little sneakers pattered across the linoleum. Titi and her nephew had a conversation in that rat-a-tat Dominican dialect unintelligible to white boys from New Hampshire, no matter how many discs we've gotten through in *Rosetta Stone*.

"Hey Lee?" said Harley, a hint of mischief in her smile. She had reached her limit for emotional discussion.

"Yeah?"

"Do you like my mom?"

I coughed. "What do you mean?"

Harley's smile widened. A cruel glint behind her eye. "You don't think she's pretty?"

"I don't think about things like that."

"'Cuz I think that she might have it for you."

I blinked my mind clear. A hard restart. Margarita? The idea was so absurd, I should have just laughed it off.

"Listen, you have to stop sneaking out at night," I said, sounding harsher than I'd intended. "Titi is on to you. The next time you do it, there will be consequences."

The silence stiffened. I cleared my throat drily. Harley put up her hands and twinkled her fingers.

"I'm really scared," she said. Again, not quite pulling off the sarcasm, seeming just a little scared.

"Just stay out of trouble, alright? And don't let her see what's in the drawer."

"Hey Lee?"

"Yeah?"

"Are you going to see her when you go to court?"

I paused in the threshold. On the opposite wall was a photograph of Titi and her late husband hiking the White Mountains of my home state. In the kitchen, she was singing Spanish songs to Jojo, harmonizing with his squeals of disapproval.

"Yeah," I said. "Why?"

Harley brushed her hair contemplatively. The knots groaned as she pulled them.

"Don't tell her that I miss her, alright?" she said. "I mean like...if she asks."

◆

The kitchen smelled of a combination of incense and simmering garlic, and slightly of bag of trash that has been tied and removed from the wastebasket. Titi sat at the table with Jojo on her lap. A pot of rice was on the stovetop; steam spit against the grease-spotted backsplash. Jojo was verging on a tantrum, eyes glassy, squirming and spitting applesauce onto his Power Rangers bib. He babbled like a tiny, fiery preacher, smacking his hands emphatically on the placemat to punctuate his points about the coming rapture. Harley had followed me into the kitchen. She found two string cheeses from the refrigerator and took them back to her bedroom. "Flaquita, would you take the trash out?" Titi called after her. But Harley had already closed the door behind her.

Like all foster mothers, Titi saved the most pressing issues for when I was just about to leave. Problems with their landlords, with Anita Flores, a recent cancer diagnosis, some new evidence that the children might have been molested: all of these conversations were only ever initiated once I'd already sheathed my notebook and begun untangling my headphones, preferably if I had five more homes to hit before nightfall, ideally if I were running late for court. For this reason, I'd usually try to make my exit quickly. Despite all these years of evidence to the contrary, something deep and possibly intractable within me still believed that if I didn't hear about a problem, it might just go away.

Right on time, Titi furrowed her brow. Her eyebrows spread their wings.

"There's something you and me need to talk about, Bubba."

Jojo condemned an offering of applesauce. He clamped his hands around the spoon and howled into it, like a prophet into a megaphone.

"Jojo's birthday party?" I said. "Don't worry, I'll make sure she doesn't know."

"Not that." She craned her neck to check if Harley's door was closed. "Outside. Grab the trash bag, will you? Good boy."

Two teenage boys joined us on the elevator. They were comically high, laughing at the buttons as they lit up. Titi asked them about their father: Was he feeling any better? Did he like her pound cake?

On the sidewalk, she and I conferred beneath a streetlight, surrounded by bags of trash set out for weekly pickup. The black bags surrounded us like a sage council of elders, leaning their pointed heads together to murmur amongst themselves. Across the street, two stray cats yowled and hissed.

"I want to get her on birth control, Lee."

I set the trash bag down beneath the streetlight. It slumped onto its side.

"Sure. I'll get an appointment scheduled with the clinic."

"Thanks."

The streetlight cast the sidewalk in a warm orange light. It wasn't quite dark out yet—the evening was a cool, electric blue. Christmas wreaths watched us from the windows. A silvery banner that hung across a nearby entryway read: *North Pole Alley*. Titi and I both looked at our shadows on the concrete.

"You have to promise me that you won't tell her."

"About the birth control?"

"That I've been reading through her texts."

"Of course."

Titi raised her arms out for a hug. She wore the same perfume as my grandmother, a sweet cinnamon. Maybe that's why I liked her so much.

"I really think you should read them too, Lee."

I broke off our embrace.

"We've been over this."

"No, I mean. There's a lot of stuff in there. A lot, a lot. More than I can tell you."

A shyness came over her. Or maybe it was guilt. A hangdog look on a hawk-like face.

"What are you trying to tell me?"

"Harley's got a boyfriend, Bubba. He's almost your age."

# 7.

**It's this memory in particular that strikes me,** ten years after all of this, five hundred miles north of Southern Boulevard. My daughter is in the car seat, still crying not to go home, but with less and less conviction. The bag of apples rests where the ghost of Margarita fled. As I pull out of the apple orchard's gravel parking lot and begin the long drive back to Lily's mother's house, I think about the pressure behind Titi's eyes that night when she'd told me about Harley's adult boyfriend. How I'd looked up at the building from the sidewalk and seen the little girl watching from her window. How I'd used not knowing what to do as an excuse for doing nothing. I was a kid back then, in some ways—in most ways, I guess. But I'm a man now, undeniably. A father. So what will I do now?

As we get back on the highway, my daughter finally calms. Now she hums the theme to *Mulan*, the only Disney movie I let her watch when she's at my house. I want her to know that women can be warriors. In fact, most have to be, at some point or another—at least as far as I can tell. Plus, the songs are catchy. In the passenger seat, the bag of apples sits upright and alert. I fiddle with the radio and tell myself that everything is alright. My daughter isn't dating any twenty-five-year-olds. She's in good hands with her mother. Tonight, I'll give Sara the apples when I drop Lily off so that they can bake a pie.

When I finally left the Bronx, I could have moved anywhere I wanted. I had no responsibilities. No ties. No bonds at all to anything. I could have moved to California, or Hawaii, or Timbuktu—it didn't matter. But while these New Hampshire winters might be dark and endless, on days like today, as the huge green hills roll up and down outside the window, as we pass stately, spired church-houses and gleaming walls of granite, and the hawks overhead careen in lazy circles and everywhere the red and orange trees shake and laugh and hiss in the golden light of afternoon, I know that I was always meant to end up exactly where I started: home.

There's a pinging sound coming from the dashboard. I'm not used to this car yet, so for a moment, I think there might be something wrong. Then I see, by the speedometer, that it's just that the gas light has come on.

"Where we going?" Lily asks, when I find a truck-stop at the next exit. I've already told her ten times. I pull the car into the port and struggle for a moment to find the button that pops the gas lid. In the port ahead there is a beat-up pick-up truck. There's a motorcycle on our right, a Harley Davidson. The guy filling it doesn't look like a real biker though. His leather jacket looks too new. Probably some Masshole who sells insurance, up here on a weekend ride.

"I'm just getting us some gas," I tell her.

Liliana eyes me skeptically.

"Where?"

"Right here, honey. This is called a gas station. This is where we get the gas for the car."

"Are we going to the rester-not?"

"The what...oh, *restaurant*" She must have noticed the sign across the truck-stop entrance that reads *Ann's Lunch.* "Oh no. I'm sorry kiddo, we don't have time."

"But I'm *hungry* Daddy. I want chocolate milk."

"Lily, I'm sorry. We have to get moving."

"I want to go to the rester-not with you! OK? Please! OK, Daddy? Can I have some some chocolate milk?"

I know I have to have her home by four. And if we're late, her mom will kill me. Still, we've got a long ride ahead of us— and Lily is relentless. She'll whine the whole ride home. Plus, there are few greater joys than watching my daughter drink a chocolate milk. It's like watching an Olympian receive the gold medal they've been working for all their life. She wants it so badly, you just can't help feeling she deserves it.

"We really can't" I say, though already I know it's only a matter of time until I give in.

"Please? OK? I said please."

"I'm just going to call Mommy," I tell her. "If she says so, then we can, OK?"

"I want to go to the rester-not, ok, Daddy? Now. OK?"

I close the door to get some silence. I take out my phone. But as I go to call my wife and let her know, I see I already have two missed calls from her. Something like irritation washes through me, but maybe something deeper. Overhead, a hawk is blown off course by  a stiffening wind. The pines along the roadside shake. It's getting colder out. I think it might snow later. I put the phone back in my pocket and open up the car door.

"Who wants some chocolate milk?" I say, lifting my little one up from the car seat. As we cross the asphalt toward the rester-not, my daughter squeals the squeal of the victorious and points a finger to the sky.

# 8.

**The Bronx County Supreme Court was a monolith of polished limestone,** rising up from East 161<sup>st</sup> Street like a mythical mountain fortress. Gilded panes glittered in the sunlight across the entrance, refracting golden glow onto the sprawling concrete stairway. There was a quote across the stone above the entrance, engraved in letters three feet high. *The Administration of Justice*, it read, *Represents the Noblest Field for the Exercise of Human Capacity*. The day of Margarita's visitation hearing, I shielded my eyes on my way past this courthouse towards my destination, the family courthouse, which was down the hill and around the corner and looked like a gigantic concrete dumpster. The day's proceedings wouldn't start till 9:00, but by 8:15 birthparents were lined up outside the door, flicking cigarettes onto the sidewalk, glaring at passing cars.

I only ever came to court to get or give bad news—and yet, a part of me did enjoy it. It made me feel legitimate, I guess, dressing up in my stepdad's blazer. At the very least, coming to court reminded me that it wasn't for my own twisted pleasure that I spent my days breaking the hearts of New York City's most impoverished single mothers. I did it for the greater good.

The seventh floor was dark and cavernous, a low-slung echoey expanse with marble floors and dirty windows. A congregation of birthparents, kids and rumpled lawyers slouched on rows of wooden pews. Margarita was already there when I arrived, dressed in one of Ty's sweatshirts and blue jeans, sitting beside her lawyer with her back straight, arms crossed, rolling her eyes in response to some advice she'd just been given. I cursed beneath my breath when I saw who she'd been assigned to. I'd been hoping she'd get Morales, a ferocious young Bronx Defender who'd once told a judge that I was so blinded by my biases that I should get a special license plate. She was the sharpest of the bunch. With Morales, Rita might have had a shot. Eli Schluss, that self-righteous little twerp, might have done her right as well. But Margarita was unlucky. She'd gotten Abrams—the same lawyer who'd represented Ms. Washington. She was a wide-eyed young woman with a perpetually exasperated expression and a gigantic orange thermos from which she was always sipping soup. From the looks of it, Rita shared my assessment of her lawyer. This was no time for sipping soup.

I sat down at the end of a crowded pew to review the report I'd written and submitted to the court, which I'd be testifying to the truth of once we got inside. *Ms. Sand has missed four scheduled intake appointments with mental health...* it read. *Ms. Sand's relationship with the subject children appears volatile and strained...* And then: *Ms. Sand, raised the bottle in her hand, aimed it at my head and squeezed....*

"There he is..." I looked up to see Margarita standing over me. Her hair was wet with hairspray, hanging down in crispy ringlets. Her hazel eyes looked golden-green in the sunlight through the dirty windows. She punched me on the arm. "I missed ya, buddy..."

It had been several weeks since we'd last seen each other. In fact, she'd skipped the last three visits—and the meeting with Harley's guidance counselor—since our tete-a-tete at the McDonald's. At first, I'd thought it might have been a miscommunication: that when I'd told her about the motion to suspend her visitation, she'd assumed this meant her visitation had already been suspended. In fact, the suspension would not legally begin until the judge granted the motion, which he would do today. I had tried many times to clear this up: I'd called her phone about twenty times and even stopped by her apartment twice, though both times all I heard inside were men's voices. Last week, I'd taken the kids shopping at the Foot Locker down the street rather than make them wait around in the Children's Future lobby for a visit that I knew she wouldn't show for. "I told you, didn't I?" Harley had said, shoving Jojo's tiny feet into a men's size 13 and filming his crying for TikTok.

"I thought I was a cocksucker," I said to Rita now, as she slipped in beside me in the pew.

"Oh yeah?"

"No—that's what you called me, remember? The last time I called?"

"Ah, well. You know how I get."

Rita sat down beside me in the pew. I turned the court report facedown on my lap. "Your eye looks better," I said.

"You ever had a bruise before, Lee? They go away, you know."

"You should be sitting with your lawyer. You can go over your strategy together. Plan out how you're going to beat me in there."

Margarita sucked her teeth in Abrams's direction. The lawyer closed her eyes as she took a healthy pull of soup.

"Her? Listen, I don't think baby girl is wrapped too tight. She's over there talking to me about the fucking constitution. I'm like sweetheart, I poured juice on this motherfucker's head. The one guy whose head you don't pour juice on! What'd I think was going to happen?"

"So, you're not mad at me?"

I'd been trying to match her glibness, but as I'd said that, my voice contained a little warble. Odd, I know: I was about to devastate this woman, to crush her throat beneath my step, and here I was, sounding like a toddler apologizing to his mother after a tantrum at the Stop and Shop.

Margarita shrugged.

"Nah, I am. You suck, Lee. But so does everybody. I suck too. Ty sucks fucking dick. Anyway, it doesn't matter. I'm gonna get my visits back."

"Is that what Abrams said?"

"That's what I said. I got a plan."

"What's that?"

"You'll see."

Her playful manner made me nervous. For a moment there, I'd thought that her friendliness might have meant that there was still hope for our relationship. Maybe, I'd thought, she had assessed the situation and seen my side of things. She would endure the court's inevitable punishment and come to understand that my testimony was not a betrayal, but the wake-up call she needed. Now, I realized that the only reason for her good mood was because she didn't understand how bleak things really were. Either that or she'd snuck in a pipe bomb past the metal detectors.

"AAAALL PARTIES ON MAAAAAARGARITA SAND!" said the court officer, throwing the double doors wide. He sounded like a train conductor. The train to hell was leaving.

My heart beat a spastic rhythm. I tapped my shoes in 7/4. God, I was such a traitor. At least Brutus believed that he was doing something noble. At least Judas was well-paid. How many more times could I really do this? I thought, for the thousandth time. Maybe tomorrow, I'd put in my notice. I could take the Greyhound up to Manchester and be working for my stepdad's brokerage by the weekend. Come next Monday, I'll be walking a retiree through a living room that needs a reno: sure, it could use a little work, but I promise you, the bones are good.

As we followed the court officer into an anteroom outside the courtroom and waited there a few moments for the case before us to clear out, I felt a tug on my elbow. Margarita hung on my arm—an absent, far-off look in her eyes.

"You ok?" I said.

She didn't realize she'd been doing it. "Sorry," she said, shaking her head back to the present.

The anteroom was filling now—my attorney and the law guardian were discussing a softball league that both their daughters played in. Abrams came in, hustling and bustling, a massive file in one arm, papers sprouting loose, cradling her thermos like a baby. Margarita stepped from sneaker to sneaker, smoothed her hair back with one hand.

"Hey," I said. "Whatever happens in there...you've been through worse than this before, right?"

Margarita mumbled softly:

"I told you. I got a plan."

When Abrams saw us talking, she gave me the same disdainful look that all the public defenders gave to caseworkers. Like I'd just said the N-word at a party.

"You ready, girlie?" she said to Margarita. "We're gonna crush in there."

The doors to the courtroom opened. The crowd shuffled forward, but Margarita didn't move. She closed her eyes a moment, breathed in deep, exhaled.

"You're fired, baby," she said to Abrams, and strode through the doors alone.

◆

Long odds inspire grand delusions. Over the years, I'd seen about a dozen birthparents represent themselves in family court. And though, I'd always admired their bravado, it usually led to the defendant being hauled out mid-diatribe by the court officers, followed by a quick, uncontested order from the judge to dismantle their family *in absentia*. So when Margarita strode into the courtroom alone, shooting me a wink, my soul slunk out the bottom of my khakis. Really, to call Part 13 a 'courtroom' would be an exaggeration—it was more like court-closet. Birthparents, caseworkers and lawyers all sat at a single table—

so close we could have shared a pizza. My attorney, DiBenedetto, dressed in an electric blue suit that seemed a little much for family court, gave me a rakish, knowing grin. This was the first of many motions that we would win together.

Hon. Judge L. Screen sat at a desk at the front of the courtroom, frowning at a stack of papers. He had a large, fleshy face with jowly cheeks and wide-set eyes that radiated incredulity, a salt-and-pepper jheri curl, and a golden hoop earring. Party Judge, Anita Flores called him, on account of the hairstyle and the earring, but the nickname didn't really fit. His gaze was deathly serious. A few months back, Party Judge and I had terminated the parental rights of Ms. Washington right at this very table. "Why you lyin' Lee? Why you lyin'?" she'd muttered over and over, holding Abrams' hand beneath the table while I spoke the truth into the microphone.

The judge pressed a button and a giant digital clock on his desk began counting backwards from thirty minutes.

"The court," began the judge, "has been informed that Ms. Sand has decided to represent herself today at this motion hearing. Is that correct?"

Margarita's voice was soft and wavering. She stared down at the table.

"Uh huh," she said.

Usually, birthparents who defended themselves came in hot, rolling their shoulders like gladiators begging Nero for more lions. But Rita stared down at her sneakers.

"Ms. Sand," said Screen, slowly, quizzically, "I do feel compelled to say this is customarily not seen as a wise choice, to defend oneself."

Margarita blinked. She breathed in heavy. 25:00, read the clock, in broad red letters. 24:45. In the few months I had known her, I'd seen her show every emotion you could think of —but I'd never seen her scared.

"I wasn't getting nothing from my lawyer, your honor sir," she said; speaking in the same dulled out, uncertain voice she used for imitations of her husband, when she'd try to make her daughter laugh: "It's like, I call her, she don't answer. I leave a message, she don't call me back. I know these lawyers is free and y'all get what you pay for, your honor sir, but I'm thinking if none of y'all want to help me at least I can try and help myself. These are my children y'all saying I can't see, after all, your honor sir."

The words hung in the air for twenty-seven seconds, according to the clock. The judge turned the pages of my court report, marking passages with red pen.

"What is the highest grade you've completed, Ms. Sand?"

Margarita twisted the end of her braid around her finger as the clock counted off the seconds. 22:15. 22:10...22:05.

"Eighth, your honor sir. No, ninth. When is it when they start teaching about all the triangles?"

My lawyer stood up. With his tailored suit and pointed chin, he looked a little like the Devil.

"Your honor," he said, "I'd like to remind the court that we have only thirty minutes allotted for this hearing. The agency very strongly requests that you make a ruling on this motion today, based on the evidence submitted by the caseworker. As you can see, his report is quite thorough."

"Thank you, Mr. DeBenedetto," Judge Screen cut off the lawyer with a prim smile. "Given that I received the report three minutes ago, I trust you'll allow some time for me to think it over."

This had been the extent of my rebellion. To send the report slightly later than I should have, as a form of protest against the System I was part of. What a badass.

"I apologize for that, sir," I said. "I meant to email it last night but..."

"That's fine, Mr. Todd. We all know you're trying very hard. But if Ms. Sand here has chosen to represent herself, it is incumbent on me to decide whether or not she is capable of doing so. We cannot hold a hearing if she does not have adequate representation. Ms. Sand, before I grant your request I want to make sure you are fully cognizant of the implications of your decision."

Margarita kept her eyes low. She pretended to shuffle through papers on the table. 19:00, read the clock. 18:55. 18:52.

"Cog-ni-what now?"

"Your honor, the report, please." My lawyer was getting shrill: "I'd like to get to my caseworker's testimony. Harley and Jojo Sand should not have to be subjected to the trauma of any more visits on account of this court's delays. The agency has no objection to Ms. Sand representing herself..."

"Yes, please, your honor, sir. I think I could do a real good job...."

The judge's eyes fell on Margarita now. She shuffled papers around on the table absently.

At last, the judge gave way.

"You know what?" he said. "It's already 4:42, and even if Ms. Sand were to decide to take a new lawyer, by the time we get somebody from Bronx Defenders down here we'll be out of time anyway. Counsel, Ms. Sand, I apologize, but I am going to have to pick a short adjourn date, at which point I will deal with any matters relating to visitation. In the interim, Ms. Sand, I want you to think long and hard about whether you actually want to proceed this way, without legal guidance, on your own...OK? I must say, you would be doing yourself a grave disservice not to explore the best possible legal options available for you and your family."

"Th-thank you, your honor sir, I w-will."

"We will resolve this matter at the adjourn date," said the judge. "I should be able to find an available slot sometime in the next few days."

Lawyers grumbled, shuffled papers, reached into their bags. Margarita kept her eyes on the court report on the desk in front of us, took out a pen and scribbled something in the margins. Maybe a note on future strategy, I thought, squinting at her loopy handwriting—some counterpoint she did not want to forget. The first letter was an *S*. Margarita felt me watching her and looked up, eyes like a magician's showing me my card. I read the rest of what she'd written: *U C K* then *A* then *D*...

◆

Party Judge's affect got more casual once he'd relieved himself of the duty of making a decision. You could almost feel him loosen up.

"Ok, ok, now, I want to leave some time to pick the adjourn date. I've got a few dates later this week. How about Thursday, 11:30-12:00?"

"No good, your honor, sorry. I'm on intake," said my lawyer.

"Right, right. How about 4:30, same day?"

"Works for me."

"Can't do it," said the law guardian, a friendly, green-eyed Indian woman whose name I can't remember. "I have to leave early that day."

"Alright then. Moving on to next week. Only time the court has available is Wednesday 9-9:30?"

"Darn. I have a trial."

"Well, the next week is Christmas week. We all know how tough it is to schedule things around the holidays. So we're moving into January now. How about January 7th? The court has the whole afternoon open."

"Tuesday afternoons are tough for me, your honor. I have my kids that day."

"How about January...oh boy. January 25th? 10:30?"

"Works for me."

"Here too."

"Ok then. The motion will be heard on—"

"My bad. I have a TPR. I could do 3 PM that same day, though. Does that work?"

"It does not. February 14th? 2:00-2:30?"

"No good, your honor."

"February 16th? 2:15?"

"Darn it."

"March 1st? 9:00?"

"I'm off that whole week, your honor."

"March 2nd?"

"That's still..."

"Right. How about the Ides of March?"

"What's that, your honor?"

"March 15th."

"No good."

"April 10th, afternoon?"

"Trial."

"May...Jesus. May 27th?"

"That's Memorial Day, your honor."

"Right, right, right..."

◆

As this drama descended into farce, I acted disappointed to my lawyer, and later too, for Anita Flores, in her darkened office lair. But internally, as the red numbers on the courtroom clock counted down to zero, as Margarita nudged my elbow to make sure I'd seen a doodle she'd drawn of what I think was supposed to be me being subjected to a sex act and crying 'WAHHH', as the judge declared—against all reason—that we would decide the matter on May 28th, a solid five months in the future, and that in the interim Children's Future would remain obligated to facilitate visitation between Margarita and her children, I was dancing on the table. I was ripping off my button-down, planting a kiss on Party Judge's cheek. And yeah, tomorrow I'd still have to terminate the Mathis family. Later that week, I'd remove a screaming Ivan Santiago from another foster home because his new foster mother had been deported. But at least for a day, the executioner was on vacation. That courtroom felt like a beach in the Bahamas.

Afterward, I walked out into the weak rays of the early winter sun and headed down 161st Street toward the stadium to catch the 4-train. The gold trim of the Supreme Courthouse glittered in the fading sunlight. Maybe, the System wasn't all-powerful after all, I thought. Maybe Harley had been wrong about her mother. Maybe I should give Estelle another call...

Margarita walked a few blocks ahead of me on the sidewalk, her red hair burning brightly amidst the fog of bobbing blue and gray winter hats. She'd gone ahead of me out of the courtroom, before I'd had the chance to say congratulations. But she didn't walk straight to the subway. Instead, she turned off Grand Concourse up 158th, walking with a new limp I knew better than to ask about, and made her way through a small park in the shadow of the subway line.

I found her past the base of a giant stone statue in the plaza—a tribute to some local civil rights figure I'd never heard of. She was sitting on a bench, feeding a flock of pigeons from a bag of potato chips.

"You following me?" she said, when she saw that I was coming.

"You really kicked our ass in there," I said, breathless. "May 28th! Can you believe it?"

She threw a potato chip onto the concrete. Pigeons scrabbled on the ground.

"That's Bronx Court for you, I guess," she said.

The wind rose, sculling dead leaves across the concrete. A cruiser pulled to the curb. A crowd of teenagers scattered like a firework. Margarita looked past my shoulder, this way and that, counting the cars honking on East 158th. The stone eyes of the overlooking statue made me uneasy. A block down, the 4-train hurtled through the sky.

I tried again to congratulate her: to say her kids would be so happy. That Anita Flores would be so pissed. But something had come over her. Her mood had shifted with the wind. As I spoke, she nodded, not in agreement, but like my words confirmed some dirty secret that she'd long suspected. When she ran out of potato chips, she tossed the bag right on the ground.

"About that court report," I said. "I know it might have seemed kind of harsh. But like I told you—if I'd refused to write it, Anita Flores would have just moved me off the case, and then you'd have some other worker. So I figured the best thing would be..."

"I don't really give a fuck what you figured, Lee."

"No, I know. I know you don't. But it's just been so long since..."

Margarita sniffed.

"I'm just one of your cases, man. I know what it is."

"That's not— "

"You know what your problem is Lee? You won't just be what you are. If you're gonna do something, do it. Don't apologize. Don't pretend. Just be a man, you know?"

I didn't know what to do with that, so I just let it go.

"Listen," I said. "There's something we need to talk about. It's Harley. I don't want you to freak out but—"

"What, Ms. Thing dating twenty-five-year-olds?" The pigeons cooed. Margarita stared up at the statue: the two exchanged stone-faced expressions. "She can do what she wants. You think she's gonna listen to me?"

I stared at her for half a minute. She returned her attention to the pigeons. Today was the most rousing victory I'd ever witnessed a birthparent win in court. But I'd never seen her so defeated.

"Are you alright?" I asked her.

"Are we done here, bro? I'm supposed to meet someone."

There was no point pushing it any further. I told her it was all right, we could talk later, and that I hoped to see her at the next visit. I turned down the street, but caught one heel against my toe.

"You know," I said, turning back. "Harley really misses you."

Margarita gave that nod again—acknowledgement but not agreement. A cold wind wrapped a strand of red across her chin. The empty bag of potato chips loop-de-looped out towards the street.

# 9.

**Up until this point, I'd felt like I had a pretty good understanding of who Margarita was.** Maybe I didn't really know what made her tick, but at the very least, in most situations, I knew how she'd react. For instance, if Anita Flores stopped by the visiting room to see how things were going, Rita would suck her teeth, or make faces at her fingernails, or ask Harley if she smelled something funny just now. Like clockwork, if Jojo ran too quickly into Titi's arms one week, the next, Rita would demand I schedule a visual check with the clinic pediatrician to look into some imaginary bruises on her baby's inner thigh. These reactions had a kind of logic to them. But in the aftermath of her victory in Judge Screen's courtroom, Margarita's behavior stopped making any sense at all. She cancelled the next few family visits—the same ones she'd just clawed back from the System's clutches. She informed her therapist that she'd been cured, then threw a lamp out of the lobby window. I got a garbled voice message from her one day, asking if she could borrow $100 from me personally—but when I called back, her phone was out of minutes. At first, I told myself that it just was some misfiring mental piston; a symptom of Bipolar II, or borderline personality, or some other mental health disorder that I wasn't qualified to understand. This wasn't the Margarita I knew, I told myself. As though I could ever really know her.

"Didn't I tell you this would happen?" Harley said one day, after her mother failed to accompany her to her appointment with the Children's Future sexual health counselor on the third floor. Titi was at a meeting with Jojo's speech therapist, so the task had come to me.

"She's self-sabotaging," I said. "It doesn't mean that she doesn't want to see you."

Caseworkers used say that all the time about our birthparents. *Self-sabotage.* I think that we just liked the way it sounded. Classy. French.

"Yeah well, you ain't seen nothing yet," said Harley.

The sexual health counselor came out into the lobby and called out Harley's name. I asked if Harley wanted me to come in with her. "That's just what I want," she said. "That would be great, Lee." Her sarcasm did land this time.

When Margarita finally called, she sounded like she'd just washed ashore—her voice was weak and wet and groggy. "I'm all fucked up, Lee. Can you come over?" she said. "I can explain it all in person."

Somehow, the call filled me with hope. Hope for what? I didn't know. Was I still rooting for her now, despite myself, despite *her*self? No. Of course not. At least that's what I told myself. She'd ditched her family for a month—just completely abandoned her responsibilities. She must have known how much that would hurt her children, and yet clearly didn't care. Still, here I was, feeling like my life had purpose again just because she'd called. Of course, this turned out to be just another of my grand delusions. When I showed up to Rita's place that night, I was the last thing in the world she needed. And afterward, when I emerged from the heat of her apartment, I felt like I might turn to smoke.

◆

All my life, I've been able to tell when I'm dreaming. In the middle of a nightmare, I'll be about to career over the edge of some cliff, or murder or get murdered by my mother, or be swimming in a giant jar of pickle juice with the lid about to get screwed on, when suddenly I'll realize: there's no need to panic, soon enough, I'll wake up on my air mattress and all this will go away. This was how I felt in the weeks that followed that birth home visit to Rita's apartment: there was no reason to be upset; none of this was really happening. Meanwhile, my eye-twitch popped up again, out of nowhere, like a birthfather on parole. Margarita's parenting class instructor called to say she'd dropped out of her Wednesday classes. She stopped bothering to call ahead and cancel visits and now just simply didn't show. "You call me next time your little friend bothers to show up," Titi told me one day in the Children's Future lobby, as Harley twiddled on her phone and Jojo chased another toddler across the carpet and the clock hit 4:15. "This is torture for them, Bub." Rita's phone was disconnected, so my only hope to re-establish contact would have been to go back to her apartment, the scene of our collective shame. If I had had the courage to face her, I would have grabbed her by her bony shoulders: "Get yourself together!" I would scream. "Don't you love your children? Don't you care about them at all?" But of course, I didn't do that. What would be the point? Any moment now, I would wake up on my air mattress, screaming, drenched in sweat, but with my soul still clean.

As Christmas passed and dirty snowbanks began to mount along the sidewalks, I found myself increasingly yearning for the life I'd had before Children's Future. Back before I started taking everything so goddamn seriously. When, right out of college, high on the thrill of being young and broke in the Big City, Estelle and I and all my other hipster friends would bop around Brooklyn and the Lower East Side, playing music and pub trivia, surviving on $5 pickleback whiskey shots and late-night pizza slices, passing out on the L-train home. Life felt so easy then, full of possibilities, without stakes. Over the past few years, I'd receded from this scene: I was too tired, I guess, and guilty, and the imbalance of carrying a full caseload in my head during weightless, carefree nights left me with this perpetual vertiginous feeling—a wobbling in my soul I couldn't shake.

About a month after what had happened with Margarita though, an old pal of mine, Jack, texted me to say he was having a party out in Bushwick. At first, I didn't answer. In fact, I'd settled in for another night of drinking Fireball on my air mattress, savoring the smell of the restaurant next door through my opened window while eating cold tortillas and watching *Arrested Development* on the TV perched atop my mini fridge. Outside my door, I heard my three roommates come home from class—and soon enough, I could hear them in the living room, sitting barefoot on the couch and having one of their self-aggrandizing roundtables about the rights of unionized teaching assistants at Columbia or whatever the fuck. Suddenly it hit me: I couldn't take this for another second. I'd been hiding out too long in this dingy, temporary hovel, a refugee from my own social circle. And for what? Wasn't all this self-loathing getting self-indulgent? And was it such an inequity to live in my own world? So I texted Jack back for the address and apologized for ghosting him the past nine months.

The party was somewhere out in Bushwick, three trains away from Morningside Heights. I was very drunk when I arrived.

I came up the freight elevator of the converted loft building and I put my wine bottle on the kitchen counter. My old friends were all together in a high-ceilinged living room with exposed brick on the far wall and flimsy Wayfair floor lamps. The soft, comforting tones of Drake came through the speaker. *Settlers of Catan* lay splayed out on a low coffee-table, but nobody was playing. The room buzzed with talk of politics and prestige TV. My old friends were all there. Liza. Dave. Schmitty. Genevieve. A few guys from that last band that I'd been in: The Plaid Diaspora. We used to play shows to, like, eleven people in lofts like this all over Bushwick. God, we sucked so hard. As my old friends greeted me with hugs and handshakes and 'Hey Todd-O, where ya been's?' I felt like an astronaut, the sole survivor of some catastrophic space voyage, finally coming back to Earth. No one asked about my job. No one asked about Estelle. Instead, we reminisced about late nights and early mornings, joked about our disappointing twenties, then moved on to gossip—did you hear that Marjorie got pregnant? And Noah finally came out.

Someone passed around lines of cocaine.

I almost couldn't believe how much fun I was having. Was this all right? Was this OK? As the wine and gossip and drugs flowed, I began to feel like my old self again. The happy-go-lucky, goofball guitarist that I used to be—my mother's happy little boy. And really—why *had* I been taking all of this so seriously, I asked myself? So some mentally unwell Puerto Rican woman in the Bronx doesn't love her children—at least not in the way they need her to—whoop-dee-fucking-do! I mean, yeah, it's sad, but—so? She wasn't *my* mother. They weren't *my* kids. No, even my guilt for what had happened with Margarita was just another posture. Self-flagellation for the sake of self-importance. Did I blame myself every time some plane crashed in Indonesia? Was it my fault if some lunatic in Texas took an AR-15 to the mall? No. Monday morning, I could walk into Anita Flores's office and say 'peace' to all the Crayola monsters tacked up on her wall. I'd take the 5-train home, and by the time I got back to my sublet, the Sands would cease to exist for me in any practical sense. They'd be an earthquake in Pakistan. A quadruple murder in Kentucky. I would never set foot in the Bronx again, unless some brunch spot opened up in Mott Haven, or I got Red Sox-Yankees tickets next time my sister visited. No, in my new, carefree life, I'd go to parties like this every Friday. I'd get a job bartending at Jack's bar, study for the LSAT in Central Park in the daytime with a new girlfriend that I met on Bumble. I would do as much cocaine as humanly possible, and it would all be fine.

This feeling lasted until the clouds of cocaine parted. But as the buzzing in my bloodstream settled to a grinding whir, I heard a whisper in my ear. I don't know what brought it on.

Maybe it was the sight of my big, dumb face in the coke mirror. Maybe she'd been lurking in the background all night, waiting, with her usual theatricality, for the perfect cue to burst onto the stage. Whatever the reason, as I looked about the party, laughing, snorting, wondering if my heart might stop, I felt Margarita's presence. I thought of her that one night in her apartment, looking through the peephole of her door as I'd stood out in the hallway. How had I looked to her? I thought of the wave of sickness she must have felt. Of her closing her eyes, steeling herself with one last Xanax from the bottle, and fumbling with the door chain to let me in. "Look who it is," she'd said, slurring slightly, dressed in a black bathrobe, leaning on one hip. "I knew you couldn't wait to see me, right?"

Back at the party I must have groaned aloud—or maybe I just sighed. My friends were looking at me funny. Liza—who used to play movie trivia with me on Wednesday nights in Williamsburg—gave me a sympathetic look.

"So how have you been holding up, these days, Todd-O?" she said. "Since... you know, with Estelle?" Todd-O had been my nickname back in college. I don't know what it is about me: everywhere I go, I get a new one.

"Es...telle?" I said, like an alien sounding out the human tongue.

Dave, who I hadn't seen in years, but seemed to have been briefed on the details of my failed engagement, seemed uncomfortable with the ensuing pause. "Have you guys tried these little shrimp?" he said, indicating three cocktail shrimps he'd collected on a paper plate. "They're really good."

For a few moments, the conversation turned to shrimp. The shrimp were good, it was agreed. How do you like the shrimp, Lee? someone asked. But I wasn't there. I was sitting at a kitchen table in the Bronx, across from Margarita. Her eyelids were heavy, her skin a pall. She kept letting out these quiet, inward, sick-sweet little girlish giggles that sounded nothing like herself at all.

"Aren't you going to record?" I'd asked her nervously, with a half-serious look at her phone. Rita stared at a space beyond my shoulder.

The radiator wheezed itself awake; the pipe above her refrigerator hissed and spit.

"You remember when Ty almost found us in here together?" she said.

I grabbed two shrimps off of Liza's plate and made them joust with each other. I made desperate little laser noises. The people on the couch cocked their heads to the side in unison. I did another line of cocaine. My chest tightened. That metallic, inky flavor dripped from my sinuses into my throat. I felt like my brain was popping open. "Cocaine is underrated isn't it?" I said. "We should really do it more."

"Are you OK?" said Liza.

I felt a sudden urge to flee. To take the bus home to New Hampshire. Or Pennsylvania. Or off a bridge into the Hudson. Any place would do. Any place where I wouldn't be how Margarita saw me. What she thought I didn't have the guts to be. How could I explain this to my friends? All these decent people, with decent thoughts and decent lives, who never have to hurt anybody. How could I make them understand? When I looked up at them, they were looking past me. Over my shoulder. Toward the door.

"Oh my gosh," said someone, with a sympathetic grimace in my direction. "Estelle!"

◆

She sauntered in like this was her apartment. Like these were all her friends. This was the first time I'd seen her since I'd packed the last of my things into the U-Haul and declined her gracious offer of what would have been a pretty pathetic goodbye brunch. Now, in normal circumstances, I would have had no desire to make things uncomfortable for her. I would have excused myself from the festivities as quietly as I had from the relationship. But seeing the way she stood now by the stereo, her hair cut short and spiky, wearing those same black jeans she'd worn the night I'd proposed to her, her fingers interlocked so lovingly, so—goddamnit—dependently with Craig's, I felt a sudden urge to make a scene. I forgot about Margarita, if only for a second. It was a relief to feel my own anguish for once. So pure. So painful. Mine.

Next thing I knew I was in the kitchen to fix a drink, and there they were again. "Look who it is," I said, and Estelle acted as though she hadn't seen me yet, that I must have imagined the three times our gazes had already crossed. The way she'd ducked her head into his shoulder made me want to stick toothpicks in my eyes and serve them to her as hors d'oeuvres.

"I just wanted to say a quick hello," I said, "so it's not weird."

Estelle gave me a brittle hug—a mannequin's embrace. Had she always felt so hollow? Craig shook my hand firmly. Yes, I thought. Yes! So awkward—so uncomfortable. Still, I wanted more. What could I do to make this worse? Puke on my button-down? Try and kiss Craig?

"It's nice to see you, Lee," said Estelle.

"How you been, dude?" said Craig.

At the time this was my life's great tragic romance. And yet, and yet—how could they be so cordial? So almost professional, like we all used to work in the same marketing department. And me too—I just stood there taking it. Why? What was I doing? Shaking their hands, grinning, laughing: Oh yes, nice to see too? Soon enough, I was asking of their recent vacation to her parents' lake house in Vermont. How was the weather? How are your parents? Did you make tender love out on the dock beneath the moonlight, your ecstatic cries echoing across the silent lake? Tell me more! More, please! More!

But it wasn't working. This pain wasn't enough to keep me in the present.

Back in her apartment, Rita lit a cigarette, took two pulls, and put it out. The radiator clacked, louder, louder. Clack. Clack. CLACK CLACK. The pipe sprayed like a sauna. "Will you just tell me what's the matter, Rita?" I asked her. "You don't seem like yourself tonight."

"Who do I seem like, Todd?"

She raised her eyes to meet mine. The stars on her face looked like a spreading mold. She got up from the table, stepping lightly on her cracking ankles, bathrobe swishing. I took out my notebook and started drawing shaky spirals. As she came behind me, I caught the whiff of strawberry vanilla shampoo. Heard the sound of something slipping. "What are you doing?" I asked, without turning. Did I already know? Had I known all along? She was on my lap before I realized what was happening, naked save for a pair of zebra-striped underwear with a little black bow beneath her belly-button. Her thighs were soft and warm and a little slick with lotion. She put her hand across my mouth to stifle up my protests. Her knees clenched my hipbones. Her palm was cold and damp. "This is what you wanted, right?" Her tongue flicked in my ear. "You gonna be a man, or what?"

"Should we all do a shot?" said Craig. I must have been standing there in the kitchen, smiling with blank maturity for a solid thirty seconds. He poured three shots of Fireball and dispensed them amongst the triangle.

Margarita moved her hand off my mouth, long nails dragging gently across the stubble on my throat. She moved her face towards mine. I tried to move, to free myself, but she had me pinned. For just a moment, not more than a couple seconds, but still a beat too long, my mind excused itself from my body, floated up with the smoke lifting from the ashtray, looked down at what was happening from a bird's eye view. Stop this! I screamed silently, as Margarita began to buck her hips gently, expertly, back and forth, back and forth—as she reared her neck to the ceiling, pressing her clammy breasts against my turning cheek, reaching between my legs with her other hand. This isn't you, I screamed. This isn't you! And, yet—and yet—who else was I? Were these not my eyes she was looking into, my lips that hers were searching for, as in her eyes, dread replaced determination, and with steady fingers, she undid the buckle of my belt and started pulling at my zipper...

With a whoosh, I returned into my body. Shoved her off my lap. She tumbled backwards, smacked the back of her head on the table. "What the fuck are you doing?" I yelled. She was sobbing now, shaking, naked, crumpled on the floor. "I'll do anything you want me to," she said softly, biting her forearm, sobbing. "Anything for them."

I lifted the shotglass Craig had poured me. Margarita cried and cried. I zipped up my pants. Wiped off her lipstick with my shirtsleeve. The radiator clacked and pounded. I ran out of her apartment, back to safety, back to my air mattress, back to a world where I could tell myself this hadn't happened. For weeks now, I'd thought it was the most hopeless thing I'd ever been a part of. But now as I stood before my ex-fiancee and her boyfriend, I saw things in another light.

"To you guys," I said.

"No, Lee," Estelle said. "To you..."

I felt a rising within me—a wild, freeing feeling. I thought of Margarita on the floor, shaking, moaning: please, Lee, please, please. Please just give me back my babies. I'll do anything you want. Now, I thought: If only I could see her again, I would tell her: it's OK. I get it now. It isn't hopeless. How could I have been so blind? This was LOVE, true love, in all its brutal majesty; heedless and headlong and full of beauty and pain and sacrifice. It was seedy, yes, but glorious. It was an honor to behold.

"Are you alright, dude?" Craig began.

Her love for them was flowing through me. It was absolute. Almighty. It was the love of every mother I had ever wronged, aching like an echo through all time.

I raised my glass to meet Craig's. Beneath the table, Margarita took my hand. I lifted her to her feet. She took my glass of Fireball and threw it in Craig's eyes.

# 10.

**Two days later, I strode through the broken door to Margarita's building,** past the tile mosaic of the Italian fishing port and stoned teenagers in the lobby. Every object that I looked at had a spinning, scintillating halo. Sparks fizzled in the corners of my vision, a brilliant, holy light. And while these may have been the lingering effects of Craig's ferocious, retaliatory headbutt, as I climbed the huddled, crooked stairs to Rita's apartment, I felt better than I ever had. Gone were the bitterness and depression I'd lapsed back into since her disappearance. Now when I thought over the grim, unseemly morass of misunderstandings that had led her, squirming and reluctant and naked to my lap, all I saw was golden light. I had to stop a few times to catch my balance in the hallway—since Craig's headbutt, narrow spaces gave me vertigo. Still, when I reached the door to her apartment, I knocked proudly, triumphantly, thinking: the second she opens up, the both of us are free.

For a long time, nobody answered. I knocked until my knuckles ached. I pounded loud enough to raise the dead. I even said a little prayer—though I've been agnostic ever since my mother made me be an altar boy. At last, just as I was starting to get desperate, I heard a stirring from within.

"Rita!" I said, into the pane. "Rita! It's me. Don't worry! I just came by to talk."

I could picture her on the other side, sharing glances with her fingernails, giving the side-eye to the door. And why should she trust me? All this time that I'd fancied myself her only hope to get her kids back, she'd thought I was trying to exchange them for a blowjob. That that's the kind of man I was.

"You don't have to let me in," I said. My voice bounced around the narrow, tiled hallway, came back around and slapped me in the head. Since the party, loud noises had made me want to vomit. "I'm here to say I'm on your side. About the other night. You've got nothing at all to be ashamed about. You did what any mother would, if they thought it would get their children back."

I could feel her looking at me through the keyhole. I could sense her fear on the other side. Her disappearance made perfect sense now. The way she'd sabotaged every bit of progress that the System had allowed. To her, my every act of lenience, every look of understanding, every supportive word, had seemed like nothing more than the leery compliments of a drunken foster father, looming in the threshold to her bedroom while she closed her eyes to pray.

"I know that maybe in your life, men might act a certain way. So why should I be any different? But from the bottom of my heart, Rita—I swear to you. My only goal is to do what's best for your children. I want to *help* you, not...well, you know. I've never wanted anything but that. To help."

At last I heard a click. The door caught on the chain.

"Rita! Rita! Thank God! Thank God!"

The door closed again. Then the lock unclasped. The door swung open.

The woman who stood before me was in her mid-thirties, wearing teal hospital scrubs and twisting on an earring. Behind her, two little kids argued at the breakfast table. The TV played the morning news.

"I'm looking for Margarita Sand?" I said.

The threshold went topsy-turvy, tilting back and forth, upside down. The lights and sounds melded to a blaring chime. I had to clutch my knees to stop from falling over. This woman looked at me in abject terror—and I remembered then that both my eyes were still black and swollen from the headbutt, cheeks purplish and yellow. I looked like a monster in her doorway.

"I'm sorry, sir," she said, through the closing door. Her accent was Caribbean. "We just moved in here last week."

◆

Margarita's landlord, a helpful Dominican woman with a leopard-print sweater and a colostomy bag, lived on the first floor of the building. When I told her I was with child welfare services and I was looking for a client, she led me into her apartment, to a cramped desk shared by a computer and a hamster cage. It must have been this woman's husband that Margarita slept with for a discount on the rent—Cenia here didn't strike me as the type. In the corner of the apartment, a bright red parrot eyed me from a golden cage that glinted in the sunlight through the window. All the houseplants were dead.

"Carrot-top, right?" said the woman, clicking a boxy mouse from 1985. There's something so pleasant about a Spanish accent on an older woman. She pulled up an Excel spreadsheet. "Your girl was six months behind on rent..."

Margarita hadn't left a forwarding address. She wasn't in any of the shelters I searched around the Bronx and Harlem, nor the unmarked, black-windowed domestic violence house in Yonkers for women on the run. I asked around with other birthmothers on my caseload who might have known her from the street, but none of them had seen her—or else just wouldn't snitch. I even tried to file a missing person's report at the precinct, but the desk sergeant just gave me that same emasculating smirk that Bronx cops always gave to white male social workers. "Some deadbeat ducking the child snatchers?" he said. "Yeah, we'll get right on that, Chief." Lastly, I called every number that I had for Ty in the casefile. But when I stopped by his last known address, a woman in a blue headwrap and blue contact lenses came to the door. "He said he lived *here*?" she said. "Piece of shit..."

One day, Anita Flores stopped by my desk. She tried her best to sound compassionate. But there's not really a delicate way to say what she suggested: "You could try the morgue."

This had long been my greatest fear. That Margarita would take the same road out as Ms. Washington. That I would drive her down it. It would be my job to break the news to Harley—just as I had to Curtis, Ms. Washington's son. "She told me she was going on vacation," the boy had told me, his cheeks imprinted with the waffle pattern of the bedspread that he'd spent the last two hours moaning into. I'd given him a hug that made us both feel worse.

"Don't get too down about it, Pea-Pod," said Anita. "I knew the second that I met her: it was always gonna end this way. I shouldn't have even let you try."

Finally, I got the call from Titi. On the phone, she was sobbing and hysterical, coming in and out of Spanish and English. At first I couldn't make out what she was saying. I figured she'd heard the news from someone in the neighborhood, or worse, Harley herself. I need you to come here right now, Lee, she said. It's over, Lee. It's bad.

I knocked on the door. Harley answered. Her face was puffy and downcast, hair in tied-off twizzles. "Did you hear from her?" I asked. "Is she...has she...." Harley turned on her heel and stomped back into her bedroom. I lingered in the threshold. To enter would make it true. One step forward—she was dead.

Titi hobbled over, her movements slow and labored. "What's going on, T?" I said. "Please, just tell me."

She motioned me into the apartment. The neon parrot-lamp on the credenza made the entryway glow pink and teal. In the hall, I stepped on a plastic truck and it snapped beneath my weight. Somewhere in Titi's distant bedroom, I heard Jojo's muffled whining, plaintive and resigned. In the kitchen, Titi flicked on the light. It took a moment for my eyes to adjust.

Her eyes were burning black. And did her face look...somehow...?

"What..." I paused, frowned... "Titi—What happened to your eyebrows?"

Titi sat at the table, her gaze tracing the placemat, her face as naked as a mole-rat. Harley peered out from her bedroom door.

"I'm sorry, Bubba. Really. But I want her out. Tonight."

◆

The settlement of half-eaten bowls and smudged glasses on the desk in Harley's bedroom had now colonized the neighboring dresser. Another two bowls had formed a convoy to subdue the natives on the windowsill. Harley sat cross-legged on the bed, with Jojo rolling happily back and forth across her lap, breaking out in periodic shrieks of glee. I stood at Harley's dresser, stuffing its contents into a red-and-purple Children's Future duffel bag some other kid had left behind.

"Bitch told me I can't see my boyfriend...." Harley explained, angrily but weakly, knowing that her reasoning was pretty thin.

I folded up a pair of jeans. I was still too relieved to scold her. As I packed up Harley's things, her defiance softened.

"She really says I have to leave?" she said.

"It's not her," I lied. "It's me. It's my decision."

I'd meant to preserve her feelings by taking the blame, since she despised me anyway. But I'd forgotten how thin these walls were: of course, she'd already heard me in the kitchen with Titi for the last forty-five minutes, begging to let her stay. I'm too old, Lee. My bones hurt. My sugars are on a trampoline,

Titi had said, resolute and unblinking, her browless face looking like a peeled potato. This little girl needs more than I can give.

All she needs is... I'd trailed off. All she needs is love, is what I'd planned to say, as if having unlimited, unconditional, saint-like love for someone else's child were a reasonable expectation. But I knew already: people can't be guilted into love. I'd tried before with Ms. Quintana when she'd tried to give back Ivan Santiago. Without you, I'd said, this boy has no one. A week later, she was off to the DR on a singles cruise.

So now all I could do was sigh and say: Who knows what she needs?

Titi gave me what I think was look of gratitude—it was hard to read her expression without her eyebrows. She reached out and grabbed me by the hand and whispered: I'm going to keep paying for her phone, though. Someone's gotta keep a look out for the kid.

Back in Harley's bedroom, I folded another pair of jeans and stuffed them into the duffel. "You have a lot of pants," I muttered, just to say something. She didn't even have that many.

"I told you Titi doesn't love me." Harley shook slightly as she spoke. The worst part was—she was right. She'd set out to prove this and succeeded. Titi was a good woman, and Harley knew that: it only made the fact she didn't love her worse. There was nothing I could say to change that. So I just folded pants.

"Where are you going to bring us?" she said.

I couldn't tell her that I didn't know. That the Placement Unit hadn't called me back yet. That the amount of thought put into her new home would not amount to much more than, "Well, who has an opening?" Still, I had far worse news than that.

"There's no easy way to say this," I said. "Jojo is staying here."

"Fuck out of here."

"I can't move him from a pre-adoptive home. Not unless it's to go back with your parents."

It almost seemed to bring her peace. Like I'd finally put away the clamps and vises and slipped the curtain from the guillotine. She leaned down and kissed her brother on the forehead. "Ha ha? Ha ha?" he said. This was the closest he had ever come to saying her name out loud.

"So I gotta count on Rita?" she said.

"I know she can do it."

"You don't even know where she is."

"Well—no. Not at this exact moment. But—"

"What if my dad could take us? He's outta jail, you know. The other day we started texting."

I thought this over for a moment. But no, no—I'd read the casefile. With his rapsheet, that simply wasn't possible. The only hope was for Margarita to emerge from whatever hell I'd sent her to—if somehow, someway, she could be found.

"Wait," I said. "You have a number for your father?"

# 11.

**The restaurant inside the gas station is nicer than I'd expected.** Some of these spots up here can get a little grody—but we must be near a ski resort. The napkin holder on our table is a gleaming stainless steel. Ski badges and novelty license plates line the walls. The place smells like fresh coffee, maple syrup, motor oil. A weathered, friendly waitress brings the highchair without me asking, plus a paper placemat and some crayons for Lily. She asks what she can start us with and, once she comes back with the chocolate milk, I let her know: "I'll have a beer."

As the waitress leaves and Lily starts to scribble jagged lines on the placemat, I glance at my watch. Already, I'm feeling guilty about our little lunch-date. Or at least I know I *should* be feeling guilty. Now that we're inside the restaurant, and I've gotten my little girl the chocolate milk her heart desired, my fit of pettiness subsides: I really should call her mother to let her know what's going on. She picks up after one ring.

"Where are you guys?" she says, voice a little frantic.

"Listen, I know I'd said that we'd be back by four but –"

"Oh, come on. I told you that Lily's got that birthday party."

"I know, I know, I'm sorry. We just got a flat tire, and I don't have a spare—"

"Lee, this isn't fair. We're supposed to be on the same page. You're either missing visits, or you don't bring her back when you're supposed to. How am I supposed to plan around that?"

"Missing visits? What—you mean *last* week? I was working! I told you that!"

"Ok, fine, but—"

"Sara, don't say I'm *missing* visits, alright? That's bullshit and you know it. Don't say it like that, please."

Across the table, Lily bites her lip, presses crayon to placemat, and draws two long, narrow ovals, filled in with faces with dots for features. Our fighting doesn't seem to bother her—or at least she doesn't let on. On the other end of the phone, Sara gives in with a sigh.

"Ok. Ok. You're right. I'm sorry. I'm just stressed. I told my sister we'd be there at four, and...well, you know how she is."

"You want me to call her? It's my fault. I'll take the blame. We're just here waiting here for Triple-A. I feel like an asshole."

"Ha, no. That's alright, Lee. I don't think that's...I won't subject you to that."

The waitress comes back with my beer. She takes out a pad to take our order—I wince and hold my hand over the phone. The waitress nods and turns around, returns to some conversation she was having with a hunched old cop at the cash register.

"Listen," I say, "This might not be the time to bring this up but... Look, I'm sure it's nothing, and I'm not making any accusations at all, OK? But...do you know a guy named Arnold?"

I can feel her tense up through the phone. "What?"

"Arnold. Lily's been going on and on about a guy named Arnold. Arnold this, Arnold that. And she seems sort of—I don't know, agitated, about it? And look, obviously, who you see or whatever, that's not my business anymore..."

"Right, it isn't—"

"But, well, when we spoke about it, I thought we'd agreed that, at least until Lily gets a little more understanding about—"

"Are you implying that I am bringing strange men around our daughter?"

"No! What? I didn't say anything about *strange* men, did I? Maybe Arnold's great, what do I know? I'm sure he's a gem. It's just that—"

"This conversation is really, *really,* pissing me off, Lee."

"Alright. Ok. Look, I'm sorry. I didn't mean it like that. It's just—this co-parenting thing. It's tricky, right? I'm still figuring it out. Ok? Maybe we can talk about it later."

"Fine. Whatever. What time will you be back?

"It shouldn't be too long. We're just pulled off at a gas station now, waiting for the guy. I'm an idiot, not having a spare."

She hangs up before I've said goodbye. Across the table, Liliana gnaws on the straw to the chocolate milk that she's already finished, singing the *Mulan* theme again, but this time changing most of the words to be about chocolate milk. On the placemat, I see her final artwork: four limbless stick figures, like heads on long spikes. Three are drawn in blue, and another, off to the side, in red. I feel a sudden tightness in my throat.

"What's that honey?" I ask.

"Just drawing," she shrugs elaborately.

"Is that..." I squint. I have that old unbalanced feeling. The heaviness in my chest, that floating sensation in my head. Like when Ivan Santiago hid beneath his bed and whispered into teddy's ears what his father used to do. I'd just stared at the bubbly letters I'd been tracing in my notebook. "Is that a...family?" I say.

Lily shrugs. My concern bores her. Would you ask Picasso to explain himself? She gestures vaguely, almost rhetorically, at our surroundings. "Is this a rester-not?"

"Yes, this is a restaurant. Lily, I want to talk about your drawing."

"Can I have more chocolate milk?"

"Who is this red man supposed to be?" I say, pointing to the stick-figure in red. His eyes are red. His teeth are red. His smile is demonic.

"Who?" says Lily, chewing on her straw.

"Is this Arnold? Tell me baby. Please, focus, Lily. Please..."

My daughter smiles at me, big and broad and proud. My heart splits in half with a violence, with all the dangers I can't prevent. All the evil that we do to one another, just because we can.

"This?" she says. "Daddy. No! That's Santa!"

My whole body loosens. I have to laugh. The waitress comes back again, and this time we order—a burger for me, macaroni for my Lily. "Another round?" she says, nodding at my beer and Lily's chocolate milk, with a wry, salesmen's smile. She puts her pad back in her pocket. I shrug and tell her OK. What the hell.

# 12.

**Home visits with birthfathers were usually more awkward than hostile.** Unlike their female counterparts, birthfathers didn't tend to see me as the worst thing to ever happen to them, nor was I the personification of all their moral failings. I was more like an annoyance. An oddity. Like a Verizon guy who'd set them up with WiFi and now, for some reason, sat down on the sofa to ask about their feelings.

When I knocked on the door of Ty's low-slung basement apartment in a sleepy rowhouse in Morris Heights, it wasn't him who answered, but a lanky, red-eyed teenager. He asked me through the door chain if I had a warrant.

"Let him in," called Ty, over the sound of barking dogs. "Fuck is wrong with you?"

The apartment was dark and hazy, billowing with smoke. My eyes were burning within seconds, and a minute later I was stoned. Two pit bulls, Bert and Ernie, lazed on a kiss-print daybed beneath an enormous television playing Sportscenter on mute. Videogames, bootleg DVDs, and Manga-style comic books with titles like *Death Note* and *Full Metal Alchemist* rose from the floor in crooked towers. The walls bore concert flyers of Bronx *bachata* DJs I'd never heard of, and the same poster of two women kissing in their underwear that had graced the walls of half the dorm rooms in my college. Behind the couch, a cylindrical fish tank bubbled brightly: zebra-striped clown fish and orange puffers and a ruffled black euclid with a spindly Fu Manchu swam in loping circles.

He told me to sit down on an ash-pocked leather sofa, and he sat opposite me on another. He wore crisp black trackpants, a white shirt with gold letters spelling *GUCCI*, and a flat Yankees hat pulled down low over his eyes. I told myself not to be nervous. To think of him like any other birthfather. Just another deadbeat Dad. Not the man who'd publicly executed the last guy to violate Margarita. The last guy before me, I mean.

"You sure you don't want something to drink, man?" he said. "I got coffee...soda...or...do you like...tea?" He sounded like he was offering refreshments to an alien—guessing: what the fuck does this thing like?

I sat up straight, remembering a piece of advice I'd gotten the last time I'd visited Mr. Santiago at Rikers. You sit like a bitch, I'll treat you like one.

"Look," I said. "If she's at all important to you, if any part of you cares at all...all I need is an address. Because if I don't find her soon, that's it."

Ty scratched his eyebrow idly. Was that an Omega gleaming on his wrist? Was I sitting like a bitch sits? I covered up my Timex with my other hand. Ty snapped his fingers at his surly teenaged friend.

"Yo Sammy," Ty said, summoning the red-eyed teenager. "Sammy boy. Take a walk, alright?"

"But I just got back..." said the boy.

"What'd you say?"

The boy moped toward the door, muttering into the collar of his parka, putting headphones in. Ty turned back to me.

"You hungry?" he said.

"No, that's—"

Ty called after the boy: "Get us two pastramis. Toasted. Extra cheese. You like cheese, right, Lee? But I swear to God Sammy, if you bring mine back with mayo again, I'm gonna lose my fucking mind..."

"I told them no mayo, T, it's not my fault that..."

"Yeah, you told them! They put mayo on it against your orders! They insisted on the mayo, right? Get the fuck out of here."

The door closed. Ty slumped back into the couch and rubbed his forehead. He pushed up the brim of his hat and eyed me solemnly. "If I know one thing in this world, Lee," he said, "it's that when that boy comes back, he's giving me a sandwich with fucking mayo."

"Is he your..." I couldn't possibly guess. "...roommate?"

This made Ty laugh. Evidently it was a stupid question, though to this day, I'm not sure why.

"Look," he said. "I know you got a job to do. If I knew where Rita was, I'd tell you. I've been trying to get it out of her for like a month. Last time I called, she just bawled me out."

"When did you last speak to her?"

"I don't know. Yesterday? Day before? She was ranting and raving. I'm this, I'm that, blah blah. You know how she gets..."

My joy came on so powerfully I had to cough to tamp it down. Rita was alive! I hadn't driven her to suicide or overdose.

She was not at the bottom of the Hudson sharing a soggy blunt with Ms. Washington. As I sat there, coughing out my glee, Ty continued with a monologue I couldn't follow—explaining where he'd been these past months, why he hadn't shown—but really I didn't care. Finally, he undid his frizzy ponytail and smoothed his hair beneath his hat. He pulled the brim of the hat up, then down, then took it off and threw it. In the corner, Bert or Ernie growled.

"Man, I'm just making up excuses," he concluded, finally. "Rita's gonna do what Rita does. But I know I should do better."

What was this? I thought. Had I—somehow, through a series of distracted nods and pretend coughing—just coaxed this man to a breakthrough? Was I somehow, all this time, actually OK at this?

"Do better...how?" I said finally. I felt like I was back in high school, baked out of my head, getting called on unexpectedly in history class and blurting out: the cotton gin?

"You got kids, Todd?"

I coughed again. Maintain, Lee. OK. Maintain.

"Let's keep the focus on you."

"Course you don't. Well, man, I feel bad for you then. Cause without kids, what's the point? Just running around for no reason. You got a girl, at least? Or a...dude?"

For some reason I'm not proud of, it felt very important to make clear I wasn't gay. "I'm engaged," I said. "To a *girl*."

"Well, when y'all do have kids, you'll understand."

"Understand what?"

"How good it feels, man. Being Dad—it's the best."

I couldn't get my bearings. Was he being…wistful? I'd come ready to lock horns with an unhinged serial abuser who'd once choked out Rita in the movie theater while the credits rolled on *Spiderman 3*; who'd once hid his piece in Harley's backpack the day the cops came looking; who had recently spent two months in Rikers for slashing an acquaintance with a fly knife on the 5-train. I had no tools for combatting wistfulness.

"I still remember when I first felt it," Ty continued, "When I really realized things were different now. I was different now. I was in bed one night, I had Rita in one arm, and little Harley in the other, like we was puzzle pieces. Both of them snoring their asses off. Just *huuh-hewwww, huh-heeeww*. In and out, in and out. And I'm just lying there, looking at their faces in the dark like, it's really up to me now. I got to be somebody."

I watched the euclid swim three laps and thought of the parts of the story I knew he wasn't telling. The bruises. How he'd left six months after Jojo came—just as Rita's depression grew claws and dragged the family down to hell. Still, these days, when my daughter buries her forehead in my ribcage and lets out her happy baby sigh, I can't pretend that I don't know exactly what he meant.

"You know," I said. "There was never even a case filed against you. You could just ask the judge to give them back to you."

Ty crossed his arms. Two handguns were tattooed on the underside of each of his wrists, shooting dollar signs up his arms. The word *RITA* was in red cursive on his neck—though he had other women on his forearms. In the fish tank, a clownfish floated casually to the edge of the glass—a spy sent by the others, pretending not to listen.

"That's kinda...what's the word...isn't it?" he said.

"What do you mean?"

"Like, because I wasn't there at all, they can't charge me with neglect..."

I thought a moment. "Ironic?"

"That's it," he said. "Ironic. Nah, man. I mean, I'm fucked up anyway you want to look at it. I don't need a judge to tell me that. Those are Rita's babies, for better or for worse."

There was not much point in arguing. Even if Ty did file for custody, Anita Flores would make me fight him tooth and nail. Plus, his name wasn't even on Harley's birth certificate—which could only make things harder.

"Well, you can still be there for them in other ways," I said. "I know Harley could use someone to talk to. Lord knows there's a lot she can't tell me."

"You talking about the older boyfriend thing? Rita called me about that. She was losing her goddamn mind."

"She told me she didn't care."

"Rita did? Bro, you can't trust anything she says. She'll always make herself sound more crazy than she really is."

"Why would she do that?"

"Because she's crazy! I don't know, man, she's living with her head cut off—I don't think she's got much of a plan. I promise you though—the day she heard that shit from Harley, she was busting heads like fucking Kojak. I tried to get the boy's name from Harley, but my little girl's too smart. She knows what I'd do to him." He paused to let that register. Then: "Ha. That was a joke."

"I wouldn't blame you." I hadn't meant to say that out loud. It was the weed smoke talking, seeping from my lungs out of my lips.

Ty gave me a look of dark amusement, as though to say: You know I kill men, right? Then: "Do you know his name?"

Jairo Del Santos, I almost said. Titi had showed me all their texts the last time I was there. Jairo Del Fucking Santos. Phone number 347-194-7832. Jairo Del Santos, who worked part-time at a moving company, who had a patchy, junkyard chinstrap beard and turtled hunch about his shoulders that had surely turned off all the girls his age. Jairo Del Santos. Jairo Del Santos. Who every night would cajole Harley to sneak out. Who'd convinced her to get herself kicked out of Titi's once she'd told the police about their relationship. I'd be doing my job, in a way, wouldn't I? By giving the fucker's name to Ty? I'd be empowering parents to protect their children—just like Anita said we should.

"Please," I said instead. "You think she'd tell me?"

Ty seemed almost relieved to have no way of knowing. I don't think he was a killer. At least not in his heart.

"She don't hate you, you know," he said.

"I don't know about that."

"Nah, she tells me you're alright. We all know you got a job to do."

"So did the Nazis," I muttered—thinking of the night I'd taken Harley from Titi's, when I'd brought her to her new foster home at Ms. Conley's. The kid had cried so hard that I'd thought that she might actually choke, while I just sat there in the dark shrugging off the glares of stuffed animals poking their heads out from the toy chest. Conley had kicked her out a week later. She was with Iglesia now. Ty looked back at me, amused.

"Hey, man," he said. "I'm sure some Nazis were OK."

I looked at him quizzically. Ty gave an open-minded shrug.

"I mean, at least compared to other Nazis. Point is—I don't think you got to be too hard on yourself, bro. I gave all my caseworkers hell growing up, don't mean I really thought my Mom had it in her to get cleanly. And believe me—the whole Bronx knows it not your fault how Rita is."

It surprised me, the sudden gratitude I felt towards him for saying that. An OK Nazi—I could take that as a compliment, right? At least compared to other Nazis. "I just wish I could get her to...I don't know... calm down a little."

"Ha, welcome to my world, bro! Welcome to the fucking circus! You should see Rita and my mom in a room together. You know how a betta fish will try and fight its own reflection? Man, my whole *life* is crazy women! Last Thanksgiving, they threw each other down the stairs!"

I laughed, choosing to let him slide on the details of that particular criminal report—the one that said he'd had Rita in a chokehold when the cops arrived, holding her over the railing. Truth is, I was enjoying the conversation. Ty was the only man on earth that I could talk to about his wife.

He pulled out a joint from a metal case in a drawer on the coffee table. "You don't mind, right? I got a prescription, I swear, ha."

"It's like if everything isn't going exactly her way," I said, "she lashes out."

Ty lit the joint and leaned back, biting rings of smoke.

"Nah, she's lashing out regardless. Rita's a warrior, bro. And you know what warriors want?"

I thought a moment. I had no idea what warriors want.

"War, man! All she wants is war. Peace just makes her nervous. You know, one time, Harley came home with an A in social studies. Proudest day I've ever had. The next morning, Rita tried to kill me."

"Like...*kill,* kill?"

"I was taking a shower—she comes in to the bathroom with the hair dryer and that crazy look she gets. You know that crazy Rita look. Like she's so pissed off it makes her laugh. She's pointing it at me like a piece. 'What's her name, motherfucker,' she's shouting. 'Who is she, who is she?' Like we didn't have an understanding! Like she ain't fucked half *my* friends! Only reason I didn't fry is 'cuz it came unplugged when she threw it."

I laughed again—I couldn't help it. Not so much at the facts, but at the way he'd told the story. His Margarita impression was spot on; he'd really nailed the eyerolls, the hair flicks. Both of them, come to think of it, did excellent impersonations of the other.

He waved the joint in my direction. Would it be so wrong for me to share a hit? A toast to new friends, new enemies—what were we? Anyway, with all the smoke in here already, I was already ripped.

"That's just the bad shit though," he said. "With Rita, I just put that aside. Because the good days...when she's dancing around the kitchen in my sweatshirt, making pancakes or whatever...man, I..." Ty gave a self-collecting grunt, a look of faint embarrassment. There was an awkward, manly silence. I thought, suddenly, of my stepdad—how the poor guy used to try to have these heart-to-hearts about his problems with my mom.

We sat there in the quiet for while.

"So... who are your teams?" I said, at last. Ty gave me the same look of gratitude that poor Ken used to when I'd change the subject. Like I'd saved him from himself. When in doubt, talk sports.

Soon enough, we were swapping thoughts about the NBA and NFL. How, to him, in a certain light, I kind of looked like a budget-ass Tom Brady, but he wouldn't hold that against me. How the Knicks really fucking suck. Maybe it should have troubled me that I got along so well with a murderer, but maybe it was fitting. I'd spent the last month thinking I'd killed Margarita, so I sort of did know how it felt.

Later, when Sammy came back with two pastrami sandwiches, I was too hungry to decline mine. Ty took a bite and threw his at Sammy, then sent him back out to buy "banana-leaves" from some cross-town bodega, which may have been some kind of code. After an hour or so, the home visit felt less like casework than one of those languorous, carefree college afternoons, when I'd skip class to share a bowl with my roommates and write songs about Estelle.

When it was time to go, I began to pack my bag up. He said he'd call about arranging visitation—and I promised to help him file what he had to in court for visitation rights, if he could stomach being supervised. We're on the same side, I said as I was leaving. We both want what's best for your kids.

"Yeah," said Ty, "but who could really know that?"

He hadn't meant to let that slip. He'd forgotten who I was. I slipped my backpack off of my shoulder back onto the couch.

"You don't think Rita can do it?" I said.

Ty looked at me unsurely. I met his gaze. There was a bond between us: two men who'd both cared for and abused her. The worst things that had ever happened to her and the only hopes that she had left. Ty returned his attention to the fish tank. Their slow circles seemed to hypnotize him. I sat back on the couch, swallowing a bite of mostly mayonnaise, staring at his upturned baseball hat across from me on the couch, the lining stained with hair grease.

"Anything I tell you is confidential right?" he said.

"Of course," I lied.

"Man, I've known her since she was thirteen. The shit she and I been through together...She's just...I wish..."

He couldn't spit it out. The fish tank glowed like moonlight on a gravestone.

"It's not like it happened all at once, you know what I'm saying? But I came in one morning man and—and I saw it all, clear. She was sitting at the kitchen table, slumped over her knee, trying to tie her sneakers. Over and over, one string around the other. She couldn't pull the knot through. And every time it fell apart, she'd give this laugh, like heh, heh. This dead-ass, snake laugh, you know? Heh heh heh. Harley was at the table, eating cereal with water, watching this like it was on TV. I could smell Jojo from two rooms away..."

Ty paused. The fish swam round and round and round.

"You ever been to the Poconos?" he said.

"The where?"

"The Poconos, man. Out in PA. The mountains. Clear air. Log cabins, for real. Whatever. When Harley was born, that's where we went to hide out from the baby-snatchers. I found us some skank motel. And at night we'd sit there listening to everything, you know, the bugs buzzing, coyotes howling, owls and shit. And I'm just thinking like, where the fuck am I? What the fuck are we gonna do now? I was a seventeen-year-old kid from East Tremont Street, living on a pillowcase of cash, with no one in the world but this wild-ass chick and her baby. And I'm in the fucking Poconos? Thing is though—to Rita, it was all just funny. She'd never had more fun. You shoulda seen her when she was younger, man. She'd take my hand and tell me: boy, all you do is worry."

There is no amount of training that can make giving comfort to another man come naturally to a white guy from New Hampshire. "It's alright," I said, when something in his voice gave way: "It's alright..."

"Nah," said Ty. "I'm trying to explain something to you, Todd."

"Explain what?"

"That that's the Rita that Jo and Harley deserve. The way she was. My Rita. Not some sick bitch laughing at her shoelace. So I had to make the call. I owed it to them, right? Cuz never in a million years would that girl let you really take them."

Some kinds of guilt get deep into your spine. I could see it in the way Ty stood, a slight curve, a stoop in the shoulders. I've had back problems for years. His confession complete, he turned and slunk out of the room, and I heard him rifling through drawers—one after another, slamming shut. A minute later, he came back with a pencil and wrote down an address on a sheet of paper.

"This is where she's staying at," he said. "Please, man. She's in a hole. You have to fix her."

I put the paper in my pocket. Ty told me to wait for him to call before I went to that address: the situation didn't sound too stable. But he didn't ask me to keep his secret—in fact, he never did. He didn't have to. From this point on, we were the Margarita brothers. And there's no loyalty more sacred than the one between two traitors.

# 13.

**At the time, I couldn't help but see myself as the protagonist in this story**—even though of course that wasn't true. If anything, I was the bad guy—the barrier to the hero's hopes and dreams. But like anyone, I could only see the world through my own eyes. I could only follow what I believed to be my own purpose, which was to find Margarita. Whether she *wanted* to be found—well that was outside of my view, off in some murky, hidden place, written on some page of the casefile that had long since slipped loose and been taken by the wind. And though she would tell me much of her story later, on our long drives up and back to Westchester, I still don't really know if everything she told me was just the way she wanted me to see her. If everything I understood about her, or Ty, or Harley or Titi—or, hell, for that matter, anyone I've ever cared about—is just what I've chosen to believe.

So just like I don't know why she'd first disappeared, or what happened to her while she was away, I also don't fully understand why, about a month after she'd gone missing, but before I'd worked up the nerve to find her at the address Ty had given me, Margarita re-emerged at last, alive and well and angry, in the new playground by the basketball courts in Crotona Park.

It was a cold Friday morning in February—Valentine's day, if I remember right. Her face was hidden by a black scarf, her eyes behind bedazzled plastic shades. All her hair save for a single wayward strand of red was tucked neatly beneath the hood of her furry parka. She crouched behind a park bench, watching from across the playground as Titi pulled Jojo out of his stroller, zipped up his Dallas Cowboys jacket and set to chasing him across the mulch. Seeing her son's breath in the cold made Margarita want to scream—that was *her* breath, wasn't it? Coming from the lungs she'd given him. She crept around the perimeter of the playground, ducked beneath a spiral slide, and hurried up the stairs of the jungle gym. On the mulch below, Titi picked up Jojo and placed him atop a dinosaur hobbyhorse. His laughter lilted back and forth, back and forth, like a saw cutting her in half, one push at a time, deeper, deeper, until at last she jumped down the stairs, shoved Titi in the back, ripped her baby off the dinosaur, and took off running.

"I never saw her coming, Lee," Titi would tell me later. "I thought I broke my ass!"

Margarita's plan was simple, at least from what I gathered: once clear of Titi, she and Jo would catch a gypsy cab to the Port Authority bus terminal, where Harley was already waiting. In a few days, they'd be somewhere like Florida, or California, or the Poconos—anywhere, really. It didn't matter, so long as it was far away from me.

With Jojo in her arms, she sprinted past the basketball courts, sneakers slipping on the ice. The path cut through bony trees. Jojo screamed and writhed, thin strings of spit streaming in the wind. With an errant fist, he knocked the shades off her face onto the path and they snapped beneath her feet.

She must have run a half mile. Her legs were aching, throat tasted like iron, nose bleeding down her lips and chin. Jojo seemed to weigh a hundred pounds. Or maybe she'd just lost her Mama muscles. The path sloped downwards, looped around the banks of the frozen pond. Tall cattails on the pond's edge hissed and swayed. She put him down to catch her breath, thinking that foster mothers can't run, won't run—they don't care enough to chase. At least, I assume that this is what she thought. Why else would she have stopped?

When she saw Titi coming, Margarita tried to run again, but her legs wouldn't take her. Her back seized. Her lungs wheezed. Her son wriggled out of her arms—or maybe she just let him go—and hobbled off back up the path, towards his foster mother, screaming in the cold. Margarita took a few steps toward re-kidnapping her fleeing child, but slipped across a patch of ice and smacked her head on the ground. When she came to seconds later, Titi was lifting her to her feet and walking her toward a bench along the banks of the pond, wiping ice and little sticks out of her hair.

"I'm sorry, I'm sorry, I'm..." Margarita cried so hard she couldn't breathe.

Titi patted her back, gently, almost lovingly, like she were her child. "It's alright," she said. "OK now, honey, OK—let it out, my love."

Finally, Rita caught her breath. Through her hands she looked up at the older woman:

"What happened to..." She paused to collect herself. "...your eyebrows?"

◆

A black crow stalked the cattails on the pond's edge. It watched the two women on the bench with interest, its eyes black and wise, hopping nimbly through the mud and slush as though to hear them better.

This was the detail that stuck out in Titi's memory later, when she told me this story. I'd been supervising a family visit between Ivan and Mr. Santiago when she'd called. "You gotta get here quick, Bubba," Titi had said. "Our friend, she runs like a little duckling..." I'd looked back to Mr. Santiago, munged out on suboxone, fiddling idly with a headless GI Joe while his son filled out his multiplication tables on the visiting room floor. He probably wouldn't hit him, right?

I muttered something about an emergency, then ran the five blocks to Titi's. She ushered me to her kitchen table and I plopped down, still sweating from my sprint. She set a rum flan in front of me; then in her staccato, rambling manner began to tell me what had happened. Like with every conversation that I'd ever had with Titi, there were a few detours on the way.

"OK, OK. Got it. A crow was watching you, uh huh..." I said at last, trying to nudge her back towards the main thread of the story with a twirl of my pencil. "And then Rita said...?"

"Did you know crows are among the most intelligent birds in North America? I swear, they pick up on emotions—this one could tell that Margarita was in pain. It—"

"That's *really* interesting," I interrupted, swallowing my impatience along with another bite of flan. "But what did Rita *say*?"

Titi frowned judgmentally. What kind of person isn't interested in bird facts, her expression seemed to wonder?

I ate a piece of flan in two bites to win back her affection. Begrudgingly, she carried on: "She didn't look too good, Bubba. Gray, not enough blood in her. Her eyes had that wolfy look, like all the junkies get."

"And...?"

"The wind was like ice. She pulled up her little hood. You know, she acts all ghetto with you, because she knows that you don't know. But to me, she's just this little girl. She's looking up at me with those big moon eyes, shaking like a leaf. She says '*Please*, Titi, *please*. Don't tell Lee, OK?'"

"What'd you say?"

Titi shrugged, unconflicted by her treachery. "I promised her I wouldn't. I told her, 'Hey I have the baby back. And you and me, we should be friends.'"

Having solidified her truce with Rita, she lifted Jojo from her own lap and placed him on his mother's. He squirmed and hiccuped. The crow poked its head beneath the mush and excavated the remains of a discarded chicken wing. A spindly ligament dangled from its long black beak. The wind whisked Rita's sigh off down the path.

"What the fuck am I gonna do, Titi?" she said.

"You has to do your services, *mi amor*. Whatever they tell you to do, you do it."

"For what? So the doctor can tell Lee Todd I'm crazy? That I don't love my babies? I went down to that psychiatrist's office! Tried to apologize, or whatever. That fat cunt called the cops!" As his mother spoke, Jojo climbed off her lap and nestled himself back into his foster mother's belly.

"Just like he is now," Titi told me, back in her kitchen, while Jojo poked at a fresh piece of flan on my plate with his little dinosaur spoon. "Where he feel safe."

"No, Papi," I said, and made a funny face that made him cry.

The cold in the park seemed to envelop the two women. The wind's breath was harsh and ragged. Titi held Rita's bare hand in her fuzzy mitten. "Let me give you some advice," she said.

"So give it."

For a long time, Titi didn't speak. She wasn't sure if she should say it. Then she locked eyes with the crow. ("Some people say that they're as intelligent as chimpanzees, Lee! The dolphins of the sky.") It raised its greasy wings above its shoulders, as though to ask: why not?

"Maybe you should give up," she said.

"Excuse you?"

"Just go away. It would be better for them."

I can imagine the look on Rita's face. The look she gives when dumping fruit juice on her enemies. When she electrocutes her lovers. Sometimes, these days, I'll be at the checkout line at Market Basket and see her face looking back at me from the cover of *People* magazine, replacing some new

Jenner, enraged but also faintly amused by my life choices: Really, Lee, frozen pizza again? Wow.

But Titi didn't care how Rita took it. She was staring at the crow.

"I've been a foster mother for a real long time," she said. "Seen all kinds of parents, all kinds of kids. What I learned is, if the kids know that the parents are nearby, they always gonna wonder why you won't come back. They gonna blame themselves. Every day, they go around with half a brain—one mind in the foster home, the other always thinking, you know, 'Why not me?' Look at your daughter, *mi amor*—a month after you stopped visiting, look what she done to me! My son Jerome though? His birthmother died back when he was a baby. Now he's a surgeon at Montefiore. Ears, nose, and throat. *Mira*— you're a nice girl. Young. You'll be pretty too, if you get rid of those tattoos. You can start again somewhere new. Meet someone to love you—not that clown that you run around with. I could adopt Jojo for you. Make sure he grows up good."

Margarita thought this over for a moment, then picked a pebble from beneath her feet. She aimed it at the crow, but the crow was ready.

"They can see things before they happen, Lee. It side-stepped the rock, so graceful, like a dancer, like a beautiful, black ballerina and—"

"Jesus Christ! Enough about the crow! What did she say, Titi? Why did you tell me this was so important?!"

Titi cut another piece of flan; it was my punishment for interrupting. She slapped Jojo's hand from my plate as he went to intercept it. If I have another bite of flan, I thought, I'll be more flan than Lee.

"It's not so much what she said, but how she said it," said Titi. "I seen that look before."

Margarita stood up from the bench, brushed her eyes with her forearm, smoothed the dirt out of her jacket.

"You can have him," she told Titi. "When I'm gone...I won't need him anymore."

The crow dropped the chicken wing onto the frozen ground, spread its wings and flew away. The flan jiggled menacingly, tauntingly on my plate. Since Ty had given me the address, I'd made excuses to myself for why I hadn't gone there yet. But now I had no choice. I could be there in twenty minutes if I sprinted.

As I stood to leave, Titi grabbed me by the hand, desperate and dismayed. "Hey—hold on a second, Bubby! Let me pack that up for you to go."

◆

The drunk in the next room must have smashed the lightbulb on his way in again that morning. The floor of the hallway twinkled in the dark. In her room, Rita took a handful of Xanax, washed it down with a glug of Pepsi from a liter long gone flat, and shot herself between the toes with what she had left in her suitcase. Her door was just a piece of thin, unfitted plywood, so she took the knife that Ty had lent her out from beneath the pillow in case her neighbor tried to force his way in again.

Her room was one of several in the basement of a vacant building. She shared a single doorless bathroom glowing greenly at the end of the hall. In her room, there was no furniture besides a mattress with a fitted sheet slumping off the shoulder, and a few stacked plastic drawers dotted with glitter and tied shut with bungee cords. Half-filled, uncapped plastic bottles lined the windowsill. Two leopard-print suitcases lay splayed open on the floor with their innards bared and neatly folded. Photographs of the kids and Ty were taped to the wall above her mattress, beneath two words written in marker: BE HAPPY. In a tank beneath the window covered by a towel, Harley's turtles floated dead atop an inch or so of brownish water.

The tithe brought her what she needed. One minute, everything was jagged edges; the next, every cell in her body was wrapped inside a velvet blanket. She was liquid; she was easy; a warm sack of water sinking slowly to the ocean floor. People think that it's a weakness, she once told me, but that's just 'cause they don't know.

She felt a pulse inside her pocket then. She rolled onto her side, took out her phone and saw a text from Harley.

*You coming?*

For a moment, the text confused her. It confused me too, when Titi first showed it to me on her nephew's spyware application. Rita lay back inside the bliss, her vision blurring now, sweat beading at her throat. The phone pulsed again and again.

*I'm where you said to wait.*

*Ma?*

*Hello?*

*You coming?*

*Really?*

Downtown, Harley boarded the 2-train north from the Port Authority. The train car swelled with noise and bodies. Margarita took another handful of Xanax. How many would it take? Ten? Twenty? Enough to fade away. Enough to make her children doctors. The world drew itself around her. She pulled the fitted sheet over her head and felt her blood fill up with light.

She texted Harley that she loved her. She sent the same to Ty. In that moment, did she finally feel it? Or did she hope that texting it would make it true? Death was coming now. Closer. Drool trickled from her lips onto the pillow. Her skin was itching, tickling, buzzing. She thought of Harley and Jojo—the best things she ever did—but did she even really do it? *I love you*—she texted again. To Harley, to Ty—to Titi even. *I love you. I love you. I love you.* Death approached, coming down the stairs from the street into the basement room, stepping carefully to avoid crunching glass beneath his bony feet. She heard a knocking on a door, the door opening, her name being called. Death was here. He'd found her, finally. She closed her eyes and sank and sank and sank. "Rita?" a voice called to her through the darkness, uncertain. Death wasn't sure he had the right room. It was so dark in the hallway. Finally, finally He had found her. Please. Come in. I'm ready.

"Rita?" I called again, soft, pushing on the plywood, my eyes adjusting to the dark. "Rita? RITA?"

# 14.

**I'm not sure I can take credit for saving Margarita's life,** since I was more or less the reason that she'd tried to end it. So instead I'll just say that when I found her in her basement room, still as a corpse and wrapped up in a fitted sheet, I called 9-1-1, and the EMTs shot the Narcan up her nostrils just in time. Then they rushed her to St. Bonaventure to pump her stomach free of all the Xanax that she'd used to chase the heroin.

"You family?" the nurse asked me when I came into her half of the small brown hospital room, rolling a leopard-print suitcase with a wobbly wheel behind me.

The room was cluttered with machinery and smelled like sweat and sanitizer. She lay with her hair fanned out on the pillow, her eyes puffed shut. I'd never noticed how thin her wrists were until I saw them in hospital bracelets. I didn't want to embarrass her with talk of foster care, so I just told the nurse I was.

"Where am..." she said, once she'd woken up, her voice scratched and punctured. When she realized that it was only me who'd come to visit, she fell back down on the pillow. "You *got* to be kidding me," she said, addressing some invisible third party. Some ghost whose joke I was.

"I brought your stuff," I said. While the EMTs had loaded her into the ambulance, I'd kicked the needles and the knife into the corner and packed her things into the suitcase. At one point, her walleyed neighbor had wandered in through the broken door dressed in fatigues and flip-flops; he'd tried to sell me a briefcase full of herbal lotions, but I told him I was good.

"You got the turtles too?" Margarita asked.

"I, uh..." Did she not know they were dead? Was now the time to tell her?

"I promised Harley I'd take care of them."

"I'll swing by later to make sure they're alright."

She nodded.

I sat down in the bedside chair. "How are you feeling?"

She picked idly at the IV implanted in her hand. A black monitor behind the bed muttered angry noises. All her lines were red and squiggly. Her neighbor through the partition coughed and coughed and coughed. She asked me for a glass of water, so I filled a paper cup from the sink. When I came back, she was sitting up in the bed. She held one hand out to take the cup—with the other, she played Snake on her phone.

"How'd you find me?" she said.

"I just kept going into random apartments. That's why it took so long."

Margarita looked at me blankly. The joke had made a joke. The snake on her screen ate its own tail and exploded.

"I told him not to tell you where I was," she said.

"Why? There's nothing to be ashamed about."

"Because I knew you'd say dumb shit like that.'"

I took this mild sassing as her way of being friendly. The faint suggestion of apology in the tone with which she'd said this insult was about as close to a thank you as I'd get.

"He was worried about you. We both were."

"That's just what I need. You two retards teaming up..."

I paused a moment—unsure how to broach what I knew I had to say. Through the partition, her roommate coughed his soul out of his body.

"Listen, Rita..." I began.

"No."

"Hear me out..."

"Uh-uh. Please, bro... Um, Nurse? Can I get a nurse in here?"

"We have to talk about it..."

"I'm not here. I'm on the beach in Florida. Oh, it's nice and sunny..."

"Look, Rita. That night in your apartment...if I ever made you feel like that's what I was after... Well, I know it must be so difficult, as a woman, a woman of, you know, color, with me for a caseworker. And I can see how, well....the humiliation, the shame of it. I can't help but feel responsible."

The muttering monitor wanted to be heard now. It had something to say. Margarita stared it back into silence. Finally, she turned back to me:

"Motherfucker, how stupid are you?"

"I'm just trying to say that I understand—"

"What—you think I tried to kill myself because you wouldn't fuck me?"

"No. No! What? Jesus, no! Of course not. I just meant...you shouldn't feel ashamed. Or...you know, disheartened."

Margarita made a show of laughing—a caustic, squeaky laugh, I guess to show the dead guy next door how funny all this was to her. Ha ha squeak squeak ha ha ha. "Damn, Lee. You got a high opinion of yourself. Think your dick so good I can't live without it?"

My stammering denials only heightened her amusement. Margarita's eyes twinkled through the haze of sedatives. You've never seen a recent suicide so tickled.

"Hey, maybe it is," she said. "Maybe I love you, Lee. It was just too much love for me to take."

"You know that's not what I mean."

"Come on, boo. Don't you love me too? If you say no, I'll kill myself."

"Are you done?"

"You know I was trying to blackmail you, right? I got the whole thing recorded on my phone. Only reason I would ever go near your ugly ass. With your eyes so close together..." She shook her head. "So tell me—what the fuck do I have to be ashamed about?"

It's not like she had hurt my feelings—that's not why I got quiet. It's not like I was stewing. Anyway, I thought, that was my whole point, wasn't it? That she had nothing to be ashamed about. Typical Rita, always has to win the argument, even when we both agree. I should tell her therapist that they should work on that.

"Then why did you disappear?" I said.

Rita shrugged. "Because I suck, Lee."

"Come on. That's not helpful."

"You're telling me."

"I mean that kind of negative thinking."

"Who cares how I think about it? Send me to all the shrinks you want to, Lee. I'm still gonna suck."

I responded with some platitude about there being good in everybody. But it wasn't persuasive. Because you can have some good in you and still, overall, suck.

"You don't believe me? Ask my kids how much good I got. Go ask Harley—she'll tell you! 'My mom sucks.'"

"Well, I disagree," I offered weakly.

"That's because you're stupid, Lee."

"The kids love you."

"Maybe they ain't too bright neither."

"Come on..."

"Even if they did, they shouldn't. Cuz I'm fucking sick of them. Harley? I can't stand the sight of her ratty ass. I swear to God I see her father looking out through her eyes sometimes. Her *real* father, you know? And Jojo—little man—he's the one that started all this in the first place. If you really want to know. Since the day he was born, I felt like a crab with no shell. This last month in the hole, at least I felt like me again."

Once again, I found myself arguing with Margarita on her own behalf. I wasn't skilled enough to overcome the disadvantage. One by one, she picked apart my arguments. Soon enough, I was hardly making any sense at all.

"Then why'd you try to kidnap them? If you're so pleased to be alone?"

"Oh yeah, I forgot. All the best mothers kidnap children. I must have missed that day in parent class. Face it, Lee. These kids are better off with Titi. At least with her, I know that they're with someone who cares about them. At least I know they got each other."

I didn't say anything for a long time. Finally I clasped my hands together and softly cleared my throat.

"Titi didn't tell you, did she?"

"Tell me what?"

The doctor interrupted us just after I got through the official Children's Future justification for separating her children from each other, but before she'd finished cursing at me. He was young and unnervingly thin, with a long neck and cool demeanor—not too much older than the two of us. He told us that Margarita's condition was stable and that, when she was ready for discharge, she'd be referred to mental health and...well, he said, with a look of dispassionate contempt in my direction, domestic violence services, given what had turned up in the health record.

"Oh no. Ha!" I laughed. "I'm not the husband..." But he had already gone.

"How could you do this to them?" said Rita, so softly I could barely hear. "How could you make them go through this alone?"

"Yeah, well I'm not the one who..." I trailed off.

"Who what?"

I knew I shouldn't say it. Two hours after a mentally ill woman tries to kill herself is not the recommended time for the telling of harsh truths.

"Who what, Lee? Say it. Who *what*, faggot?"

I think I was still mad she'd called me ugly. She could call me a faggot all day and it wouldn't bother me—but I knew for a fact that my eyes were not *that* close together. One thing about idealists: we tend to be a little vain.

"Who bailed," I said.

For a moment, I thought she might actually try to bite me. Her eyes had knives and forks. Given the chance, she might have chewed the skin off of my face and spit it in the trash bag hanging from the IV pole. Instead, she did something far more unsettling. She sank into the bed, turned onto her side and began, quietly, to cry.

I must have made a hundred birthmothers in the Bronx cry by now, a hundred times each, at least. I had put in my ten thousand hours. I was a master in my field. I knew exactly when—and, crucially, for how long—to avert my eyes. When to ask, gently, if they'd like a tissue or a glass of water, to nod solemnly along as they tried to catch their breath, to affirm their right to their emotions, their sadness, but never, ever, apologize. But Rita crying? I was not prepared for it. It didn't quite compute. I felt like I was seventeen again, walking in on Ken weeping in the kitchen the day he found out that Tom Petty died; I shared a look with the heart monitor as though it were my older sister, like: did *you* know he was such a fan?

I don't know how long this went on for. Five minutes? Maybe thirty. I sat there, helpless and unnecessary, exchanging looks with the equipment, until at last a knock came on the door. Ty was here, dressed in a puffy jacket wet with snow, face whipped reddish by the wind outside, carrying a bouquet of frozen roses, dripping as they thawed. His hair fell down his shoulders in wild, knotty brambles. Harley stood behind him dressed in sweatpants and furry boots, calm and resolute and playing with her phone. This was one of the only times I ever saw the two of them together. Usually, they'd hang out without me knowing—unsanctioned, unsupervised, unbothered by the System. It was easier for us all that way.

"Yo, Lee! Heil Hitler, baby," he said.

We shook hands with a clasp of the hand, turn of the wrist, clap on the back. After however many years now in the Bronx, I finally had the handshake down.

"You shouldn't have brought Harley here without me," I said.

Ty slapped me on the shoulder as he walked by me towards his wife.

"Who am I talking to? Your twin?"

"Relax, Lee. Ms. What's-her-Name is downstairs," explained Harley, showing off for her parents by being rude to me.

"Morales," I said.

"Nah, that was last week. This one is, like, Henriquez. I think."

Ty pointed with his roses to Margarita's suitcase. "You moving in?" Water splattered on the floor.

"I'm not in the mood, Ty," said Rita.

"Maybe you should take some more Xanax, then. I heard it's good for that."

"Fuck you."

"Guys," I said, motioning toward Harley. "Come on."

"What, you trying to spare Ms. Twenty-five-year-old's feelings? She's a grown-ass woman! Aren't you, Harley? At least that's what her boyfriend thinks."

"He's not twenty-five, Dad. He's nineteen. And we're just talking."

"That sounds fun. Can I just talk to him too?"

"Don't listen to your father, baby," said Margarita.

"I can't understand him anyway," said Harley.

"See what I put up with, Lee? These women and their craziness...."

Ty sat down at the bedside. Harley held her mother by the hand. I hovered by the doorway like some new boyfriend at Thanksgiving, hoping I wouldn't have to say much. Of course, I knew, I should have made Harley leave. The whole point of Children's Future's was to prevent foster kids from being exposed to scenes like this. Traumatic scenes. Memories about their parents that they can't forget. But what memory will hurt her more, I wondered, when she looks back on all this later? That of seeing her mother in this condition, or of some random dead-eyed white guy preventing her from being able to see her mother in this condition?

Margarita touched her hand to Harley's cheek.

"You don't know how good it feels to see you again, baby."

"It's good to see you too, Ma."

"No, you don't know, baby. You're the best thing that I've ever seen. I didn't think that..." Margarita was overwhelmed again.

Ty tried to ask me if I'd seen the Knicks game last night. He flicked his lighter rapidly, manically: flick, flick, flick.

Harley held her mother's wrist, seemingly unfazed. "I know Ma. It's alright."

"It's not alright. It was a mistake. All of this. I didn't mean it. It was just reaction to the medication. The psychiatrist got me on all the wrong levels. It's not like I gave up."

"I know, Ma."

"I don't know what's wrong with me. To leave you like that, waiting. It ain't right, baby."

"It's just one of those things, Ma. You didn't mean it. I know."

"I'm going to make it up to you. This point on, OK? I'll do every damn thing they tell me to. Therapy, drugs training, I don't give a shit. You think I'm going to let this...ho over there break up our family? Hell no...Give me six months. That's all I need. Can you give me that much time? I swear, the night you and Jo come back, we're getting pies from Ray's..."

"Pepperoni and mushroom?"

"Damn right, and with extra cheese too."

"And breadsticks?"

"Two things of breadsticks, baby. All the breadsticks in the Bronx. Though last time they fucked my order up. I'm just trying to say that it's about you. Whatever you want. You and Jo. I'm not having no more slip-ups. No more Margarita days. Ok? I know I owe you that much. I know that you deserve a better me."

"You don't owe me, Ma."

"You believe me, right? Cuz, I swear to God, this time I mean it."

"I believe you."

I saw Harley's foster mother in the hallway now, scowling at her watch. It *was* Henriquez, the fusty retired librarian in her mohair bomber hat. When she saw me, she raised her hands in disbelief. She was one of Anita's favorites, the kind who'd call the agency if I was any more than fifteen minutes late for a home visit.

"Harley," I said... "I think it's time we let your mother get some rest."

"Shut the fuck up, Lee," said Rita.

"He's right," said Ty, standing up. "We all gotta get going..."

"I'm talking to my daughter."

Harley took her mother's hand. "Ma, there's something I've got to tell you."

"Anything, baby. You can always tell me anything."

Harley nodded, thinking it over for a moment. Henriquez tapped on the door, smiling irritably, 'Holaaaaa.' The monitor prattled on about Margarita's vitals to the ceiling. The dead man next door listened closely. At last, Harley leaned down and kissed her mother on the cheek.

"I'm sorry, Ma."

"For what, baby?"

"I don't think I can see you anymore."

◆

"She doesn't really mean it," Rita said, after they had gone. The room was dark now, save for the glow of the TV playing local news on loop. There'd been a fire in a deli down in Soundview. A protest somewhere downtown. She held the roses to her chest and sniffed them, one by one.

I agreed. "She's just emotional right now."

Rita sneered into the bouquet.

"You don't think I got it in me either, do you?"

"Of course I do."

"You're a piece of shit, Lee."

"Uh-huh."

"You think you're some nice fucking guy, don't you? Yeah, I suck. I'm a pig. But you, Lee. You think you're pretty swell."

"That's right. I do think that. I'm swell."

"You're gonna regret coming after my family. You know that right? You don't know who you're fucking with. All of you will. You, Anita Flores, fucking Titi. And if you think I'm giving up, you got another thing coming, boy. Nah. Time I'm done with you, you'll wish to God you'd let me die."

It was late now. The lights in the hallway had gone dim. The nurses changed shifts. I had six missed calls from Anita Flores about another case—some foster mother had gotten picked up for shoplifting, something dumb like that. I muttered that I should get going soon, but as I placed my notebook in my backpack, Rita turned from her side to face the ceiling. Her chest swelled, her breath rasping through the damage in her throat. On the TV, the newscast cut to sports.

"Hey Lee?" she said.

"Yeah?"

"Can you stay 'til I fall asleep?"

# 15.

**As it turned out, this time, Rita wasn't lying.** At least she wasn't yet. Maybe it was the brush with death that changed her. Maybe it was how close she'd come to never seeing her kids again. Maybe, as she once let slip and then denied, Ty was paying for her new apartment in Eastchester on the condition that she stay clean—"so you can tell that heifer that calls herself the *housing specialist* she don't have to work too hard, alright?" Whatever the reason, she arrived on time to the next visit with her eyes bright and present, hair dyed a shade of midnight blue which she swore to God was violet, tied up in a topknot like some kind of psychedelic samurai. She brought a bouquet of flowers for Titi, because: "I'm not the type to shove old ladies. I mean, I don't want to be that type." She gave her therapist cash for the smashed vase in the lobby. Soon enough, she had enrolled in a new substance abuse program and anger management class through her St. Bonaventure suicide counselor, which she swore was "better than those scumbag System classes you sent me to, buddy. At least this one has bagels," and finished not one but two different parenting courses at the Salvation Army on Arthur Avenue, explaining: "Don't I got two kids?"

Of course, for my part, I was thrilled to have her back. As the weeks went by, I felt increasingly vindicated: justified, hell, even a bit absolved. Yeah, maybe I was willing to overlook some issues that I wouldn't have with other clients. But it was working, wasn't it? After all this time, finally—something I'd done worked.

◆

One Tuesday, I was walking from the 5-train on Freeman Street to the agency and found Margarita and Ty idling in the bus lane in Ty's blacked-out Camaro, smoking cigarettes and blaring Fetty Wap. The bassline shook the windshield. Inside, Rita gesticulated wildly, slapping the back of her pink glove into her palm to punctuate some punchline she'd been building towards. Ty leaned back against the driver's side window, sipping an Arizona Ice-Tea through a straw, shaking his head like he'd heard this one before. I knocked on the glass. Rita smiled at me through the tint—delighted to be caught. Ty turned down the music.

"Oh shit," she said. "It's Dad!"

"Yo, Adolf, get this lunatic away from me," said Ty.

"You're just giving her a ride, right?" I said. "Tell me that you aren't back together..." I'd already explained to each of them that, given their DV history, it would be much easier to give Margarita the kids back if I could testify that the two of them were not together. Now they both looked at me, either confused or feigning it.

"*Tell me* that you're just giving her a ride..." I said again.

Rita caught my gist first. She giggled like a teenager.

"Me? You think I'm with this guy?" she said. "This my Uber driver." She slapped Ty on the shoulder. "You know, I thought you looked familiar..."

I coughed into my collar so they wouldn't see me laugh.

"I've been keeping Wednesday afternoons open for you," I said to Ty. "If you want to visit with them on your own..."

Rita slapped him on the shoulder with a pink leather glove. "Please. You think I'm letting this greaseball around my kids without my supervision? You should see the dirt underneath this motherfucker's fingernails..." She opened the car door with a ch-chunk, then turned and leaned back in through the window "Come get me at six?"

But while, to me, Margarita's re-emergence seemed like a miracle, Anita Flores didn't see it the same way. "You know, they only ever get themselves together once it's already too late," she told me at our weekly one-on-one, squinting at my notes on Rita's progress in the System on her glowing computer screen, her transition lenses going dark. And the day after I submitted a report about Rita's latest negative drug tox, Anita made me move her visits with Jojo from Visiting Room 9 into Room 11, a slope-ceilinged, airless hovel that doubled as the file room. It was the room we used for hopeless cases, for mothers that we didn't think would show. Ms. Washington, for example, before she'd killed herself, used to not visit little Curtis there every Thursday. The little guy would sit on the metal folding chair for the mandated thirty minutes, staring at the clock while I read him Dr. Seuss. Now Ms. Washington haunted the room she'd never visited in real life, hoping that her son might come to see her. At least that was my personal theory on why it was always fifteen degrees colder than the other rooms and smelled like gin and wet cigarettes.

Usually, an unexpected change of venue was the kind of thing that Rita would give me shit about. I expected a big fight. But the day I brought her and Jojo into the file/visitation room, she didn't seem to care: "As long as I get to see my little monkey man," she said, pulling Jojo from the beige file cabinet he'd been attempting to scale and then blowing a raspberry on his stomach. "You could make me come to Mars and I'd still show up on time—unless the bus screws me again."

Jojo received the raspberry with skepticism, looking down his nose at his reddened belly like: What was the point of that? As she came back down for more kisses, he barrel-rolled across the thinning carpet, making lilting, inquisitive motor noises with his lips: *Bbbbbbb?* he said. *Phlbbbb?*

Rita pulled him on her lap and tried to calm him down with pictures on her phone—"and here's me with your Daddy, here's a new playpen that mommy bought for you, here's...oops! That one's not for babies..."

Jojo dove off his mother's lap, landed face-first on the floor, and started screaming.

"Chill, little man!" said Rita, pulling him back to her by the ankles. "Am I that bad?"

Jojo rolled onto his other side.

Rita's laughter grew self-conscious. He wasn't a motor anymore. He was all human, all Sand: unaccountably dissatisfied: "Chill! Chill, baby! Please chill for Mommy? Please?"

"Titi told me he's been like this all day," I lied, hoping it might comfort her. She propped herself over him on her elbows, gold *RiRi* pendant dancing on a dangling chain, and pressed her nose to his.

"He doesn't like her food I bet," she said. "Oxtail and nasty-ass goat curry and whatever other voodoo shit she feeds my baby. I'd be a little fussy too."

"Maybe he had too much juice before she dropped him off," I said.

"She feeds him juice? You know that shit is mad unhealthy right?" She said this without a drop of irony.

Jojo kicked off his Transformer shoes and wriggled his way to freedom, crawling elbow-to-elbow like some hellbent Navy Seal. Then he rolled back beneath his mother, giggling and grasping at her chain. Margarita nuzzled his nose again, but this time, her affection seemed to cross some line. You never know with babies. His laughter turned to cries mid-hitch. He pointed an accusatory finger in her face, and shouted *N-N-N-N!!!* At last she carried him over to the bookcase. The two picked through the remains. By this point in the day, the bookcase had been stripped clean by caseworkers who needed them for other visits. All that was left was a squat book with thick, cardboard pages about a mole who befriends a mouse. Even Jojo found the plot far-fetched. He flapped his arms in disapproval, slapped the book out of her hands. Just when her frustration seemed on the verge of welling over, Margarita had an idea. She dug through the baby backpack Titi had dropped him off with and pulled out what she'd been searching for: a plastic jar of applesauce and a little rubber spoon.

"Two-prong approach, Pea-Pod. You read, I feed."

I stiffened slightly when she sat close beside me on the shallow couch.

"Come on, don't just read it," she said, sticking Jojo on my lap. "Ty used to do these funny voices..."

I tried a vaguely Spanish accent for the mouse that I worried might sound racist—but Jo and Rita laughed. She reached over with her spoon hand to point to each of the drawings—"What's that, baby? Who's that little Mexican mouse talking to?" And, with a teasing smirk at me, as applesauce fell in globs from her spoon onto my lap: "I'm sorry, boo—I'm dripping all over you."

"I'm sorry, am I interrupting something...?"

Anita Flores stood in the threshold, rapping her rings against the metal jamb. I snapped the book shut. Rita scooched away from me on the couch, pulled her son off of our laps onto her shoulder.

"What does she want?" Rita said to me.

"Don't you two look like you're having fun?"

Anita wore a black pantsuit with a blue carnation pinned to the pocket, dark blue lipstick; her silver hair chrome in the sepulchral light of the file/visitation room. She pulled up a plastic chair and smiled as warmly as one can while wearing bluish lipstick. I figured she must have just come up from her car because her floral perfume had afternotes of mint and cigarette. Either that or Ms. Washington had drifted in to say hello.

"Gosh, isn't he cute..." Anita said.

Rita snapped Jojo into his car seat; she'd once told me that if she met Anita on the street, she'd lift her by the hair-bun and throw her in the dumpster. I gave her a look to let her know I'd prefer she didn't.

"Yeah, he's getting big though," was all she said.

"Look at those cheeks."

"Uh-huh."

"De-lish."

Margarita nodded warily. The scar on Anita's throat peered out beneath a muslin shawl. The still-pending suspension hung unmentioned between them. They were both too smart to bring it up.

"This can't be easy on you, can it?" she said to Rita. "With all that's going on with Harley?"

"We're just on a little break," said Rita.

"Still, I'm sure it hurts. I'm a mother too, you know."

"So?"

"So, I know what it feels like to see your children suffer."

The night she'd sworn off visitation, Harley had gone back to her foster home in Richman Plaza and cut up Ms. Henriquez's mohair hat with a pair of kitchen scissors. A few weeks later, she'd convinced a foster sister to take a shit in Ms. Antonelli's oven. Her latest removal incident wasn't strictly her fault—I don't think she understood how much diabetics need their insulin. Now her latest placement—with Ms. Kingsley—was already on the rocks. If I had to remove her again, her next move would be to a facility: some group residence like Children's Village or, more likely, Mount Pleasant, where the Bronx's most frequently rejected teenagers swapped cigarettes and HPV, and one-eyed human traffickers hung around the McDonald's by the Metro North on the lookout for fresh runaways.

"She knows how to handle herself," said Rita, brushing a strand of violet from her forehead. "I always taught her that."

"I'm sure you did."

"I did!"

"I believe you!"

"Good."

The two women eyed each other like bloodied grizzlies, lowing at the sky before another charge. Anita rolled a gold-rope bracelet from her wrist up to her sleeve. Margarita cricked her neck.

You know," said Anita. "You and I have a lot in common."

"Mmm-hmm?"

"Did you know I was a foster kid too? Way back in the Stone Age. You had Ms. Baldassari too, right? On Webster Ave? She was old when I was there—she must have been a mummy by the time..."

"She the one who smelled like cheddar cheese?"

"Yes! Ha! I think it was her skin condition. Whenever she'd try and make us go to church we would hide her prescription perfume."

"Me and this kid Andre used to pretend we was possessed by the devil. Write fake Latin shit on the walls in lipstick. One time, Baladassari made us see her priest."

"That's bad. You're bad!"

"Hey Flores?"

"Yeah, hon?"

"I don't really like to talk about the past."

"No, no. Me neither."

"So what'd you bring it up for?"

Anita chuckled gamely. She'd rarely had the pleasure of a worthy adversary.

"What was your mom like, Ms. Sand?"

"Why?"

Anita pulled her chair a little closer. As she spoke, she tugged at the bracelet on her wrist, spinning it round and round.

"Everybody thinks you're some kind of orphan, right, when they hear you're in foster care? Like you're all alone in the world, picking pockets in Times Square. But it wasn't like that for me. My mom was always coming around. Checking on me. Telling me she loved me. We would be together soon. And we almost were, a few times. 'Cuz she could keep it together for a little while. But deep down, I knew that wasn't really her. Some new guy would come around and, well… When you've seen what we have—it's not like you forget it, right? But she still made me pretend that I believed her. Still had to go through the same bullshit every time. And that's what I hated most, you know? Not that she didn't love me—because she did. Not that she was so damn weak. But having to believe in something that I didn't really believe in? That made it feel like my fault, somehow, every time she'd let me down. Like—what did I expect? Like I must be fucking stupid. Did you ever feel that way?"

Margarita shifted in her seat. She rocked Jojo gently back and forth in the car seat, eyes fixed on her baby's face.

"I just said I don't like to talk about the past."

Anita nodded like she understood. Of course. Of course. But, a moment later, she continued:

"I would have understood, I think. If she could have faced what she was. What she wasn't. I would have respected that. At least it would have taken it off me. In the end, we might have ended up with a real relationship. She could have been a kooky grandma to my baby. And I would kill to have that now."

Anita touched two bony, quivering fingers to the dolphin tattooed on Rita's wrist now. Rita stared at the fingers touching her but did not move.

"See, Rita—can I call you Rita?—we're almost nine months into your case. Way more than halfway through. I know you've done some therapy. Some parenting classes. And that's great. I'm so, so proud of you for doing that. But Harley isn't even visiting, is she? And I get the sense that Lee here has been telling you some happy stories lately. Some hopes. Some dreams. But he doesn't know this life like we do, does he? Like Harley does. And even this little munchkin over here. He knows it too. So really, who are we benefitting by making this go on? Maybe it's time for us, all of us, to be honest with ourselves."

As I listened to this conversation—the faint menace in Anita's kindly tone: I thought, How could I have ever thought that Rita and I were in control? That any of this was up to us? Anita Flores had run this place since the crack days. She'd known a million Margaritas. A million Harleys. A million Jojos. A million me's. She was all-knowing. All-seeing. She was God with blue lipstick and Louboutins and Parkinson's.

Finally, Rita spoke:

"You're talking about a 'conditional surrender,' right?"

"That's...Oh. Yes. That's right. Has this already been discussed?"

"This motherfucker over here has been on me for weeks to sign your paper. Says right now, I got no chance."

"Lee has?" Anita looked at me. God seemed confused. Her Louboutin's were fake. "You have?"

I looked from Rita to Anita. Anita back to Rita. I felt like Margarita's shoelace, the night that Ty called in the case. Looped around myself and pulling to a knot that fell apart.

"Yes?" I said.

"And I tell him the same thing every time, don't I, Todd?—If Harley wants me to, I'll sign whatever. But I gotta know for sure that she really doesn't want to come home. Like for real, for real. 'Cuz when I was a kid, my mother couldn't be bothered. I don't want my baby to ever think I just gave up."

"It's not something we'd rush into, hon."

"Maybe Lee could talk to her about it again? So she knows she's got the controls?"

"Sure. You can do that right, Lee? Ms. Sand, I have to say— this is...this is progress. Great progress. It might not feel that way." And then, with a wink in my direction, "And please, don't hold it against Lee, OK? It was his job to try and make you sign."

After Anita had clopped out of the file room, thwarted and impressed, Margarita put her jacket on.

"Is it fucking freezing in here or is that just me?" she said, with an exaggerated shiver.

"What was that about?" I asked.

Margarita pulled the furry hood above her head. "If you keep being easy on me, she's gonna take you off the case."

"I would have brought it up earlier, but I didn't think...Rita—that was an act, right? You're not really thinking of surrender?"

Rita nuzzled Jojo's head. The boy woke up with a yawn. Rita took advantage of his dazed state to get her kisses while she could. She kissed him on the head, cheeks, stomach, butt, again and again and again.

"You know," she said. "I don't even remember what my mother looks like anymore. All I got is bits and pieces. But I turned out alright without her, didn't I? I'm not perfect, but I'm here. So I can get myself a whole new outlook at therapy. I can get a job at Walgreens. I can love my little girl so hard it scares me. But if Harley really thinks that she don't need me—who am I to say she's wrong?"

There wasn't time to argue. The visit was almost over. Soon we'd have to head down to the lobby and hand her baby back to Titi. I looked down at my Timex and told her that we only had a few minutes left. On the wall above the doorway, the clock hadn't worked in months.

◆

Not too long after our case conference in the file/visitation room, I explained to Harley the concept of conditional surrender.

We had the conversation while seated on a plastic-wrapped sectional in a dark and dusty living room in the apartment of Ms. Kingsley, on the 37th floor in the River Park Towers. *Plastic Surgery Addicts* blared at high volume on a gigantic, incandescent TV screen. Harley sat in cannonball position, knees pulled to her chest, hoodie pulled over her head. Through a frosted window smeared with finger-grease, the criss-crossing highways of the Bronx glittered; the borough looked like a skeleton in golden chains.

"So I'd be adopted by who...Ms. Kingsley?" said Harley, pulling tight her hoodie-strings—with an incredulous nod at the dull-eyed and imperious woman sitting two cushions over, paying more attention to the stains on her mumu than the specifics of this conversation.

What could I do but shrug? As far as fosters mothers went, Kingsley was not one of the good ones. In fact, I'd tried to close her home twice already, once the previous fall for spending the money I'd approved for Xavier Dujon's back-to-school clothes on the TV currently lighting up the living room, and again for continually allowing her thrice-convicted brother to sleep in the spare room after he'd failed the Children's Future's background check. Each time, Anita Flores had overruled me. "What Lee...?" she'd said, fingers struggling with the child-lock on her pillbox, "... you think we've got old ladies lining up on Southern Boulevard who want to take in violent teenagers?"

Harley repeated the proposition, slower this time: "You're saying my choices is Rita or... Ms. Kingsley? What about my dad?"

Kingsley interrupted without taking her eyes off of the TV. Her interpersonal style was a charming blend of listless and impatient. She spoke with a sing-song accent that would have sounded almost beautiful if she weren't such an ugly person:

"If you've got no more questions for me," she said. "I'd like to take my bath now."

I did my best to ignore her. "Your dad is not considered a resource at this time," I told Harley.

"But Ms. Kingsley is? You know she has an extra bedroom she doesn't let us into? Every night I gotta listen to Marcus and his nightmares."

"That room is for my son, Mr. Lee. When he comes back from Iraq."

"He *been* gone, Lee! For like five years already..."

"I swear to God, this little girl..."

I wouldn't say I was relieved at how poorly this was going. But I can't deny that a part of me was looking forward to telling Rita about it later. To see the relief in her eye, the nodding of her violet head, a punch on my shoulder that I'd pretend didn't hurt.

"Kingsley," I said. "We talked about this last time. You can't have children of both genders sleeping in the same room. Clean it out, or I'll have to remove them all."

Ms. Kingsley crossed her arms across her mumu. A fat gangster in repose. Of course, she'd been a foster mother long enough to know I had no leverage. To answer Anita's question: no, we did not have old ladies lining up on Southern Boulevard to take in violent teenagers.

"I'm going to take my bath now. Thanks."

"You know why this bitch is always bathing, don't you?" Harley asked as Kingsley shuffled barefoot towards the bathroom.

Actually, I had been wondering about this for some time. It seemed like every time I came here, Ms. Kingsley was about to take a bath. "Why?"

Harley cupped her hand to her mouth to make a microphone. "Because she's fucking DIRTY."

The bathroom door closed. Kingsley turned the water on. Satisfied her joke had landed, Harley returned her attention to the plastic surgery addicts on the TV. I knew I shouldn't leave the matter hanging: even with Kingsley clearly not being a viable permanency option, it was my job to document Harley's thoughts about the possibility of becoming legally freed. From the kitchen, the blender whirred; one of Harley's foster sisters, Empress, mixed fruits and vegetables for the miracle cures she sold down in the plaza. An older teen, Angel, wandered in from the bedroom, shooting at zombies on his phone with the sound on full blast. From the bathroom played the kind of mellow jazz music I'd only ever heard on hold with my insurance provider.

I had to shout to hear myself: "IS THERE ANOTHER ROOM WE COULD USE?"

"Shut up, Lee. I want to hear this."

For the next few minutes, we watched a young man explain to a team of doctors how he'd like them to make him look more like an elf. They shaved the man's nose and ears to pointed edges—afterwards his satisfaction seemed a little forced.

"Alright, let's go," Harley finally said. "This show's mad random."

In contrast to the clutter in the living room, the bedroom looked like a barracks. There were two sets of narrow bunkbeds on either side of the room, separated by a makeshift nightstand: a metal folding chair bearing empty bottles of nail polish and comic books with nail polish stains across the cover. The window by the bed was covered in Saran Wrap to trap the heat. Two more children had been placed in the home since I'd last been here. The walls were white and empty. Kingsley didn't allow them to put up any personal effects because "it's just more cleaning once they leave."

When we came in, a chubby boy with messy braids was doing his homework on a top bunk, dressed in a T-shirt and basketball shorts. I recognized him from Children's Future; I'd once found him sobbing in the lobby, and I'd let him play with my phone until his mom got there. "Hey...bud," I said now, a little awkwardly; I could not recall his name.

"You're Todd, right?" he said. "You know my worker—LaDawn?"

"LaDawn, sure! She and I are friends."

The boy had big front teeth pocked with brownish-yellow calcium deposits.

"She told me you're a pussy," he said.

I smiled tightly at the little bastard. I had tried to buy LaDawn a drink at the latest Children's Future happy hour. "Rum and Coke, please," she'd said, and then with an elbow to Lisa, the sociotherapist from the third floor: "Oh, and Lee? Make sure it don't go...flat."

Harley snapped her finger at her foster brother. "Yeah well, at least he don't wet the bed, Marcus."

"I don't," the boy said. Harley assured him that he did. They went back and forth on the matter, his denials becoming decreasingly convincing, until finally he hopped from the bunk, tried to slap her, missed, then ran out and slammed the door behind him. Alone together now, Harley and I sat on opposing beds, hunching our backs beneath top bunks.

"Listen," I said. "Your mother wants me to tell you that, first of all, she loves you, but she also knows that you are your own person. And that this situation—your life, I mean—it's all in your control."

Harley thought about this for a moment. But as she ran the proposition over in her head, considering my words, her lips curled toward a smirk.

"You and LaDawn was smashing right?" she said at last.

I tried again. "What I want, what your mother wants, is for you to be happy...but I don't want you to feel as though you're under pressure to answer me a certain way, so..."

"Did it not work out because you're not over your fiancée?"

"....what's most important is that you feel heard and listened to and..." I coughed into my hand: "Who told you that? LaDawn?"

"Nah, Titi told me. She said your ass got dumped."

Titi was such a gossip. I'd told her that in confidence, three chamomiles deep.

"Titi never told me you two were still in contact."

"Yeah, sometimes. Just on Facebook."

"Well, I didn't get dumped..." I lied.

"It's OK, Lee. My love life's not so hot neither."

Harley nibbled on her fingernail. Clearly, my checklist would go unchecked today. I wrote *SC undecided on surrender* and sheathed my notebook in my backpack.

"Do you want to talk about it?" I said.

"Not really," she said, sassy suddenly.

"You're the one who brought it up."

"You wouldn't understand, Lee."

"Actually, if there's one thing on this Earth I am qualified to talk about, it's a not-so-hot love life."

Harley fiddled idly with the slats on the underside of the top bunk. "It's just my boyfriend..."

"Jairo?" Fuck—I was not supposed to know his name. "You know how Titi is," I explained a little hastily. "Get some tea in her, that old bird sings like a canary."

"If I tell you something—you promise you won't run and tell my parents?"

"Anything you tell me, it stays within this room."

"You promise, Lee? Cuz if they find out..."

I promised.

The kid let out a long exhale. "Well, you know how guys are. But I didn't want to yet. So it was over. Just like that. I couldn't live without him, though. I like talking to him—he don't just see me like some little kid. You know—I'm not some scared, poor little foster kid. Wah wah wah. You know? So now I'm like: Why don't I? Who cares? It's not like some movie where it's so important—"

Before Harley could arrive at the revelation I was dreading, we were interrupted by Ms. Kingsley in the threshold, looking like a mug shot on the local news with her hard black eyes and slicked-back hair. Her pink puffy bathrobe and matching slippers with kitten's whiskers on them made this effect more unnerving.

"You little THIEF," she yelled.

"Huh?"

"Where's my hair-straightener, thief?"

Harley rubbed her eyes with her shirtsleeve.

"Fuck outta here," she said.

He wanted to...what? I thought. Wasn't sure she wanted to...Oh, shit. Oh, right.

Kingsley's eyes narrowed. Sometimes, her melodic accent could make her irritability come across almost playful. But this was an illusion.

"Where is it then? Tell me where it is, girl."

"Did you check up your butt? I know you got a lotta space..."

"I told you, you take my things one more time—you're out of my house so quick..."

"Ms. Kingsley, please," I said. "Harley and I were having our one-on-one..."

"I do a lot for the agency, Lee. And all you do is give me thieves."

This triggered something in me. Some righteous rage that must have been hiding deep within me all these years. I meant to tell her off, once and for all. To call her a crook. The kind of parasitic grifter that robs these kids of the care they need. But as I stood up, I smacked my head on the top bunk, and in the resulting ringing silence could only think to say:

"Why don't you get back in the bath, Kingsley?"

Kingsley looked confused. My retort hadn't really landed.

"But...I'm done with my bath?" she said.

"Take another one then."

"Why would I take two baths?"

"Cause you're dirty," muttered Harley, with a sigh, less like a joke this time than a lamentable, undeniable conclusion. In the intervening minute, she'd collected herself—walked back from whatever brink she'd finally worked the nerve to step toward. Now, she observed the conflict between her foster mother and caseworker with the weariness of a much older person. Like she was some jaded New York City teacher and Kingsley and I were hopeless teens.

The foster mother told me she was going to report me to Anita Flores for undermining her authority in front of the children. I swallowed all the anger shaking in my throat and said that was her right. When she'd closed the door behind her, I unzipped my backpack.

"Alright," I said. "Give it to me."

"I didn't steal it," said Harley. "I just borrowed it."

"Yeah, well, if she finds it in here, your next stop might be Mount Pleasant."

"You think I give a shit?"

"Yes, I do."

Harley begrudgingly retrieved the hair-straightener from beneath the bed. It was heavy, pink, and looked like gigantic salad tongs that ended in metal heating plates. I wrapped the cord around it and placed it in my backpack. On my way out, I would apologize to Kingsley, then ask to use the bathroom and hide it beneath some towels. That was my plan, at least.

"What were you about to say?" I said, zipping up my backpack. "Before? About your boyfriend."

For a moment, Harley seemed to be working up the nerve again. She gave a big sigh, closed her eyes, and held her head up by the temples, all the classic symptoms of an impending confession. Then, instead she took out her phone and started texting.

"Harley?" I said. "You were saying?"

"Huh?"

"What did you want to tell me? About your boyfriend? He's trying to force you to do something that you don't want to do?"

*Tick Tick Tick.* The tap-dancing of a spider. *Tick Tick. Tick.* "Huh? Ha ha. What?" She giggled loudly at her phone now, HA HA HAAAA, in that self-conscious, showy way of pre-teens trying to make passers-by imagine how must fun they're missing out on.

"Is it...sex?"

At last, she tossed the phone onto her pillow.

"Ew, Lee. What? Oh my god! No. It's just this party coming up," she said. "He wanted me to go. I said no. But now, I think I'm going."

"A party?"

"Ya-huh."

"That's what you wanted to talk about? A party that you don't want to go to? That's what you made me promise not to tell your mom?"

"Yeah, but like I said. I changed my mind. I'm going."

What I said next, I wish I had sold better. Maybe it would have made some difference. The thing is, even as I said it, I knew she'd think I didn't mean it. That there was nothing I could say to make her trust me. Did that mean that what I said was insincere? Maybe not entirely. But, if I'm honest with myself, I didn't quite believe me either.

"If you feel like you're being pressured to do something you don't want to do," I said, writing out my cell-phone number on a piece of paper from my notebook and handing it to her: "I want you to call me, OK? Anytime, any place. Don't worry about bothering me—I got nothing going on anyway. If you ever feel in danger, I'll come pick you up. No questions asked."

For a moment, we were silent. Through the door, I heard Kingsley asking Empress if she'd seen Harley take her hair-straightener—but Empress didn't squeal. Angel saved the human race from the zombie apocalypse occurring on his phone—*POW POW POW*. At last, Harley started back on about my failed engagement, eyes glinting with that Sandian mischievousness that she was getting better at the longer that she stayed in care. Did I still love my fiancee? Had she cheated on me? Was I *so* sad about it?

On my way out, I forgot to re-hide the hair-straightener. I had too much on my mind. The tongs bounced inside my backpack the whole subway ride up to Titi's—patting me on the back with every step I took, as though to say: this is a good idea, Lee. This is you looking out for the kid. Isn't this what parents do?

Titi opened the door with two bright red eyebrows drawn onto her face at far too sharp an angle. It was like she had a mental block when it came to how eyebrows are supposed to look.

"Blanquito!" she said. "What are you doing here?" Jojo was on her hip, clad in a new bright orange New York Knicks onesie Rita had brought for him last week. I tickled his little toe and he screamed and kicked me in the stomach. "I've got chicken and rice going," she said. "Hope you brought an appetite!"

I followed her into the apartment—thinking, should I do this? Is this some kind of violation? Yes.

"Do you still have the way into Harley's phone?"

# 16.

**The texts didn't give me the whole story.** Some I got from Marcus—Harley's bed-wetting foster brother—when I cornered him a few weeks later. Harley told me some of it herself, over a game of checkers in a dingy rec room, long after we'd run out of things to say. Some of it I got from Rita, much later, on one of our long drives home. Still, eventually, in the course of reading through Harley's texts on my brightly-colored, freshly installed ParentInfo 2.0 app—texts to one friend named Celestine, her mom, her dad, her boyfriend, her boyfriend's friends, etc., thousands of them, one after another, *ping ping ping ping*—I found what I'd been after. And since then, it's been after me.

Not all the time, obviously—it isn't my trauma. I wasn't even there. It's not like I've spent the last ten years haunted every waking second. It just comes up sometimes. I'll hear a hiss in the pines behind my condo complex, and suddenly I'm not in my room anymore, but back on Ms. Kingsley's plastic-wrapped couch, my eyes tracing the various Jesuses on the wall. Or I'll hear the burbled whining of my teakettle, right before the shrieking really starts—and by the time I reach the stove I'm running down Southern Boulevard, the warm winds from the subway whipping overhead while snowflakes swarm and swirl.

It even happened the night my wife divorced me, in the back booth at the Chili's in West Lebanon, New Hampshire, not too long ago. I'd been sipping on a Jalapeno CoronaRita as Sara worked through her little speech—I couldn't give her what she needed, she said, I drank too much, and was never fully present: love shouldn't have to be this *hard*. She was right—of course she was. After we'd met on Bumble, we'd only dated for a few months before she'd found out she was pregnant, and we'd been in couples counseling almost ever since. And though I'd done my best to love her the way she deserved—and she did deserve it; she was great—it was a love that lacked conviction. I wanted it to work so badly, and yet, for reasons even I don't understand, I never gave it all I had. So, that night, as I sat back against the booth in the Chili's in West Leb, with the Celtics playing the Denver Nuggets on the TV behind my wife's head, the game heading into overtime, pawing idly at the iPad that they insist you order with even though it kept freezing and rebooting, I knew that this was all my own doing. I'd brought about the one fate that I'd feared most—that my daughter, too, would grow up in a broken home. With uncertainty. Without me there to make sure. Because of me, again, *again,* an innocent little girl would be cast headlong into whatever the void might have in store for her.

The waitress came with my fajitas then. They were sizzling when she brought them, hissing and steaming and crackling on the cast-iron pan they serve them on. I felt it happening, in my head, my heart, my soul. The pines. The kettle. That hissing, *Ssss Sss Ssss.* No, I thought. Not now. Not *now.* I touched my wife on the wrist to tell her that I understood where she was coming from, but also to ground myself to something in this Chili's, to someone, to cling to something physical and present. "I know this isn't what we wanted," Sara was saying, crying softly now, graciously, though I could barely hear her. "But they can't say we didn't try."

I gave a pleading look to no one in particular. What was I pleading for? Who was I pleading to? To the onions and green peppers and blackened chicken screaming on the pan? To Sara, to let us live out our dead-end marriage? To the past, which keeps dragging me back toward it—to make me look, to make me see? The rising steam fogged my glasses. I begged it to stop. At least, let me be present once. That was all so long ago. Let me live my life. Why should I have to relive it? I wasn't even there.

But the hissing didn't listen. It never does. I'm pretty sure it never will. Soon enough, it was all I could hear. I started talking quickly, pressured, trying to drown the sound out with my voice. I told my wife that I would still be a good father, we could stay friends, that no matter what, we will always love each other, in a way, because we'll always share the most precious person in the world and *SSSsssssSSsss* and I am going to make sure of it and *SssssssSSSs* and *SssssSSSsSSS*.

I closed my eyes to collect myself. But when I opened them I wasn't in a Chili's; I wasn't even me. I was back in a foster home off Tremont Ave, nine years ago, looking out through Harley's eyes, like I'd done so many times before and since, looking up at the diamond pattern on the underside of the top bunk in a barracks-like bedroom in the Bronx, trying not to hear the hissing of the pines, the kettle, of the meal the waitress brought me on the night I got divorced, of that same awful sound a hundred ways, a quiet, angry, constant whisper growing in the dark above the upper-bunk:

*SssSSsssSSsssssSSSSssSSSSssssssssssssssssssss.*

◆

Harley punched the mattress overhead. Was that...she thought. No. Oh, come *on*.

"Marcus!" she whispered.

Four children shared one bedroom in Ms. Kingsley's house. Harley and Marcus on the bunks on one side, Angel and Empress on the other. Above Angel, Empress lay on top of the sheets in her mesh shorts and the sandals she never took off. The snare drums in her headphones sounded like someone tapping a piece of paper gently in the dark. The moonlight cast a glowing square on the hard floor between the bunkbeds.

*SsssSSsssssSSSsssSsssssss.*

"Marcus!"

The smell permeated the room now. The wet stain spread. Harley figured it would only be a matter of time before it started raining urine. She jumped out of the bed and shook the boy awake.

"For real, Marcus?" she said.

The boy opened his eyes.

"What?" he groaned.

"It happened again."

"No it didn't. I swear. I'm dry."

"I *heard* you."

"You can't *hear* pissing, Harley."

"Then what the fuck's that smell then?"

Marcus exhaled a long, doomed sigh.

"Come on," said Harley. "Get up. Be quiet."

She took some clothes out of the dresser and led him to the bathroom.

"You're not going to tell Angel, right?" he said, coming out of the bathroom dressed in basketball shorts, his boxers in a plastic bag.

"If he gives you shit, I'll tell homeroom how we caught him jerking off."

"Kingsley said she'd kick me out next time I ruin her sheets."

"When she goes out, we can take them to the laundromat. You can stay in my bed tonight."

Marcus's eyes bugged. For a second, Harley didn't realize what she'd said.

"Yeah right, Marco," she said. "No. I'm going out."

Marcus's relief was total.

"Oh yeah?" he said, nonchalantly, playing it as cool as one can while dangling a shopping bag of pee-soaked undies by one's side. "Where you going?"

Harley took the bag from him and tied the handles shut.

"To a party," she said.

◆

Harley got dressed in the bathroom, squeezing into a pair of jeans Rita had brought for her at one of their early visits. *Hey sexy mama!* her mom had said while Harley tried them on in the Children's Future bathroom—*hey ma, yoo can I get yo' numbaaaaaa sexy mamaaaaa*. Now, she took a couple of selfies, texted them to Jairo, despaired at the lighting, then perused Ms. Kingsley's cabinet for some makeup she could steal. She hated the way her hair looked—frizzy and greasy from her unwashed pillowcase—but she couldn't risk the noise the shower would make. Where had Lee Todd put that damn hair straightener?

"What are you guys gonna do?"

Marcus had come back from the bedroom. He stood in the bathroom door.

"How long you been standing there?"

"I have to pee."

"Again? Bro you gotta get that bladder checked."

Marcus shrugged.

"What are you looking at?" she said, irritated now. "Go the fuck back to sleep!"

Marcus was at his most annoying when his feelings were hurt. His softness; the damp, sad look in his eyes. That brown stain across his front teeth. The way that he was fat and skinny at the same time and had that hunched, scared look about him, like a dog who knows you're gonna kick him, and it just makes you want to kick him more.

When she got her makeup right, she crept out into the living room and scanned the room for signs of Kingsley. Candles burned on a wooden TV tray in the corner near the door. Eucalyptus plants strained out of their vases, brushing her as she walked by. There were a thousand different pictures of Jesus in the hallway. Happy Jesus, sad Jesus, Black Jesus, white Jesus, thoughtful Jesus being nice to Judas, sexy Jesus eying the camera, his little gown slipping off his shoulder. Harley reached for the lock on the door and turned it as slowly as she could. She felt the gears of the door unclasping. The door clicked open.

"You think I could come too?"

She turned to see Marcus standing in the living room, his glasses crooked on his face, dressed now in cargo pants too tight in the crotch and a T-shirt too loose at the neck. Kingsley never bought the kids new clothes. He stood there in the flickering candlelight with his hand on his hip. He even stood annoyingly.

"Go the fuck back to bed. For real."

"Are you gonna have seeeexxxxx?" said Marcus, batting his eyes.

"Yeah, I'm meeting with your mama."

"My mom's dead, you know."

"Shut the fuck up, Marcus."

"Come on, let me go with you."

"Shhhh—"

Harley thought she heard something stirring. What would she do if Kingsley caught her here, sneaking out again? I'll hit her with a flying kick to the stomach. If she takes away my phone, I'll kill myself.

"Look," she said now, "it's not your scene, Marco. It's gonna be all Jairo's friends. The kinda guys that hate you. The kinda guys that stole your backpack and took a shit in the pocket. Remember?"

"They were just playing around. I'm cool with all those guys."

"You can't come, Marco."

"Well then I'm gonna tell..."

"Boy, if you even think..."

"MS. KIIIINGSLEY."

Harley grabbed him by the neck of his T-shirt. It gave a little as she pulled.

"Alright, alright. But you can't come dressed like that. Go take some of Angel's clothes from the dresser."

A moment later, Marcus came back out of the bedroom dressed in their foster brother's clothes, wearing a big Dallas Cowboys football jersey and jeans so big the cuffs scraped the floor. Harley hid her smile with her hand. She led him out the door into the hallway, down the steps and down the street, thinking about old days, how she used to have to bring her brother with her everywhere.

◆

The party was in a crumbling house in Crotona, with sleepy boarded windows and a front porch that slumped into the snow. Big snowflakes cruised through the slanting streetlight, landing softly on her cheeks. She and Marcus stood together on the curb, sharing a long and nervous feeling.

"I still have to pee," Marcus informed her.

"Remember what I told you," she said. "Don't say nothing weird. Don't correct nobody's English. And don't tell nobody you're my brother neither, because you're not. You heard me?"

Marcus breathed into his hands to warm them. A voice came down from above:

"Yo Har-leeeeee."

Jairo popped his head above the edge of a plywood board covering half of the second floor window. It made her stomach flutter just to hear him say her name. He leaned halfway out of the house.

"Climb the fence and sneak around back."

Harley responded with all the coolness she could conjure. She wasn't a kid tonight. There was nothing to act kiddy for. Still, she must have smiled a little too brightly, or let a lilt into her tone, because as she helped Marcus over the fence and they slunk across broken glass and dogshit scattered across the driveway, her foster brother turned back with a grin, his voice filled with equal parts delight and phlegm.

"Ooooooooooooo," he cooed. "Ooooooo ooooooo ooo ooooooooo."

Inside, the walls were rotting and covered in graffiti. Stairs to the second floor caved in at the middle into a pit of wood and splinters. The living room walls were stripped down to the studs. Ten kids sat on metal chairs in a circle around a charred piece of floor, all bundled up in jackets, hoods and gloves, drinking from brown paper bags. Blunts dangled from their mouths and glowed orange at the tips. Music played from someone's phone.

A fist clenched in Harley's stomach. Why hadn't anybody said hello to her? The boys in the circle continued blowing smoke. The girls talked amongst themselves. Was it because she was younger? Most of them were in high school already. Harley looked to Marcus, who stood in the corner, picking his nose, eating it. She remembered a piece of advice that Rita had once given her: Don't let anybody see your nerves.

"What up, Tina?" she said, squeezing a girl's shoulders as she made her way around the circle. "What up, Toon," she snatched a wonky-eyed boy's hat. "What up Titty Boy! Honk honk!" She grabbed the chest of a fat boy through his jacket. She said hello to Jairo's best friend, Stacks. He had Chinese tattoos up his neck and a lazy eye, and no matter how nice she was to him, all he ever did was stare.

There weren't any chairs left in the circle. For a moment, that old sadness resurfaced—why are there never places for me nobody likes me where's Marcus let's just go. Finally, she found herself a spot leaning against the wall, behind where Jairo sat. She poured herself a plastic cup of juice and vodka and drank it down where she stood.

"You a vodka girl? said a voice on her other side—Stacks was beside her against the wall. Was that his hand on her back? Whatever. Jairo was talking to some older girl, so whatever. She put her hand to his chest and said she was an anything girl. "Here you go then," he said, and handed her another drink, his hand tracing down her back, lower, lower, lingering on her belt for just a moment. Then he walked away. Harley's heart threw punches at her sternum. Could anybody see her nerves? Nah, she thought. I got it. No one sees them.

Alone now against the wall, she drank this drink more slowly, watching the faces of the others to gauge what reaction they might want from her. HaHAhaHA, she said, when she figured it was time to laugh, that's crazy you buggin' like oh my god yo wowwww.

Marcus was engaged in his own struggle, hovering by the far wall, taking a break from looking at his phone every so often to laugh way too hard at some joke he didn't understand. He ambled between circles, stepping over nails and glass on the stripped, rotting floors, shifting a can of beer between his hands, looking down at it every so often, eyes filled with concern, as though he'd just been informed it wasn't supposed to go down his throat but up his ass.

As the night went on, Jairo continued not paying her any attention. He was talking to some girl she recognized from the Dunkin Donuts on Boston Road—cream and sugar, she thought, that's what I should call her. No, I'm not that funny. No one would laugh. What am I even doing here? I didn't want to come. She and Marcus should just go home—"home"—back to Ms. Kingsley, back to the pee-stained bunk beds where they belonged. If they left now they could get home by midnight, away from all these people who could never understand, back to their candlelit apartment full of Jesus and TV and mean Jamaican prison guards.

Marcus caught her eye then. He gave a nervous smile. Harley nodded, drank the rest of her drink, and took a step in his direction. Come on, little brother, she'd tell him, let's go "home."

Then she felt fingers through the belt loops of her jeans. If it was Stacks, she'd have to tell him off. I was just being nice, bro. But no. Thank God. Jairo took her hips in both hands and pulled her onto his lap. She leaned her head back into the warmth of his chest. The time was now. Ready. Not? She crooked her neck around his to whisper into Jairo's ear.

"You want to take me upstairs?" she said.

Jairo grabbed her by the hand and pulled her toward the staircase. Harley waved goodbye to the room.

The bedroom upstairs was empty save for a pillow fort leaning against the corners of the far walls, composed of mismatched couch cushions, covered by a sheet. The moon poured through the window and made a silver spotlight on the floorboards. It was cold enough to see her breath.

"Yo, get out," said Jairo, stomping on the creaky floors. There was some rustling, some muted giggling, and a minute later a boy and girl crawled out from the fort, looking sheepish, holding their shoes and fixing their hair. The boy muttered something to Jairo, then turned and slapped him on the butt on his way out. He didn't say anything to Harley. But she didn't care. She was drunk enough now. Jairo's swagger from downstairs had dissipated entirely. He clutched at the back of his neck. They stood on a piece of moonlight for a long, cold moment, watching their breaths collide.

When Harley couldn't take it anymore, she sprang. She grabbed the back of his head and kissed him so hard their front teeth clicked. She pushed her tongue into his. She grabbed him around the waist and pulled him down on top of her. The two of them pulled at their belts and crawled together across the brittle floorboards, through the entrance of the fort's hanging sheet. Inside, it was darkness. She took her cellphone and placed it face-up on the floorboards: "I want to see you," she said. He was on top of her now, his shoulder pressed against her nose, breath smelling like potato chips; she counted the flowers printed on the sheet. In this dim light they looked like gray bouquets.

Margarita had always told her it would feel like getting stabbed, but now she knew that wasn't true. That was just to scare her. It wasn't so bad. She could stand it. She liked to stand it. She closed her eyes and gritted her teeth and dug her nails into his shoulder, and let the pain run through her. It was bright, it was good—the pain expanded within her, burning through the fog, leaving her alone, here, with him, the purest version of herself. Her vision enhanced. Her senses jumped. Jairo breathed heavy and ragged. The pain shot from her stomach, up her spine, and straight out through her lips. I love you, she said then. Yeah. Good. Ow. It's not bad. It's good. I'm not scared. No kid shit. I—ow—love you. She said it aloud again. I love you. I love you. I love you.

When they were done, Jairo eased himself out. Harley pulled up her jeans as quickly as she could so he wouldn't see the blood. Margarita had told her there'd be fountains of blood, gushing, exploding from you like a volcano, baby, so you better not. But there wasn't. There was just a little.

"I was good, right?" said Harley, finally.

Jairo rubbed his eyes. His breath was slow and deep. Harley pulled herself into the crook of his arm. He stiffened slightly. Her eyes had adjusted to the cellphone light. She saw now that the gray flowers were really pink and purple.

"Yeah," she said. "I was good."

Jairo was far off, wide-eyed, unblinking.

"Wait here," he said. "I'll be back in a second."

He pulled up his pants and crawled out of the fort. Harley listened as his feet creaked across the stairs. The pain was starting to accumulate, building back up, not bright now but dull and aching. She'd hoped to feel more different. New. But here she was, still Harley, thinking: was that it? Was that how it's supposed to go? And where had he gone? Did he regret it already? Was she not good? How could you even be good? To her relief, she heard footsteps coming back up the stairs. Elbows and knees crawling across the wood. A head poked through the sheets.

Harley jolted upright.

"What are you..." she said, covering her chest up with her arms—"...what are you doing here?"

Stacks didn't say a word. He crawled through the darkness, and then he was on her. His breath warmed her neck. She was paralyzed, a bump on the floor. "J said you were up for anything," he said, his hands pinning down her shoulders. Outside, she heard more footsteps coming up the stairs, crowding outside the bedroom. Planks creaked beneath the weight of many feet. His drool was in her hair. Some laughed. Others listened. What's so funny? Ha ha ha. Where was Jairo? Where had he gone? Where was he? There he was. That was his laugh. His voice. Who's next? Mackey? DJ? Then Marcus's, thin and high and terrified. "Hey, what are you guys...". A tussle, a small boy thrown against the wall. Don't let them see you, baby. Don't let them. Harley closed her eyes and counted flowers on her eyelids.

◆

On the walk back to Kingsley's, the snow turned to sleet. The streetlights made the black streets shine. A police car slowed as it passed on Southern Boulevard, then flicked its lights and drove away. Marcus walked ahead, one hand to his back from where he'd landed on the floor; he kept asking if she was OK. "Shut the fuck up Marcus," she told him. Because she was. Who cares? She liked to feel this way.

One foot went in front of the other. Puddles of slush and ice. Her legs hurt. Her bones hurt. At the corner of East 180th, she made a snowball and threw it at Marcus. It burst against his jacket. "What—you gonna tell your Mama?" she said, and tried to force a laugh. Marcus looked at her like she was a ghost.

◆

The next day at school the rumors started. "Choo choo," one girl muttered from the back the classroom in Social Studies. "All aboard," called another, as Harley passed her in the hallway. Harley laughed along. It didn't bother her. Why should it? Halfway through biology, she packed her bag and left.

"Is everything alright, honey?" She was in the nurse's office now, lying down on a brown cot, reading a cartoon poster on the wall about an anthropomorphic bottle of hand sanitizer dressed up like a cop and arresting the germs that cause a cold. It smelled like microwave pizza in this office. Stale bread and old tomatoes. The smell got inside her clothes. Her brain. She spat onto the floor. She pulled her legs into her chest and curled up in a ball. That stale smell. Oh god.

"Do you want me to call your parents?"

◆

I picked her up an hour later. I didn't yet know the extent of what had happened. All I knew is that, for some reason, at

3:30 AM that morning, she'd texted Margarita for the first time in three months. *I miss you*, she'd said. And at 8:00 AM, Margarita responded, sensing something through the phone: *What's wrong baby? Are u OK? Call me.*

"Not feeling good, huh?" I said when Harley got into the car. And later, after a long and loaded quiet: "Hey—you never told me. How did the party go?"

Harley texted someone. I felt the vibration in my pocket. "Maybe it's something you ate..." I said.

When we pulled up to Ms. Kingsley's apartment. I put the car in park and reached into my backpack. "Almost forgot," I said. I pulled out Ms. Kingsley's hair straightener.

Harley looked at me with confusion and disgust, like I had reached into my backpack and handed her a rotten fish.

"Kingsley's still at work, right?" I went on, oblivious. "So when you get upstairs just hide it underneath some towels or something. I've had it on my desk for like a week now. Are you sure everything's alright?"

That night, Harley and Marcus sat on the plastic-wrapped couch together in the living room, watching *Plastic Surgery Addicts* on TV. This episode was about a woman who wanted to look like a lizard. The doctors sliced a slit into her tongue, dyed the whites of her eyes yellow, and implanted horns at each temple. "What kinda lizard has horns?" Harley asked Marcus. "A chameleon," he said, "I think."

Harley's phone went off. It was her mother again.

*Are u ok?*

Harley didn't respond. How did she know, she wondered? Did somebody tell her? Ms. Kingsley came into the living room then, dressed only in her fuzzy bathrobe and kitten slippers. In her hand, she held the giant metal tongs of the hair-straightener. She clacked them together like a lobster claw.

"What's this?" she said.

Harley sighed. "I don't know."

"You thought I wouldn't notice that it somehow just reappeared? Like magic, huh? Girl, you're just as dumb as you are sneaky."

On the screen, the lizard-girl held a mirror to her face. She flicked her forked tongue with delight. Harley's phone buzzed again. It was Margarita—three times in succession. *Xo Xo xo* and *Can you call me?* and *I miss u too baby more than u could ever know I was just tryin to give space if that's what u needed.* Her phone vibrated over and over: *zzz, zzz, zzz.*

Kingsley shut the door to the bathroom. Her bath was almost ready. The water had been running for a while now. Her mellow jazz was playing: a saxophone hitting raunchy 7ths. Harley thought of Kingsley's naked body, sloshing in the suds. Choo choo, she thought. All aboard. It wasn't so bad. It was fine. She could stand it. She texted her mother: *40 Richman Plaza, apartment 37D—can you come pick me up right now?*

"What are you doing?" called Marcus, from the couch, as she picked the lock to the bathroom with a wire hanger. Kingsley lay back in the clawfoot tub, eyes closed, candles burning, drifting off to sleep. The hair straightener lay beside the bathroom sink. Harley made sure it was plugged in. The saxophone hit a flat note and held it—the backbeat came in soft. *Tsk tsk-tsk tsk.* When she saw her coming, Kingsley tried to stand, slipped and fell back, still half-in the tub. *Tsk-Tsk tsk.*

The saxophone scaled an octave, squeaking on its way, bending off the note. A heavy plunk, a blue flash, the music cut, then total darkness. Once the thrashing stopped, and Kingsley's screams dwindled down to painful whimpers, the only sound Harley heard was the straightening iron cooling in the water, a low hiss in the darkness.

*SssSSSssSSSSssSssSSSssssSSssssSSSssSss* it went. *Ssss SSSSSsss. Ssssssssssssss.*

# 17.

**Coincidence of coincidences:** the two EMT's that loaded Kingsley into the ambulance were the same two that had narcan'ed Margarita back to life just a few months before: a wiry woman with a shiny ponytail and an impossibly jacked Asian guy. They didn't recognize me as I passed them on my way upstairs. Anita Flores was in the living room already, sitting on the couch with the three remaining foster children, coordinating a pizza order and trying to find a movie they all could watch together. Two police officers leaned against opposite doorway frames, flirting with each other. The bathroom smelled like a pot roast.

"You got any idea where the kid mighta run off to?" one of officers asked me—sipping on a can of Sprite. I said sure and gave the wrong address.

Anita Flores wore a loose blue cocktail dress, pearl earrings, and stilettos. She smelled like white wine and Chanel No. 5. "Really, Lee?" she'd sighed, when I'd called to tell her what had happened. "Why is it always when I'm on a date?" In Kingsley's apartment, she somehow had the children laughing already. She was good with things like that.

"One of my foster mothers used to keep our couch all wrapped up too," she was saying as I sat down on the couch beside them, shifting weight to make the plastic groan. "Used to drive me crazy."

"One time I spilled a glass of milk on the recliner," said Angel. "Ms. K made me sleep out on the fire escape."

Anita glanced accusatorily in my direction, as though Kingsley's unfitness as a foster parent was something that I should have reported to her six times instead of five. "She wasn't very nice to you guys, was she?" she said.

Angel wouldn't admit one way or another whether he cared if anyone was nice to him. To him, he said, it was all funny. Empress changed the subject by telling a story about how Harley had once filled Kingsley's shampoo bottle with mayonnaise. Marcus stared into a distance that the cluttered room did not permit.

"You should have seen her flopping, Mr. Lee," he said. "Harley didn't say a word."

Empress did her best imitation. She lay down on the floor, held out her wrists and shook them: "Bzzz AHHH bzzzz-bzzzz."

"H-h-h-h-h-h Harley n-n-n-nnooo," said Angel, joining in, chattering his teeth, pulling his hair back from his forehead.

Marcus wasn't laughing. He kept his eyes low on the floor. "They're just showing off," he muttered to me, fiddling with the ankles of his mismatched socks. "They weren't even here."

Anita was scrolling through Kingsley's Netflix account: "I've seen that," she said. "That too. Oh, that was terrible..." Based on the algorithm's recommended titles, it seemed Ms. Kingsley watched mostly true crime: *An American Murder*, and

All-American Killer, and Murder in America. "Oh...look, Frozen!" said Anita, clicking onto the Kids tab. "I've heard that's good."

Empress groaned.

"I swear to God, even when Harley's gone, she's still gonna make us watch that fucking movie."

Marcus pulled on my sleeve.

"If she dies, will Harley go to jail?"

"Of course not," I said, though I had no idea. Kingsley was alive but not moving when I'd passed by her body on the stretcher. Her eyes were closed, one arm over her eyes, breathing into an oxygen mask.

"But you're going to send her up to Mount Pleasant, I bet."

"We have to make sure she's somewhere she can be safe."

"My big brother's up there too, I think—you know a big dumbass named Lance?"

I did know Lance. He and I had once played pool together during a lockdown in the Mount Pleasant rec room—some kids from the Blue Wing had been trying to escape. I told Marcus he was doing well.

"Can I talk to you?" Anita said, once the kids had settled on an episode of The Office that they'd all seen a hundred times before.

I followed her into the Jesus hallway. She wobbled on her heels. Anita always drank too much on first dates.

"We need to find her before the cops do," she said. "If we can get her up to Mount Pleasant, they won't arrest her. But it's such short notice. We'll have to say she's in an acute mental health crisis."

"Attempted murder doesn't cut it?"

"Please. You don't have to be crazy to want to kill Ms. Kingsley. No, let's get her to my buddy at St. Bonnie's..."

"The Psych ER?"

"Yeah. Any idea where she might have run to?"

Yes, I thought. "No," I said. "But I can call her mother."

Anita gave me a chilly look.

"Birthmom? Baby girl with the face tats, right? She's not gonna tell you shit."

"She might. You never know. She can be reasoned with, remember?"

Anita gave a tilt of the head, a smirking frown, as though she had no recollection whatsoever of our meeting in the file/visitation room. Although to be fair, she supervised almost a thousand cases.

"I'll believe that when I see it," she said. "But hey, you're the birth-mom whisperer, right? Go with God, Pea-Pod."

◆

Since Ty had started paying her rent, Rita had been living up in Eastchester, on the third floor of a high-shouldered Victorian she called "The Purple Palace." The house was flamboyant in its decay, with bulbous turrets and splintered balustrades and unplugged Christmas lights wound around the pillars of a shallow, cluttered porch. The railings and gutters were slightly different shades of purple and the lawn had not been mowed in years. In a fairy tale, it would be where the witch lived.

Rita opened the door before I'd even knocked. Her hair was its natural black for the first time since I had known her, tied up in a sloppy bun that popped up from a purple headband. She wore SpongeBob PJ pants and one of Ty's enormous sweatshirts.

"She's not here," she said.

"I'm just here to talk."

"You here as my friend or as my caseworker?"

It was the nicest thing she'd ever said to me.

"Let's not make this worse," I said.

I followed her up a huddled flight of stairs blocked partially by a wheelless racing bicycle and a kitchen chair with amputated legs. A pair of men's sneakers were in the entryway, nestled together like lovers on a Sunday morning, but Rita said they weren't Ty's. "He's off in one of his ghostly phases..." she began. "I ain't seen him in like a month."

Inside, the floors were covered in wall-to-wall wheat-colored carpeting, even in the kitchen. I told her I'd have to search the house for Harley. I opened closets, the cabinets beneath the kitchen sink and either side of the refrigerator, the linen closet in the narrow hallway. Rita's bedroom had only a bed, hamper, a dresser and a closet full of knee-boots and shimmering dresses. It's such a viscerally inhumane feeling, to search a home for a little girl in hiding. Is this how the Nazis felt, I wondered—the ones with consciences at least? The ones who were OK, at least compared to other Nazis? Still, my general air must have been more inept than genocidal, for Margarita didn't seem to fear me in the slightest. While I quietly ransacked her home, she sat on a beanbag chair inside a playpen, surrounded by a scattered ring of toys, making the kind of small talk that we would on any routine monthly visit.

"Did I tell you I got a little daycare going?" she said. "My cousin's son stays here on Wednesdays. Neighbor girl on Friday nights. I bought them all this shit to play with, but all they want is my phone."

I threw open the door to the closet beside the TV. An ironing board fell down and thwacked me on the shoulder. It didn't seem like the time to remind her that birthparents with children in the System are legally barred from providing childcare. Anyway, I'd told her that before. So I went with: "How's that been going?"

The next closet was behind the couch, packed to the gills: paper towels rolls, boots and jackets, an unstrung acoustic guitar, an dining set still wrapped in plastic, but not one foster child. Back in the TV room Margarita was cleaning up the toys in the playpen. She slammed the toy chest shut.

"It's fun," she said. "Gives me somebody to talk to, so I don't go crazy all alone. And you can tell little kids anything. The other day I told them I'm a famous singer—my single's called '2 Hot, 2 Heavy,' but with the number 2's. They were just like, 'Oh yeah? Cool.'"

In the bedroom, I got down on all fours to look beneath the bed. Margarita hovered in the doorway.

"What you think about these carpets, Lee? Ty told me if I pull them up, there might be hardwood floors."

"Mmm-hmm."

"And—hey, look," she said. "No broken pipes spraying mist everywhere. Nice digs huh? Feel like I'm living at the Ritz."

I got up off all fours.

"It will be much better if you give her to me than to the cops," I said, finally.

My forwardness offended her. This was supposed to be an amiable raid. Margarita sniffed.

"I'm not giving her to anybody."

I went into the other bedroom. There wasn't any furniture other than a mattress on the floor. The light in here was broken—the light from the hall made my shadow look gigantic on the bare, white wall.

"I know you're trying to be a good mother," I said. "That's not what this is about."

"Trying? Fuck you, Lee."

"Harley needs serious help. Professional help. We have to get her somewhere safe."

"Help, huh? Professional help? You're talking about medication, right? Load her up on lithium so that she don't care where you send her? What happened to the 'substance free' shit you're always trying to sell me on? How we should just accept ourselves? Nah, Lee. You just want your girls on the right drugs, huh? So you can push our heads below the table?"

Margarita flicked her hair as she said this, eyes twisting with that same mocking look I always seem to get from women once they get to know me. She sat down on the sofa and kickstarted her knee, up and down, up and down, up and down.

"You know that's not what happened," I said.

"Maybe not. But I got the clip saved on my phone, buddy boy. And I can make that shit look like whatever."

"Do it then. See if your next caseworker puts up with half the shit that I do."

I gave her back her eyeroll and she gave it back to me. We played catch this way for a while. I continued my search in the bathroom. Harley wasn't in the shower. She wasn't in the towel closet either. Maybe—no—beneath the...sink?

Rita's ankles cracked as she followed me into the bathroom, her bare feet sticking on the tile, leaning with her arms crossed against the door.

"What are you trying to do to me, Lee?" she said, desperation coming into her voice.

Perhaps unsurprisingly, Harley was not hiding beneath the bathroom sink. Crouching still, I spoke over my shoulder.

"I'm trying to help you."

"So help me."

I felt her coming up behind me now, just a foot or so away. She took her hands from her PJ pockets and put them on her hips. As I turned and stood, our eyes connected for a moment. I'd always thought her natural hair was black—but this close, it was dark brown. She wasn't wearing her usual amount of too much makeup, or those fake, long, spider's-legs eyelashes, or that heavy blue mascara—it was just her, unadorned and unencumbered, staring straight through me. Suddenly, I felt light-headed. Flecks of light darted like golden minnows on the white walls of the bathroom. The bathroom walls seemed to contract. Rita took another step towards me, her forehead coming up just to my chest. Her lips twitched briefly, then parted again. Before she got her next words out, I found the ones that I'd been searching for. Just in the nick of time.

"I know that Harley trusted you in coming here," I said. "And I know that's precious to you. But Anita Flores is waiting outside. If you don't tell me where she's hiding, the System doesn't care that it's out of love, or loyalty, or that you're trying to protect her—it just means you won't comply."

Rita broke her gaze from mine and sucked her teeth. She crossed her arms, and leaned back against the wall, a little hissy now.

"You wanna talk about complying? What about my parenting class? My therapy? The pills that dry my skin out and make the whole world taste like pennies? You know I made Ty move out just so I might have better chance to get them back. But what was it all for, if all it did was turn me into the kind of mom who rats on her own daughter?"

The ledge of the bathroom sink dug into the small of my back. The golden minnows flew away. I felt more sane with every second.

"It was for right now, Rita. All of it. For this exact moment. So that when it matters, even when it hurts— especially when it hurts—you'll do what's best for her."

She thought it over for what felt like fifteen months. Then gave a little nod. Slowly, she took the headband from around her wrist and stuffed her hair back into its bun. She opened her eyes wide and nodded in the direction of her bedroom.

"Look man," she said. "I know how much you love hide and seek. But you're never going to find someone that isn't here. So maybe you should stick to hiding..."

Of course, I thought, once it finally clicked. How could I have been so stupid? How could I not have looked there first? Maybe I wasn't cut out for the SS after all. Himmler would have sent me to the front.

I didn't go directly into the bedroom. I made a show of searching behind the couch, outside in the hallway, slammed open and shut the cabinets in the kitchen one more time: "Fine! Don't tell me!" I said. "I can search this place all night."

In the bedroom, the hamper in the corner creaked. It was not the same one that I'd hidden in all those months ago. This one was plastic. I sat down on Margarita's unmade bed.

"Come on kid," I said. For a moment, the room was still. Then the sheets stacked atop the hamper slid gently to the floor. Harley emerged from a grave of clothes, sweatshirts and underwear tumbled of off her, her skin slick with sweat, her hair matted to her cheek, her eyes swollen, unrepentant.

"Did I kill her?" she asked.

"Last I heard, she's in the ICU."

◆

Outside, Anita Flores had the engine idling. Margarita followed close behind us, down the stairs, over the walkway, eyes downcast, hands in the front pocket of Ty's sweatshirt— Where are you taking her, Lee? she asked. Please, Lee. Please. Just tell me where you're taking my baby.

"To the hospital," said Anita out the window, as Harley suddenly fought against me, straining against my grip, kicking me in the shin with her heel. "Fuck you, Lee," she said. "I'm telling Jairo about this, faggot." I opened up the backseat and forced her in.

"They'll need to put her under observation," Anita added.

With the look that Rita gave her, I worried she might reach in through the window and snap Anita's glasses in half. That'd be just like her: to throw away her good graces in the moment that she'd earned them. But she didn't. Instead, she took a deep breath. She rapped her fingers on the driver's side window.

"Can I ride with you guys?" she said.

Anita shook her head and hit the gas. The tires groaned across the gravel.

"Nice work," she said, as we pulled off down the street, leaving Rita in the rearview, cursing in the cold. In the backseat, Harley dialed Jairo and left a message: Would he round up Stacks and some of the others to storm the hospital and set her free? *Don't you love me?* she said. *Don't you love me? Don't you care for me at all?*

"How did you find her?" said Anita. The streetlights striped her face.

I checked to see that Harley wasn't listening. She was crying too hard to hear.

"I told you Mom would do the right thing," I said. "She called me as soon as Harley showed up at her house. I guess she's one of the good ones after all, huh?"

We turned onto Southern Boulevard. The subway rumbled overhead. The lights turned red to green. Confined between the subway ramparts, the street looked like a hallway that would never end.

"Typical birthparent," said Anita. "Just when her children need her most, she stabs them in the back."

# 18.

**The Psychiatric Emergency Room at St. Bonaventure Hospital** looked and felt like the inside of a microwave: a buzzing windowless cube reeking of stale humanity and disinfectant, walls white and pocked with gunk. Patients lay about the room, stretched out on worn pleather recliners bolted to the floor. One woman paced back and forth, her hair tied back in a pristine white braid, asking over and over why she had been forsaken by somebody named Israel. Is-RAY-EEL, she screamed, full of phlegm and anguish: WHY ME? WHY ME? IS-RAY-EEL WHAT HAVE I DONE? A nebbish man in spectacles shadowboxed in the corner. I'd seen him before on Southern Boulevard, challenging the old men who sat on lawn chairs outside the candy store to knock him out. In the far corner, a man with blue contact lenses and his head shaved and tattooed with a giant Mercedes Benz logo pulled up his gown, squatted low to the floor, and took a shit. Patients fell into fits, cheering, celebrating, applauding. Others jeered. They all seemed like they knew each other.

 This was not the first time that I'd had to bring a kid into the Psych ER. Maybe twice a year or so, when some kid ran out of foster mothers and we couldn't find another bed, we'd have no choice but to get them admitted here for a day or two until a spot would come open at a long-term lockdown like Mount Pleasant or Children's Village. Of course, none of us felt great about this tactic—but what else could we do? The System wasn't so much a system, but a bunch of turning gears. Anita used to let the kids sleep at her apartment for a night or two until that came out in an audit and the lawyers lost their minds. So this was our best solution: stashing children-in-crisis at St. Bonnie's.

Anita had convinced her date to give the night another chance, so she'd dropped Harley and me off at triage. A security guard had escorted the two of us down three hallways toward the Psych ER, then locked the door behind us like we were a pair of chicken nuggets getting nuked for someone's lunch.

"Yo," said Harley, more concerned than frightened. "That guy just...shitted..."

Margarita had caught up with us just as we were passing intake, just in time to make an earnest attempt at convincing anybody who would listen that she didn't know me, Harley didn't know me; I was just some strange man who'd broken into their apartment and demanded to take her daughter to the hospital. It may say something about society that every medical professional we encountered took the word of the mumbling white guy with wrinkled khakis and an eye-twitch over that of the woman who was obviously the child's mother. On the other hand, Rita did look a little ragged with her frazzled hair and PJs. And in a battle of credibility, the tie goes to the one without the face tats.

Rita and I sat cross-legged on either side of Harley's chair. The floor was hard and sticky. We didn't speak at all, except for once, about an hour in, when I asked how she was feeling and she said I made her sick. Evidently, we were pretending that she hadn't tipped me off to where Harley had been hiding. Knowing Rita, she'd convinced herself of that by now.

Eventually a passing nurse took notice of my exaggerated sighing—I'd been channeling my mother at the Olive Garden when the waitress is slow with the bread rolls— and informed us we could expect to see the doctor within...she checked her clipboard...a couple hours.

"Hours?" I said, with a haughty look toward the Sands, intimating a common cause between us. Harley put in her headphones. Margarita turned away. Really, the wait time wasn't any longer than usual. I just wanted them to think I disapproved.

The nurse's manner was placating but assured. She wore pink Crocs with tie-dyed Grateful Dead teddy bears dancing in a conga line across the straps.

"The shelters fill up when it's this cold out," she explained. "So the rest of them come here. Your daughter will be seen as soon as we can get to her."

"ISRAEL? WHY HAVE YOU FORSAKEN ME, OH ISRAEL!" shouted the white-braided woman. The shadow-boxer growled Frank Sinatra lyrics. The man who'd shat stood up and paced about the room, arms up and victorious.

"Isn't there another room we can wait in?" I said. "Don't you have a separate wing for children?"

The nurse nodded towards the two patients on either side of Harley's recliner: a little girl with two eyes swollen shut whose only companion was a stuffed-animal penguin, and a teenage boy with Ace bandages wrapped around his wrists being fed General Tso's chicken by his softly weeping mother.

On the wall behind them was a piece of construction paper. *CHILDREN*, it read, in bubbly letters. The nurse patted me on the shoulder.

"Sir," she said. "I feel your pain, believe me."

At this, Margarita perked up. She had spent the last two hours trying to make up for the past few years with Harley, kissing, holding, hugging, reassuring her daughter: I got you, she kept saying, don't you worry about none of these crazy people, 'cuz I got you. A part of me had hoped she would get mad enough to pull a Margarita Special. To yell her head off and make a scene and threaten everyone until they moved Harley up the waiting list. But instead she just looked up, squinting in the harsh light from the ceiling. I'd never seen her this serene.

"You don't like being a nurse?" she said.

The nurse shrugged. Good days and bad, she said.

Margarita leaned her head against the wall. "'Cuz I think that I would like it," she said. "I think I'd be pretty good."

◆

Later the nurse brought Harley a fruit cup and a Styrofoam plate of roast chicken and rice. A square-jawed army vet frisbeed his dinner at the wall. Israel demanded a vegan option. Every so often, the nurse would re-emerge from an office in the back and come so close to saying Harley's name—only to then decide at the very last second to announce someone else.

"Harley Sand?" she almost said at 7:30.

"Ok, let's see. Harley Sand?" she almost said at 8:45.

"Harley Sand, we're ready for you now," she was as close as humanly possible to saying at 10:15.

"Ma," said Harley, finally, her voice a little froggy.

Margarita's hair twisted in a ream around her neck. She picked at the ends with chipped fingernails.

"What is it, baby?"

"Can I ask you something?"

Margarita sat down by her side again.

"What was it like, the first time that you..." Harley trailed off.

"First time I what?"

"You know..."

Margarita blinked. "Electrocuted somebody?"

Harley closed her eyes. "No, Mom. Had sex."

Rita cast a startled, wary glance in my direction. I couldn't really give them space, so I pretended to be asleep. I closed my eyes tight and tried not to think about me and Harley's conversation in Kingsley's barracks the night I'd stowed away the hair-straightener. The night she'd needed someone, anyone, to talk to, and all she had was me.

"I've never had sex, baby. I'm waiting for Mr. Right."

"No, really, Mom. Come on."

Blue squares glowed in the darkness of my eyelids. How had Harley put it? It's just this party coming up. My legs went numb on the hard tile. I thought of Jairo's grubby chinstrap. My toes were filled with pins and needles. I'd known she was in trouble, hadn't I? I'd sensed it. And all I'd done to stop it was give the kid a phone number that I knew she wouldn't call.

"Why?" said Margarita, warily.

Harley fought back tears. "I just need to talk to somebody."

"Tell me what happened, baby. Now."

"Nevermind. Nothing. Forget it. I knew you'd be like this."

Rita calmed herself. She exhaled a long, shaking breath. "It was the worst day of my life."

Harley nodded.

"But you were OK after? I mean—it all worked out alright?"

The sounds of the Psych ER spun around them. A nearby patient took off his socks and threw them at a passing orderly. "Y'all don't be throwing socks now!" said the orderly, his voice booming like the voice of God. The nebbish boxer bounded over toward Israel, took her by the wrist and sang-shouted 'I DID IT MYYYYY WAY...'. I kept my eyes shut tight. Rita squeezed her daughter's hand.

"It worked out fine, baby."

"Really?"

"You know, for most people, the first time's not so great...."

That was when Harley gave her Mom the details. The whole story, start to finish. When I couldn't stand to hear any more, I woke up from the slumber I'd been faking, rubbed my eyes, stood up, and staggered off without a word. I should have known. I could have stopped it. She could still just be a little kid. I flashed my Children's Future ID at the security desk and they buzzed me out into the hallway. Of course, it was against the order of Bronx Family Court for me to leave the Sands together. But were we really in the Bronx anymore? No. This was the Republic of the Psychiatric Emergency Room. Judge Screen had no sovereignty. It was lawless. It was free.

In the long and low-lit hallway, a janitor mopped up the floor, rapping along to the music in his earbuds. A tiny, birdlike woman pushed a veering cart full of laundry, cursing in Russian at its broken wheel. Down the hall, the elevator door awaited like the gates of hell. I walked toward it, slowly at first, but speeding up as, with each step, I grew less certain. There was nothing I could do. Nothing I could have done. Nothing—was there? If you ever want to talk, you have my number. And she'd just sat there nodding like, yeah, Lee. OK. Sure.

Two nurses sat at a bench opposite the elevator, eating cafeteria salads beneath a gold-framed portrait of a stern old man wearing a little boy's bow-tie.

"Do you know which floor is the ICU?" I asked.

◆

Ms. Kingsley's feet and hands were wrapped in heavy bandages, her eyes purplish with lids weighed down by pain meds. The room was dark, lit only by a nightlight and the television. I slipped past nurses chatting in the hallway and in through the curtain like a mortal chill.

"Whatchu want?" she grunted, less surprised than I'd expected. Had Anita told her I'd stop by? There were no flowers or gifts or get-well cards—in fact, no indication that she'd been visited by anyone who wasn't paid to be there. Fitting, I thought, for a woman who'd spent so much time living off of lonely children's paychecks.

"I just wanted to stop by and assure you that the agency is taking care of Angel, Precious and Marcus. We've moved them to a temporary foster home until you can recover."

Kingsley's chest heaved, returning stale air to its source. An alarm was sounding in the hallway, but no one seemed to heed it. There was a chair beside the bed. The ghost of her son sat there, maybe: upright and vigilant. I say that because that's where she was looking, mournfully. She cursed when I sat down there.

"Did any of them ask about me?" she said.

"Of course. We're all very..."

"Don't lie."

I shrugged. "Then no."

Kingsley pursed her lips.

"That's what I get for giving my life to the ungrateful. But that's the job, I guess. I don't do it for the thank yous."

She said this like a challenge, begging for me to contradict her, to invite further grievances. But I did not take the bait. I wasn't here for conversation. My mind was off, soul off, nothing there behind my eyes. Being inhuman is like riding a bike: once you learn the skill, you'll always have it if you need it.

"I'm hoping you can find it in yourself not to press charges."

"You got a lot of nerve, Todd."

"Of course, what Harley did was inexcusable, and she'll be disciplined appropriately. But she has enough going against her right now, don't you think? And you know what happens to these kids, once they get a record."

Kingsley gazed down the slope of her nose at me: an ailing empress on her deathbed. What has this mad servant had the gall to ask the Queen?

"For twenty years now, I've told the agency to give me its hardest cases. Do you know why that is, Lee?"

"Because of the higher board rate?"

I would never say that kind of barb if I wasn't either drunk or this exhausted. The graves of Kingsley's eyes sprouted poisoned flowers.

"Because I know what they need," she said.

"What's that?"

"The world is hard, Lee. Maybe not for white boys. You might think I'm just some mean old banshee. But I've seen it all a hundred times. Once these kids leave my home, it's them against the streets. Only chance they got is if they come out swinging."

Kingsley crossed her bandaged wrists over her chest, satisfied that she'd convinced me. I guess, maybe, there was a valid in point in there. On the other hand, I've found that most people craft their personal philosophies to justify what they were going to do anyway. That's certainly the case with me.

"Got it," I said. "Children don't need love."

"Oh, please. When I was younger, I spent years loving these kids up—baking cookies, going to teacher conferences, how are you doing honey, how do you feel? And you know what happened? Nothing. They felt a little better and got swallowed up the same. No, Lee. The best thing we can do for that little girl is let her know she ain't that special. These streets don't give a fuck about you. You want dinner? Learn to cook. You want money? Make it. And one thing's for goddamn sure. You don't want a record, girl? Don't commit no crimes."

A nurse came into the room. Black-haired, dark-eyed, with henna flowers on her hands and a glittering stud in her nose. She asked me who the hell I was and what the hell did I think that I was doing—that Bronx 0 to 60 never failed to take me by surprise. Ms. Kingsley told the nurse I was her nephew— "See, I told you, someone cares about me after all." The nurse looked a little touched. Still, I had to go, she told me, a little more gently now. Come back tomorrow though, OK?

"You can tell yourself whatever you want, Ms. Kingsley," I said, turning toward the door. "But if you don't call the precinct and tell them that what happened to you was an accident, I'm closing down your home for good."

◆

By 1 AM, the Psych ER had fallen mostly silent. The children's section was empty. Margarita sat on a recliner vacated by the triumphant pooper once he'd been snowed with Haldol and rolled up to the wards. Harley lay snoring one seat over with her head tilted back, mouth agape. On my way back from the ICU, I'd put a dollar in the hallway vending machine and two packs of peanut M&M's had come tumbling out. I could not believe my luck.

"How are you feeling?" I asked Rita. I sat down on a recliner of my own, which faced the wall directly. Her skin was pale in the buzzing lights. She looked exhausted, wan and frail.

"I was supposed to protect her," she said. "That's my job."

I swallowed. "No, Rita. It's not your fault—"

"It was your job too, man," she said.

She wasn't looking for an argument. It was just a matter of fact.

"If I ever find out those boys' names," she said. "I'm gonna pull their throats out through their mouths."

The lights seemed to darken. Or maybe that was just my brain powering down. My thoughts grayed out into nothingness. Margarita rubbed her eyes. We sat there like that for a long time—an hour maybe. Maybe longer. At last, she held out her hand across the divide between their two chairs. I poured a handful of M&M's into it.

"How much longer, you think?" she said.

"I don't think they even have a psychiatrist," I said. "I think it's just a joke."

"Ha, yeah."

"Like on Punk'd. Remember Punk'd, on MTV?"

I was talking just to talk. Talking not to think. Rita stared me back to silence. I opened my second bag of M+M's—the lucky one, this time.

"If this was on TV, you'd be fucked," she said, after a while. "White guy fucks up a poor family in the Bronx? I'm pretty sure the audience would take my side."

"Who would you want to play you?"

"I'll play me. Who the fuck else could tell my story? Plus, I always wanted to be an actress. Did you know Marilyn Monroe was in foster care too?'"

"I told you that."

"No you didn't."

"Fine," I said.

M&M's cracked between two sets of teeth.

"All I know is, if we're going to sell this script to Lifetime, you've got to get my kids back, right? 'Cuz people like shit based on a true story. And nobody wants to watch a movie where some bipolar bitch beats the hell out of her kids, some stranger takes them from her, a little girl gets raped, and nobody learns a thing."

I looked away.

Margarita's teeth stopped mid-crunch. "Not that I did beat the hell out of them..."

She drifted back into some memory. I scrolled through Harley's texts until my phone died. Across the room, two patients jumped up from adjacent chairs and started arguing, bumping their chests together. One man accused another of stealing his hospital gown. The other man countered that it was in fact the accuser who had stolen *his* gown. He slapped him across the face. The other kicked him in the shin. A crowd of orderlies swarmed.

Two cots down, Harley stirred, awakened by all the shouting. She looked around with wide eyes, blinking away her dreams. Margarita went back to her daughter's side. For a long time, I listened to them muttering between each other, Margarita saying to go back to sleep, baby, there's nothing to be afraid of; it should be any minute now. Harley said she didn't care, it didn't matter. She inserted headphones and turned onto her other side. Margarita sat back down next to me and pretended to look at her phone, which was also dead by now.

The two of us sat like that for a long time, mourning our departed phones together.

"When May 28th comes," she said. "Do you really have to tell the judge everything I've done?"

I pressed my foot into the wall. My shoeprint stared back at me. Clay-colored squiggles on a pallid white. God, these floors were dirty.

"It's all in the case notes," I said. "Anita's already read them. There's nothing I can do."

"Maybe you could make it sound a certain type of way, though. Like yeah, I got my bad ideas and my little great depressions, whatever whatever, but you of all people, Lee, you know I would do anything to get them back."

Our eyes grazed, like strangers' hands on the subway—we pulled back just as quickly. I made a little laughing sound that sounded like I'd choked.

"Can I ask you a question?" she said. "After all the shit we've been through. Everything that's happened. Why do you still like me?"

"Like you?"

Her eyes came back on me—a lingering, inquiring stare: the stranger's hand was creeping closer. She tied her hair up into the tight bun, twisting black strands around the center. Around, around, around.

"I don't mean it like... I'm not trying to be, like..." she trailed off. "But, I mean, today. You and me, you know? Don't tell me you don't feel it. You like me, don't you, Lee?"

I ground my foot across my shoeprint, creating a feathered effect across the wall. My mind was sodden, useless.

I tried to scour my memory for some reason, some acceptable answer, some root cause I could explain. But all I found within myself were screaming children peeing themselves in the lobby as the clock ticked passed their visit time; and birthmothers moaning in the courtroom, going limp in their chairs, carried through the double doors while their lawyers stuffed papers into files; and Harley pressing the razor to Titi's eyebrows; and Kingsley's charred and heaving cruelty, her chest going up and down, up and down; and Ty's eyes going black as he stared at the Thanksgiving turkey, reaching for the carving knife; and Harley, poor Harley, doomed little sweet, cruel kid...

I looked back to Margarita. Her eyes pulled me towards her: closer, closer, out of control, into pools of swirling hazel...

"We have the same birthday," I said.

Margarita blinked. "What?"

"March 3rd, right? Same year. Pretty wild, huh? Since the moment that I saw that on the casefile, I thought: this is the one I help."

Margarita didn't say anything for a long time. She stared down at her fist. For a second I thought she might hit me. But then she shook her head and smoothed her hair back with her hand, her laugh incredulous and musical—like someday, with a lot of therapy and medication, I might not be so crazy.

"How have you never told me that?" she said.

I cleared my throat, preparing for another explanation. But I thought better of it, and just let the silence ride.

"You even got me a cake and shit. You watched me and Jojo eat it in the visit room...And still, you never thought to say...?"

I know, I said. Ha ha. I know, right? Weird.

Rita's laughter slowly, reluctantly sputtered back into the silence, and I felt her eyes on me again. A moment passed. I hummed a nonsense melody. My heart was a slamming gavel—calling for order, getting none. She reached her opened palm into the space between us. Did she want me to...take her hand? I stared straight forward, pretending I hadn't seen it. Rita wiggled her fingers at me. I couldn't ignore her any longer. I turned again to face her. Rita, no. We can't. "Ahem," she said, her eyes wide and impatient.

At last, I realized what she wanted. I poured more M&Ms into her palm.

Around 2 AM, a door opened along the back wall, and the nurse emerged again, her clipboard pressed to her chest. She made her way in our direction. Rita and I stood up together.

"Beatriza Gonzalez!" the nurse called. Behind us, Israel stood up, patting down her skirts, wrapping her long braid across her shoulder.

Margarita cursed. Harley rolled onto her other side. I walked over to the wall and pressed my forehead to it. There were just a few patients left now in the ER: hunched over, babbling, spitting on the floor. Two orderlies played cards at the security desk, throwing down one after another: *thwip thwip thwip*. Margarita draped her sweatshirt over her face. At last, I closed my eyes. And at some point after we had drifted off together, a psychiatric nurse practitioner woke up Harley, spoke to her privately within a quiet, little office, and determined her to be insane.

◆

The next morning, after the Mount Pleasant van had come to take Harley to her new home, Margarita and I walked out together through the entrance, shoulder to shoulder, staggering, squinting in the sunlight, a little stiff, a little awkward. The air was harsh. A wet snow was falling. The sky above was gray and splotchy, like a wet paper towel stretched thin over the Bronx. Rita hugged me when her ride came. A hard-eyed older man with a fitted Yankees hat in a low-slung Chrysler idled in the cab lane. From the hostile look he gave me, I got the sense they were involved.

"Who's this guy?" I said.

Rita's plastic fingernails dug lightly into my shoulder-blade. She gave a self-reproachful laugh.

"You know me," she said.

"I'll see you Tuesday, right?" I said. "We can drive up to Mount Pleasant together."

"Yeah, Lee. Sure."

She started toward the car. The sunlight reflected off a nearby windshield and flashed into my eyes. I heard the chunking of the door lock. Maybe I was just exhausted. Or I'd left my mind somewhere in the Psych ER. But as I stepped out in the street and was nearly hit by an ambulance pulling out after a drop off, I felt, suddenly and unaccountably, that I might never see her again.

"Rita!" I called. The car stopped. I ran after her. I leaned my head in through the window. Her eyes were big and red—faintly irritated. Her new man scowled—he had a scar across his lip, a hunched, haunted look about him. Rita could really choose them.

"Jairo Del Santos," I said.

"Huh?"

"That's the kid's name."

The ambulance leaned on the horn. I rapped my hand on the window and said again I'd see her Tuesday. Margarita closed her eyes and nodded. Then she elbowed her new boyfriend on the shoulder: "What the fuck are you waiting for? Let's go."

# 19.

**Sara has been calling ever since Lil and I left the diner.** If I didn't need the phone to play Spotify, I would have already turned it off.

On the road, it's getting dark. A wet, slanting snow has begun to fall. With no cities for a couple hundred miles, the stars come out in full force. We go miles without seeing any other cars out on the highway. It feels like the two of us are hurtling alone through outer space. In the car seat, Lily's snoring, her light-up shoes flashing in the rearview each time she stirs her feet. She looks just like my mother when she's sleeping—something about the almond shape of her eyelids, I think, or the way how, with her mouth agape and head thrown back, she looks half in the bag. As my nerves begin to fray, and the little voice inside my head begins to clear its throat, I search through my Spotify for a song to fill the silence. I scroll until at last, I find it: our song. As soon as I press play, that opening funk riff struts out of the speakers, glitzing up the darkened car. *Ooooh,* exclaims a high-pitched voice, dripping with innuendo. In the backseat, Lily stirs but doesn't wake. I drum my hands on the wheel and start to sing the lyrics. God, I fucking love Prince.

Songs come in and out of your life, like old friends you don't need to see that often to stay close with. I don't think I'd heard 'Kiss' for ten years, until, a few weeks back, it popped in for a visit. Since then, I've probably played it once a day. It was a Saturday afternoon, and Lily's mother had just dropped her off at my new condo. My little girl took one look at my undecorated white walls, my white carpets and pre-fab furniture, my clothes in piles on the floor—and at me, this new, bleary-eyed, reduced version of her father, in my sweatpants and my hangover, crouching down on the floor in my entryway, my arms extended for a hug. "Are you sad, Dada?" she asked, eyes welling, speaking in this shy voice that broke my heart. "Mommy says you're sad. I don't want you to be sad." I held her close. She was a limp noodle in my arms. "No!" I said, in my brightest, fakest voice, hugging her tight now, kissing her cheeks, feeling a wild desperation grow. "How could I be sad? Daddy's happy! Daddy's so happy that he gets to see you!"

But Lily wasn't buying it—my little one is so emotionally aware. She lay down flat on her stomach and began to cry. I felt like the kitchen was on fire. How could I put her out? What kind of father was I to let her see me in this state? To make an innocent, carefree toddler feel suddenly responsible for the well-being of a thirty-five-year-old man? It wasn't right. It wasn't fair. And what the fuck had my wife been telling her, to make her feel this way? My first thought was: food can make this better. There's no emotion food can't fix. So I made her a grilled cheese on the stove. But she wouldn't eat it. Next, I turned on *Muppet Babies* on TV. That was her favorite. Still, Lily wouldn't budge from the floor. "I want to go home, Daddy," she moaned. "I don't want to play with you..." That's when, out of nowhere, "Kiss" started playing in my head. The chorus, specifically. *You don't have to beeee rich...* For a moment I didn't recognize the melody. Was this some Cocomelon song, burned into my brain from the last time I saw Lily? But then at last, it clicked. Hey! Prince! Good to see you, buddy! How ya been? I took out my phone and found the song, buried deep within my 'Summer 2014' playlist, and connected it to my speakers. As the beat kicked in, Lily's whining quieted. My spirit flooded with happiness, a sense of possibility, of hope—next thing I knew, I was standing over my sobbing daughter, bobbing my head to the rhythm.

Lily brushed her hair out of her eyes, a smile spreading reluctantly across her lips. "No Dada... don't dance," she said, because she's always hated when I dance, but this time it was too late. I'd already seen that spark in her eye. Next thing she knew, I'd lifted her from the floor and we were spinning together, strutting around my dirty-but-still-antiseptic condo, with me singing in my high falsetto. *You don't have to be beautiful...* I bit my lip and made my most serious sexy Prince face. Her protests turned to squeals, her eyes began to shine, and soon enough she was shrieking along: *You don't have to be rich to be my girl. You don't have to be coo—ooo—oool to rule my world.* And from then on I knew that we could do this. We would be all right. She was still my Lily. I was still her dad. My joy was so intense that it didn't matter that we were dancing alone together across the thin white carpet of a one-bedroom hovel in a drab apartment complex in New Hampshire. I was not some failure of a man, some loser of a father. *Ain't no particular sign I'm more compatible with...* And she was not some helpless little kiddo. *I just want your extra time and your...* As long as we're together, I thought—making exaggerated smooching noises at the moment Prince demanded them—nothing bad can happen to us. And when my lower back started grabbing and I put her back down on the carpet, Lily still wasn't done. She had a lot more dance left in her. She started doing a spinning, pointing, kicking dance, like the hokey-pokey on Adderall. All flying limbs and fingerpoints and giggles—she can be such a little ham. And as I stood there watching her spin around, flapping her elbows, cackling like a little madwoman, I saw our whole life together unfolding. With each of her flailing rotations, she gained five years. I saw her first day of school, her first heartbreak, her as a difficult teenager, *Dad shut up, my godddd,* then, her as a young woman, home from college, the two of us binging on ice cream and *Arrested Development* and her not thinking it's quite as funny as I do, but laughing to appease her Dad. God, I thought, what will I say at her wedding? Would I talk about this exact moment? Is "Kiss" too sexual to be a father-daughter wedding dance? Maybe we should go with something classic like Sinatra. Who cares! I can figure that out later. Afterward, I'll stand up in front of everyone and give the kind of speech that will make a grown-up version of this little goofy, gap-toothed, spinning toddler turn red and tear up and say 'awww Dad' and know how much she's meant to me. Or maybe she won't get married at all! I have no expectations for her. No pressure. There's no need to go the conventional route if she doesn't want to. I'll be just as proud—hell, maybe even more so—if she grows up to be a wildflower.

Because that's the beauty of it. There's no one way to live—no matter what any System tries to tell you. You can do what you want! Don't let anybody tell you different! These are the kinds of things I tell my daughter now—on our Saturdays alone. Not that she understands what I'm saying. Or that I do either, for that matter. Still, isn't it my job to tell her everything I know about the world? Don't take it all too seriously, I tell her—that's always been your Daddy's problem. Don't get bogged down trying to make a difference—it's all just vanity, and in the end, where does it get you? Who does it help? No, my little darling nugget, my tiny madwoman, my brassy, sassy little buddy, I tell her: if you can do anything in life, have as much fun as you can. Blast your music. Dance.

Now, whenever I see that shyness coming back over her, I play her all the songs I loved growing up—songs that were already old when I first heard them, but for whatever reason, struck a nerve and made my quiet life feel, for the first time, like something wild. Something huge. Songs my friends and I would blast in my mom's LeSabre as we'd drive through country roads on lonely teenage Friday nights, passing around a water bottle full of vodka, screaming along to Led Zeppelin, to Jimi Hendrix, fake gyrating to Prince. Don't join the choir or chorus class with the nice girls who want to sing nice songs, Liliana, I tell her while we spin around the room together. And don't just slurp up whatever sludge Disney slops into the trough. No! Fuck that, baby! Feel that kick drum in your spine! Feel that guitar howl. Be my little funky diva queen! My electric sweetheart gypsy Mama!

The other day we started really having fun. I made just the right faces to get her goofy dance really spinning, really filling up my cold condo like light, like heat. I blasted "Purple

Rain" so loud that the elderly couple next door slipped a passive-aggressive note beneath my door. As Prince plugged his guitar into God and the music launched into the stratosphere, Liliana fell to her knees and held her hands up to the sky with a dramatic flair, not knowing any of the lyrics except *Purple rain, purple rain,* which she'd later tell me sounded very silly. She looked up at me then, to make sure I was laughing, and I swear to God, I saw a memory forming in her eye. A little click behind her pupil. At two and a half, this would be about that time, right? When the brain's recorder turns on? Dad, she thought. You are Dad. You are my crazy Dad. If only I could make time stand still, I thought. If only she wouldn't ever get any older. We could live forever in this cold condo, Daddy and Lily. Lily and Lee. Nothing will ever happen to her. I can protect her from uncertainty, from fate, from cruelty. She can always trust me to keep her safe.

A knock came on the door then. Her mother always came back from the nail salon right when Lil and I really got the party going. Right when Daddy-Daughter time lifted off the ground and my heart leapt into hyperspace.

Usually, my wife and I kept things copacetic. With no real bad blood between us, no cheating, no debts, no abuse, everything was usually cordial, even friendly. But this day, something in her mood had shifted. There was a distance in her eyes. "We've got to go," she said to Lily. And to me: "Why don't you have her ready?"

I could feel her judgment. As she came into my condo, I could see her eyes counting my deficiencies. Running down a checklist in her head. Maybe lately I hadn't kept the place as clean as I should have. But I was still moving in and...why the fuck should I feel the need to come up with excuses anyway? She was my daughter too—why should I have to answer to anyone?

"Have you been drinking?" she asked.

"No, of course not. Have *you*?"

She motioned toward the mostly empty whiskey handle that stood guard by the sink, but then seemed to think better of mentioning it.

"What, you think I'm slugging whiskey at 3 PM on a Thursday?" I said. "Christ, Sara. We were having a dance party. Is that OK? Do you *approve*?"

Sara gave me a look that was both earnest and evasive. Searching for an answer that she didn't want.

"Are you sure you're doing OK, Lee? I'm serious. I know this hasn't been easy on you. You can always talk to me."

"Oh, fuck you," I said.

I don't know where it came from. Somewhere deep within, I guess. Or someone. Lily began to whine, sensing the shift in energy. For a moment, Sara looked shocked—but quickly, resolve replaced the hurt look in her eyes. Like I'd just confirmed some decision she'd been waffling on.

"I'm sorry. I didn't mean that," I said.

"Lily, come on honey."

"Sara—no, let's not do this. Please? Please?"

It may not have been a major argument, but I could feel that something had just changed. As she rushed our daughter out of my house, depriving me of my goodbye hug, I could feel new lines between us being drawn. And I realized now the consequences would be out of my control. *Everything* was out of my control. The door closed behind them with a click, and here I was: alone again. Without control.

I poured myself a drink. Flies buzzed near my whiskey bottle. Another episode of *Muppet Babies* started up. God, I hate that opening song. This was *all* just a fantasy, I thought. This happy life. This Dad thing. Me giving out dumb advice. Any time I had with Lily was borrowed, lent out only at her mother's discretion, at her mercy. And how long could I count on that? What happens when Sara remarries? Will Lily dance with her stepdad, too? What will be *their* song? Christ, how will she turn out without me? What if my little girl grows up to be some bland little Disney princess, or some half-plastic duck-lipped idiot on Instagram? What if she turns out like her mother: a real estate agent in the same town she grew up in, who has never had to fight for love, who doesn't even think that you're supposed to, who mistakes Prince for Michael Jackson, who never goes on her own adventure to the Bronx or the Poconos or Timbuktu or wherever, who thinks living is just another errand to get done on the way home from the nail salon? What if she gets turned against me? What if she turns out like the girls who hang around the Market Basket in their PJs, strung out on pills and fentanyl, sipping Dunkin Donuts iced coffees in November, stealing avocados out of people's carts?

Through the window, I could see Sara in the parking lot shoving my little girl into her car seat, snapping the buckles over her legs. Lily was crying, screaming at her mother, her little scrunched-up face going from red to purple. Sara slammed the door shut and leaned a moment against the car, looking up at the endless sky above them, her breath like steam shooting from a broken pipe.

In the car now, I turn up "Kiss." I need the music in my spine. In my soul. Take me away, Prince. Take me to some far-off, funky place. In the car seat Lily wakes up. "Dada—I've gotta go bathroom," she yells, from the back of the dark car, face flashing in the glow of her sneakers. All that chocolate milk back at the diner must have run right through her.

Reluctantly I turn down the music. "Now?" I say.

"Now, now, now!" says Lily.

A few miles later, I find a rest stop up a little hill that overlooks the highway. Up here, New Hampshire lays splayed out beneath us, a few glittering lights within a vast, dead universe. There is not a single car on the road below us—no one else for miles. The trees up here are naked, stripped down to the bone. They look arthritic, brittle, like Anita Flores' fingers. A stiff wind stirs dead leaves across the parking lot, which is completely empty save for a pick-up truck parked beneath a single streetlight on the far side. Feeling a little jumpy, a little spooked, I run around to the back of the car and carry Lily towards an unlit one-room rest area. As we come up on it, I fear the door is locked—but when I pull the handle it swings open.

Inside, the lights are off. There is an unplugged vending machine, a map dispenser on a wooden table, and a bathroom. When I turn on the light, I half-expect to see some trucker passed out on the floor, or a pack of coyotes maybe, or some pervert jerking off into the toilet. I don't know: something wild, something waiting. But no. The bathroom buzzes blandly. Dead moths hang in the frosted window wells. We get to the toilet just in time.

Afterward, we emerge triumphant, hand in hand, back out into the night. For just a moment, the whole universe feels completely silent. But as we head back to the car, my phone buzzes again.

"Is that your phone?" Lily asks, as I lift her up onto my hip.

"Yes, honey."

"Is that Mommy?"

"No."

"Where's Mommy?"

"She's at home."

"Are we going home?"

"Yes, honey. We're almost there. OK?"

For a moment, I worry this might turn into a whole thing. That this is when the meltdown happens. But it doesn't. My little one is so resilient. "Okaaaay," she says, with a sigh, resting her head on my shoulder. Is there any better feeling than when your kid falls asleep on your shoulder? It's the feeling of being completely indispensable. Of doing exactly what you're meant to do, at least in this one moment. When we get to the car, I put her in her car seat and start the engine. The snow is picking up now. I look out across the empty parking lot, the swirling wind, the shaking, naked trees, the stars which seem to have multiplied in the past few minutes, like an army emerging from the cover of darkness, charging now, barreling down upon us. Across the lot, the solitary streetlight shines down on the pickup truck. I wonder if there's anyone inside it. Are they OK? Should I check?

"Are we going home?" says Lily, groggily, not concerned so much as curious. "Dada—where we going?"

# 20.

**Mount Pleasant Residential Treatment Facility** was a half
dozen one-floor brick buildings spattered like broken teeth
across a heathery hillside in a sleepy Westchester hamlet an
hour north of the Bronx. A broken streetlight overlooked a
gravel parking lot that housed a fleet of white vans used for
field trips and court appearances. Inside, the hallways were
yellow and narrow, decorated with resident artwork and panic
buttons behind recessed glass and glittery posters and double
doors reinforced with steel. After lunchtime, the cafeteria
served as the visiting area for families and caseworkers, so in
my memory, the whole place smells like hot dogs.

Family visits were on Tuesday nights. Often, they went
poorly. Harley would sit in the cafeteria crying, complaining
about her roommate, begging to come home. Margarita would
go to change Jojo only to discover the diaper rash from last week
had not abated—"What does Titi do all day?"—and we'd all ride
back to the Bronx in silence. But if the visit went well, if Harley
seemed happy and Jojo behaved, Margarita would talk my ear
off the whole ride home. In the car I'd have to rent each week
for the trip—usually a Hyundai—she'd sing along to the radio,
and, during commercials or the occasional stop at Burger King,
tell me stories from her life, her childhood in foster care, the

joys of growing up wild on Webster Avenue, what doing heroin feels like, and why every time you think you've left the void behind you, that just means you've fallen in. How since a few days after giving birth to Jojo, she'd felt like a microwave pizza—scalding on the outside and frozen in the middle—and it was just since she'd met me that she'd begun to think it might not last forever.

On one of these rides, I noticed a billboard advertising an apple orchard a few miles off of the highway. The sign showed a flannel-clad father hoisting his child up to pick a hanging Red Delicious.

"Hey—you think that'd be fun for the kids?" I said. "I could get Harley a day pass from Mount Pleasant. Bring Jojo up from Titi's. We could all go apple-picking."

Margarita put her feet up on the dashboard. Traffic on the Saw Mill Parkway slowed to a crawl back to the city.

"What's that?"

"They give you a bag and you go around picking apples right off the tree."

"Then what?"

"What do you mean? You eat them. It's fun."

"You really like apples, huh?"

"Well, no. Not really. It's not really about the apples."

"What the fuck are you talking about then?" said Rita, but with her little crooked smile to let me know that she was fucking with me.

She turned back on the radio. It was her turn to pick the music, and so, as usual, Beyonce was playing. *All the single ladies! All the single ladies! Oh Oh Oh...* On the horizon, the sun sank through orange, pink, and bluish clouds.

"Alright Lee," she said. "You really want to take us? We can go."

◆

The last hour of every visit was devoted to family therapy. Because Harley never behaved for long enough to win back her cell-phone privileges, these sessions were now the only window I had into her psyche. Not that I ever learned much. Harley may not have despised me anymore, but it's not like we were close. We weren't friends, we weren't enemies. To her, I was something like an unrelated uncle who'd been widowed by an aunt that no one speaks of anymore.

Harley's therapist was a young and sincere woman with a wide gap between her front teeth and an accent fresh off of the Metro North. Her office was small and colorful, all pinks and blues, with a window leading out into the courtyard and a poster on the wall of a cartoon duck dressed up like a psychiatrist, saying *I am NOT a Quack*. No matter what you said, she'd smile and nod before responding, even when she disagreed—so in my memory, her golden feather earrings are perpetually swinging.

As we began one session, Jojo sat on his mother's lap and frowned—arms crossed, curmudgeonly, like in his opinion, we all talked too much about our feelings.

"You know I used to do my therapy in this same little office?" Margarita said. "You were still inside me, Harley. Getting therapized in the womb!"

This factoid didn't interest Harley. It did not strike her as symbolic that she'd returned, like some kind of salmon, to the place where her parents met. She gestured toward the window: "Oh shit, there goes Keion," she said. Outside, in the courtyard, a lanky teenaged boy with green hair and a miniskirt had ripped a low branch from a birch tree. He swung the branch against a naked tetherball pole. The branch cracked in half. The boy whooped. Two staff members prowled the perimeter, coordinating an ambush. Harley banged on the window to try and tip him off that he'd been flanked.

The therapist turned to me.

"So, Lee," she said. "Margarita tells me the kids might be coming home soon?"

◆

On May 28th, I'd told the judge that while Margarita may have at times demonstrated poor judgment, she had undeniably made progress with regards to her mental health, parenting, anger management and substance abuse services, and thus, in the view of myself and the agency I represented, visitation was no longer a threat to the children's well-being. Not only would I recommend dropping the initial motion to suspend visitation, I said, but the agency would like to explore unsupervised visitation, with an eye toward weekend visits and a possible trial discharge, assuming all went well.

Judge Screen peered down from the bench, eyes cutting over the top of my report. A 'trial discharge' was the holy grail of child welfare—a conditional return of the children to the care of their birthparents. In almost five years at Children's Future, I'd never even gotten close.

"Anita Flores is aware of this plan?" said Judge Screen.

"Yes, sir."

Beneath the table, Rita gave me a thumbs-up that I prayed to God nobody saw.

"She must be getting soft in her old age," said the judge. "Don't tell her that I said that though. Well, Mr. Todd, this all sounds fine to me. I have to say, it's refreshing to hear you come to me with good news for a change. But I do still have some questions..."

I knew my lies would not stand up to his scrutiny. I wondered if anyone would believe my impression of a heart attack. Which arm is it I should say the pain is in? Or is it both? "Sure," I said.

"Not for you, son. Ms. Sand—I want you to congratulate you on the progress described to the court today. I know this can't be easy on you. It truly warms my heart to see a young person get her life together..."

Margarita looked up from her phone. She was dressed in a huge, heavy black-and-red sweatshirt, and jean shorts ripped across the thigh. No matter how many times I advised her to dress nicely for court, she'd show up looking like it was her laundry day.

"Uh-huh," she said.

"But as hard as this is now, it is going to get much more difficult when the children do come home. All the new skills you've learned in your classes and your therapy—your kids will put that to the test. Every time they don't want to wake up for school. Every time your daughter snaps at something innocuous you've said. When your baby won't put on his socks. When you're working yourself to the bone pay for soccer uniforms just to find out your daughter quit the team a month ago. Your ability to respond to little stresses like these will determine the health and safety of your family. So, in the next few months, as we continue preparing for a possible reunification, I want you to look long and hard at the various people in your life, and ask yourself: Does having them around make my job harder or easier? Because the task before you will be the hardest thing you've ever done. And you can't afford to let anyone make it any harder. Is that clear?"

"You're talking about my baby's father, right?"

Judge Screen smiled primly. Margarita fiddled with the hood strings of Ty's old sweatshirt.

"Your honor—soon as I get home, this sweatshirt is going in the oven. I'll cook up all his jackets too, if that's what makes you happy."

Afterward, Margarita hugged me in the elevator. My lawyer gave a quizzical look. "What the fuck you looking at?" Margarita said, showing him the zebra stripes across her middle fingernail.

Outside, we walked together toward the subway at Yankee Stadium. A pair of young mothers pushing strollers passed us on the sidewalk. Margarita leaned in to the strollers and rubbed their babies' bellies. "I want to eat them!" she told the mothers, who gave me frightened smiles and picked the pace up down the sidewalk. Rita watched them turn the corner, wiping tears from her eyes with the sleeve of her sweatshirt.

Later, as we got off the 5-train and made our way up Southern Boulevard together, the sun filtered down through the train tracks overhead and splashed the street in light. Dogs barked a celebration. Bachata blasted. Shirtless teenagers wheelied down the street. The Bronx was in bloom, I thought! The Bronx was reborn! Paris in springtime has nothing on the Bronx!

"Hey, you like pizza right? I'm buying," she said.

I wouldn't normally let a client pay—but the one time I'd refused Rita before, she didn't talk to me for two weeks. We sat down at a plastic table inside a Checkers on 174th Street. People kept coming in and out. Rita folded her slice in half and held it up between us. We clinked our crusts together.

"To being single," she said.

She took a bite and burned the roof of her mouth—she always ate too quickly. She made a comic show of fluttering her hand in front of her mouth, funneling air onto her tongue, breathing sharply in and out, in and out, in and out, until finally, she got the laugh that she was after: mine.

"You gonna be alright over there?" I said.

Rita winced and shook her head no. "You know, I really did think that we could make it work."

"Who's we?"

"Me and Ty, retard. I haven't even seen that boy in like a month. You know how he is. 'Baby, I'm sorry, I'm trying to be better,' he says, like that it's own excuse. Like he's got no control. I'm like: OK bro, don't be sorry, be better. Do something. I did. Right?"

I heaped red pepper flakes onto my pizza. It sweated onto its paper plate.

"At least this way we don't have to lie about it to the judge," I said. "You're better off, really."

"Damn right I am. I could yell my number out the window and find myself a better man in fifteen minutes." She slapped me on the shoulder. "Hey, you're better off too, without your ho-ass fiancée, right? Whatever happened to her anyway?"

"She got engaged. To the same guy she left me for."

"That bitch! I can't believe her. Damn, that's too soon, bro."

"You know what? I'm OK with it."

"Hell yeah you are, baby! Hey, look at us, Lee. Two strong, independent women."

I rolled my eyes. "Mmm-hmm," I said. Rita sang her favorite song.

"'All the ladies, that's independent, throw your hands up at me...'"

I gave a short laugh. Rita smiled, delighting in annoying me. She hummed the second verse into her soda. Through the swinging door, I watched the afternoon settle down into the evening—one of those hazy summer nights when the South Bronx really hums. Teenagers sat out on their stoops, blasting music, flirting, vaping, racing remote control cars across the street whenever traffic slowed. Cops leaned against the side of their cruisers, eating packed lunches from Tupperware containers. Old men outside the candy store on the corner of Jennings smacked dominoes onto plastic tables. A humid breeze rippled through apple blossoms and summer dresses. It's nights like this one that I wish I could go back to now. To be young again—is it that simple? To sit inside a pizza place on 174$^{\text{th}}$ Street with Rita Sand and be twenty-six together.

"Hey Rita?" I said.

"Yeah?"

"Did you ever tell Ty what I told you? About, you know. With Harley?"

Rita pulled the sleeves of the sweatshirt over her hands, the hood over her hair. "Nah," she said. "I don't even remember you telling me anything, to tell the truth." She took another bite of molten pizza and sucked her coke down to the ice.

◆

The therapist couldn't come right out and voice her objections to the court ruling, at least not in front of the family it was theoretically her job to reconcile. But as I explained to her the plan of trial discharge, I saw the flash of an alarm behind her eyes. For the first time all session, she stopped nodding her head. Outside the window, Keion broke the branch in half and passed the two halves from hand to hand.

"I told you," said Rita, with a harsh look at the therapist.

"We're all on the same team, here, Ms. Sand."

"So what's that make this? A game?" Rita gave me a smirk, proud of her wordplay. The therapist's feather earrings bobbed and bounced.

"I meant that we all want what's best for Harley."

"What's best for Harley is that she shouldn't be having sex!"

"Ma," said Harley.

"And she should be getting better grades. What's this 'D' shit? You know she was the smartest girl in class when she was little? Her 3$^{rd}$ grade teacher told me she was special. I was like, 'Duh!'"

Harley pulled up the hood of her sweatshirt. "I told you she got ADD," she muttered. Margarita reached out and mussed her daughter's hair through the hood. Harley slapped her hand away, so she did it again and again, until finally, Harley laughed, just for a second, just until she caught herself and whined stopppp.

Outside, Keion lay flat on the overgrown grass with a staff member's knee pressed into his back, laughing hysterically. "I can't...I can't...!" he screamed. "You're crushing me!" They lifted the boy onto this feet—he went limp in their arms, wailing at the sky. "My daddy's coming for your asses!"

For the rest of the session, the therapist touched upon Harley's feelings of guilt surrounding her mother's substance abuse. She was a good therapist, gentle but assertive.

Later—months later—at our last monthly meeting, after Harley had shuffled back to the girls' wing, the therapist and I would share a joint inside her office: "To tell the truth, I don't care what they do to me either," she said when the smoke detectors started flashing. "I take the LSAT next week."

◆

After we'd gone over the tentative discharge plan, Harley had another meeting: a one-on-one with her psychiatrist, who every month would up her Zoloft. We all said our goodbyes. Jojo wasn't due back to the Bronx until late because Titi had an appointment with her endocrinologist, so we had some time to kill. "You think I could show Jojo around where his mom and dad grew up?" asked Rita. The therapist lent us her ID card to give us access to the girl's wing.

It was a single hallway, quiet except for two girls in baggy khakis making out against a water fountain, unbothered by the slump-shouldered staff member sitting on a folding chair nearby, swinging a lanyard on her finger. A window at the end of the hallway gave a view into the gravel parking lot, where two boys were letting out the air to the tires on a  dirty white van.

Margarita ran her hand along the checkered tiles of the wall, sneakers squeaking on glossy hallway floors, fingers tracing over glittery posters the girls had made about being beautiful and resilient and stronger than their trauma. Everything was just like she remembered, she said, just a little smaller.

These days, Jojo was getting close to talking. As we made our way around the grounds, he babbled up a stream of vaguely Spanish nonsense words he must have heard at Titi's. Ito, no me cito, me me me quito, he said, as Rita led us into a dilapidated rec room and told a story about the time she broke a pool cue over Quiana St. John's head for trying to get too cute with Ty. Dito, me cito? Jojo repeated, like a question this time, as we walked through the cafeteria and Rita showed me the exact spot where a teenaged Ty had come right up to her with that look in his eye and a slash in his fade, stuck his hand out and said, "You from the Bronx right?" Quito, quito, me yo, Jojo insisted, shaking a tiny fist at a bush in the courtyard and fiddling with his mother's earrings as she sat down on the same picnic table where, twelve years ago, she and Ty decided, once and for all, that it was them against the world. She slumped like a Neanderthal and launched into her best Ty impression: "'Rita, you'll see, I swear to God, baby, I'll be uhhhhhh everything you ever wanted.' And you know the thing with Ty is, I can know he's lying, and somehow still believe him."

Finally, we came to her old dorm room. There was a picture of Matthew McConaughey ripped out from a magazine and taped on the door. Jojo leaned back within the cradle of his mother's elbow. She knocked on the door, and while we waited, told us about the first time she'd walked through it, at thirteen years old, carrying a red-and-purple duffel bag in her arms and Harley in her stomach. How her Children's Future caseworker had placed a hand on her shoulder and said I should have known, I should have...and promised to visit once a week, even though they both knew she wouldn't. How Margarita had laid down for the first time on that hard mattress, bare because she didn't bother with the fitted sheet, and looked up at the ceiling. She listened to the crickets chirping their numb welcome through the window. Her caseworker's car turning its wheels across the gravel in the parking lot. How a stillness came upon her then. Margarita closed her eyes within it, held her belly close. Let it be a girl, God, she thought. A girl, please. A little girl...

We stood outside that door a good five minutes. Margarita tried the knob, but it was locked. FUCK OFF a girl's voice shrieked from within, at last. Margarita yelled it back. We turned around and headed for the car.

The therapist was waiting by the double doors. She asked if I had a moment. I told Rita to go ahead. I watched her and Jojo cross the empty parking lot towards the Hyundai, the boy burying his face into his mother's shoulder, Rita touching a hand gently to the back of his head. In the heather further up the mountain, fireflies alit. I unlocked the car from a distance. The therapist and I stood together at the main entrance, leaning back against opposing arms of a wheelchair ramp. She held out her hand, and I gave her back her ID.

"I think that was therapeutic for her," I said.

"Listen," she said. "Half of my kids never even get a visitor. So it's not like I don't get it."

I puffed my chest a little. And, with an air of self-congratulation, told her that I wouldn't go out on a limb for just any family. That of the hundred or so cases I'd had, this was the only one I'd risk it for.

From the car, Rita honked the horn and yelled out the window that she was hungry. I gave her the finger.

"It's just..." the therapist trailed off. Her earrings danced like hanged men. "What are you going to do about the baby?"

# 21.

**To this point in my time at Children's Future,** I had personally transported eleven newborn children from the maternity ward directly into foster care. And every time I'd done so, I'd left a vanquished woman in my wake. I thought about this a lot in the months after we had Lily. The awful things I used to have to do. I'd see Sara sitting up with the baby, moonlight coming through the window onto our bed as she cooed into Lily's little ears, and suddenly I'd be struck with a vision of Ms. Esposito looking pallid in the maternity room light, her hair in frizzy waves, breasts still out from her first and last attempt at breastfeeding, not even bothering to pull the blanket up when she saw me come in. 'My baby, My baaaaaby,' she said, in a baby's voice. The nurse watched me with a scowl as I took the baby in my arms. Next thing I knew, I was in that wide-walled, low-ceilinged St. Bonaventure hallway, the screams from the baby in the car seat in my hands getting louder with every step as I speed-walked towards the elevators, across the parking lot, outpacing the whispers of my conscience asking: What the hell are you doing, Lee? This isn't what I meant at all.

Of course, none of these mothers ever got their children back. Inevitably, their severe postpartum depression would lead to relapse or psychosis, followed by a gradual disengagement with their other children, disappearance, and, in a couple of cases, suicide. And though each time I told myself that by taking the infant from its addled mother, I had reduced its chances of getting shaken to death, or sold into sex slavery, or thrown into a dumpster—at night I still stared up at the ceiling from my sagging air mattress, smelling all the flowers in the maternity ward, muttering into the darkness: My baby. My baby. My baaaaaaaby.

We did offer another option for expecting birthmothers. We called it, with a straight face, 'family planning.' Of course, like any liberal, I supported a woman's right to choose. But few of the birthmothers I cajoled to get abortions shared my progressive values. Was it so different from forced sterilization the time I'd pressured Ms. DelCarmen, an immigrant from El Salvador with three tattoos of the Virgin Mary, to get her baby scraped? Really, I'm not sure. Afterward, she joined a popular Bronx cult called 'The Holy Chosen' and ate a poisoned batch of oatmeal.

◆

"You gonna finish with those fries?" Rita asked me on our way back from Westchester, after we'd sat down in the same booth that we always did, in the back of a Burger King off the Saw Mill Parkway. Jojo was on her lap, dissatisfied with the menu, ever the gourmet. He reached into a glob of ketchup on her paper tray and smeared red all over the windows. The Whopper that I'd ordered rested limply in its cardboard tray, as appetizing as a fetus.

"You know that you can always tell me anything," I said, pressing my palms into my cheeks.

Margarita took a fry off my tray and pondered its existence.

"You tell me that, like, every day," she said.

"This time I really mean it. Anything you might want to get off your chest. I can work with it. I promise."

Our eyes met. Rita crossed her arms over her stomach. Her heavy sweatshirts made more sense now.

"I'm not back with Ty, alright?" she said. "Jesus, what are you, my boyfriend? Me and him are done."

I wouldn't have told me either. It would have been parental negligence to tell a guy like me the truth. I looked at Rita with a hurt, prying expression that she didn't seem to notice. She rolled her eyes and nodded at my Whopper and asked if I was done with that.

◆

The next day, I went straight into Anita Flores' office. She was sitting in the dark, ensconced in Burberry, enjoying a lunch of tea and popcorn. The air was heavy with the scent of Chanel 5 and get-well flowers. Recently, she'd had to switch her Parkinson's meds and the skin around her eyes looked ashen. Her bony fingers curled so badly she hid them beneath her desk. Still, she wore her illness well, dressed it up in pearls and pumps, her silver hair fanned out in ornate spikes from her hair-bun. This job could take her heart and her soul—she'd once told me, five amaretto sours deep at Happy Hour—but it could never take her style.

"I'd like to move the Sand case to trial discharge," I said.

According to the Mount Pleasant therapist, Harley had told her Rita was only ten weeks pregnant. If I could convince Anita to give her blessing toward a trial discharge before she realized Rita was pregnant, the judge might allow the new baby to come home.

"The...Sands...?" said Anita, wincing through her headache. I saw myself reflected in her transition lenses and thought: God, my head is huge.

"Young mom. Red hair that's blue now. Face tats..."

Anita nodded without recognition. My head seemed to inflate.

"Her daughter electrocuted Ms. Kingsley..."

Anita squinted at some email on her computer. "Sand, you said? Hold on a sec, OK?" She left me alone in her office, holding one hand to her aching back as she departed. The Crayola monsters on the wall observed me with their reddened eyes, their jagged teeth, their hungry smiles. Flo-Flo is my hero, one was signed. Mommy + Willy + Me was inscribed beneath a picture of three goblins floating in a black pool. I looked down at my phone.

A moment later, Anita came back cradling the casefile. It was bursting at the spine. The word SAND was scrawled in my handwriting across the cover, like some warning of an ancient curse.

"Harley's been in three fights since we last moved her," I said. "She's failing out of school, which isn't easy given that, up there, they mostly just watch movies. Are we doing anybody any favors to make her stay on Mount Pleasant any longer than she has to? Because we both know how this goes, right?"

Anita wasn't listening. She pored through the casefile, through reams and reams of printed progress notes— transcriptions of my handwritten observations that I typed into our dated, glitchy electronic record on a monthly basis. This was the System's official record of the history of the Sands. Margarita's life, according to some white kid from New Hampshire.

"And what about Jojo?" I continued. "You know I love Titi. But she's seventy-six years old with diabetes. If she adopts him, he'll lose two mothers by the time he's ten."

A page quivered between Anita's fingers. I spoke as steadily as I could.

"She's completed three months worth of parenting classes. She has her own apartment and pays the rent on time. She's tested negative for every substance except Xanax and Methadone eight weeks in a row. And most importantly, she loves these kids, Anita. It's the real thing this time. I swear to God."

The silence lengthened, twisted. Slowly, my boss began to read:

"October 6th," she said, "CW accompanies BM Sand and FCs Harley and Jojo to Burger King for a community supervised visit, BM falls asleep face-first on the table..."

It took me a beat to remember I had written it. But then it hit me—an image of myself, in my stupid tiny cubicle, with my stupid giant head, eating a pack of BBQ sunflower seeds and typing out each word. The program had kept buffering. I remember spitting into a plastic cup and thinking: Why do I keep eating these?

"That was so long ago..."

Anita carried on:

"October 18<sup>th</sup>: CW accompanies BM and FC's to the park to have a birthday party for Jojo, BM starts crying because she forgot to bring the cake, tells CW 'I can't take this bullshit' and walks off. November 4<sup>th</sup>: CW makes surprise visit to Birth Home, hears BM inside with an unidentified man. Another man is waiting in the hall."

"Right, right. Turned out that second guy was just there to fix the pipe above the refrigerator. I was wrong to think that was a euphemism. I must have written that part too, right? The damn system probably glitched out before I hit 'save' on the note..."

"December 2<sup>nd</sup>, collateral contact with Bronxcares Psychotherapy, BM Sand discharged from Mental Health services after throwing a lamp through the window of the lobby. December 6<sup>th</sup>: Family visit, BM encounters FM Gigante in the lobby, calls her a 'dirty-ass Dominican' and spits in her face. December 13<sup>th</sup>: BM Sand sexually propositioned CW during a BHV. December 23<sup>rd</sup>, missed Christmas visit, BM did not answer phone. December 30<sup>th</sup>, missed visit, BM did not answer phone. January 6<sup>th</sup>, missed visit, BM did not answer phone. January 13<sup>th</sup>, 20<sup>th</sup>, 27<sup>th</sup>..."

"OK! OK! I get it! Jesus!"

Anita looked up from the case notes. She took a sip of tea. The steam from the mug hazed up her glasses. She rubbed them on her shawl.

"You've been here what Todd? Two years? Three?"

"Almost five now."

"You know, when you first started, I thought you wouldn't last a month."

She closed the file and peered at me through the rising steam like a sniper through the fog. I wasn't sure what she was getting at, so I just nodded and said, "Yeah."

This was about the reception I'd expected. After all, this was Anita Flores I was talking to: the Vampire Queen of Southern Boulevard, who'd led this place through the crack days and the children of the crack days—who hadn't merely endured Parkinson's, the deaths and disappearances of however many children, two stabbings, and an attempted expose in *The New York Times* that would have brought the whole place down—no, she relished these burdens, bore them with style and grace across her shoulders, like her pink pashmina shawl. If I've been lied to a couple thousand times, I thought: How many times has she? It would be hubris to think that somehow, of these thousands of schemes she'd spent a lifetime staring through—somehow, I, Lee Todd, Pea-Pod Todd, some white hipster idiot from New Hampshire with functional alcoholism and a mild-to-moderate white savior complex, could be the one, at last, to finally get one over...

"What did I tell you about trying to feel her pain, Todd?" she said.

"I don't know what you mean," I said.

Anita smiled at me, not unfondly.

"Yes you do. Course you do. You wish this was your life, don't you? That it was you with something to lose?"

"Why would I want that?"

"At least all the other little white kids have the sense to quit after a year or so. They realize that they'll never get it, or maybe they don't want it after all, then fuck off to law school, medical school, whatever other grand plans await them."

"Come on. You know I'm not like that."

"Oh no. Not you, Lee. Not Pea-Pod! He's different."

"Can we have a real conversation here? Or do you just want to mock me?"

"Oh, now you want to talk real? Oh, it's real talk now? Where was this real talk when you were going behind my back with Judge Screen to give the kids back to that woman? Coulda used some real talk then!"

"Who told you that?"

"A little fucking birdy, Todd. You know LaDawn saw your girl in the visiting room two weeks ago, sucking on one of Shantal's lollipops, coming in and out of consciousness, while you're just sitting there singing to her son like you're his daddy? Bet you didn't tell the judge about that, did you?"

Fucking LaDawn, I thought. Who would have thought one sexual off-night could affect so many people? No, I couldn't let that happen. It would be too silly. Too absurd. I thought of Margarita in the birthing ward—six months in the future. Her eyes taking me in as I cross the tile, clutching her new baby to her chest. I thought of Harley, sneaking down from Mount Pleasant some summer night, the crickets screaming, knocking on the driver-side window of some idling Toyota Avalon and asking 'can I get a ride?' Of Ty rolling through Crotona, spotting Jairo on the sidewalk and knowing, once again, it's up to him.

"You're full of shit, Anita," I said.

The Crayola monsters on her walls gathered up behind her, gnashing teeth, screaming battle cries: *Marry Xmas, 1998* and *I luv u Ms. Anita* and *We R One Children Future Happy Family!*

"Excuse me?"

I thought back to the first day that I'd met Rita. When I'd asked the God I don't believe in for someone to believe in. I closed my eyes and tried to change their color, thinking: hazel, hazel, hazel.

"You think that just because you've been divorced three times, and your son moved to Alaska, and you've got Parkinson's disease, that that somehow proves you care?"

Anita took me in, incredulous.

"I've given everything I have to these people."

"Yeah, but what did you actually give them? Because all I see is pain."

She scoffed. And for a moment, I thought she wouldn't, but then she did. She bit.

"What do you know about pain?" she said.

My eyes drifted to the scar on her throat. I gave my most dismissive prep-school shrug. Pain? Ha. It was some old song I'd never heard. Some fusty classic. I was Margarita, rolling her eyes at the idea that I'd like Prince. Anita sat back in her chair and waited out a passing tremor. If she could have stopped her hands from trembling, she'd have squeezed the breath out of my throat.

"Whatever happens to these babies," she said, "you can always move back to where you came from. Maybe you'll think about us all from time to time. But me? I'll be on Southern

Boulevard with a baseball bat in case Mr. Santiago breaks his order of protection. I'll be in the Webster Houses Christmas Eve. I've been in the System since the day my mother's boyfriend got bored with the belt and took up a broken bottle, and motherfucker, I'll be here 'til the Bronx burns down again. So don't get it confused! This isn't your case. And Margarita's not the mother of those children. Ever since the day those kids signed their name in Shanti's sign-in book, their asses belonged to me."

I waited for a long time. I wanted to give off the impression that I did not know what to say. But I'd had my next line loaded since I'd first walked in the door.

"Are you telling me that no matter what Margarita did, she was never going to get her children out of foster care?" I said.

Anita paused. Usually, she weighed her every word. But she was too mad. Too sick. Too tired. Speak, I thought—goddamnit, speak!

"I'm saying, you could tell me Ms. Sand was Mother Mary in disguise, I wouldn't give her Jesus back. In fact, you know what? Fuck it, Lee. Tomorrow morning, I'm calling up the lawyer. 'Cuz now I'm thinking it's time we terminate that bitch's rights."

There was no point in arguing any longer. I told Anita that I understood her position. I was sorry for the nasty comment about the divorces and the Parkinson's, and that, despite what I'd said, I had more respect for her than anyone I'd ever met—which to this day is true. Lastly, as I stood to leave her office, I put my phone back in my pocket, and turned it off 'Record.'

# 22.

**My plan was pretty simple.** At 10 AM on August 20th, I would walk into Part 13 in the suit that Ken had given me for Christmas and testify against myself. I'd sit at the same lacquered desk where'd I'd spoken the fate of Esposito, Jackson, and Washington, and I'd tell the court the Sands deserved another chance. Judas had been born again. If all went well, Judge Screen would order a suspended sentence on the TPR, giving us another year to prove her case. Afterwards, when Anita would try to fire me for insubordination, I'd threaten to send the recording of our conversation to the reporter from *The New York Times*—whose business card was still buried somewhere in my desk—unless she let me see this through.

At first, Rita didn't get it. We were driving back from another visit at Mount Pleasant. Jojo was in the back, in the car seat, smashing the heads of two Power Rangers against each other. Earlier, Harley had told Margarita that she felt it was her own fault that she'd been taken into foster care, that she was defective somehow, that she didn't deserve a family that would love her. Now, Margarita's face was puffy, pensive, and she didn't seem up for the good news that I'd given her. I explained the plan again.

By the time I'd finished, we were idling in the Hyundai outside the Purple Palace. On the front lawn, a pair of pigeons splashed within a dirty-water bird bath. A big wheel bicycle peered out above a bank of weeds. By the wrought iron fence, two teenagers traded cash and Pokemon cards. Rita fiddled with the door lock.

"So," she said, "at the end of all this, after all the work I've done, all the shit the System put me through, the reason I get my babies back is because Lee Todd went off his meds?"

"Huh? I don't take meds."

"Maybe that's the problem."

I couldn't understand why she wasn't more excited. I'd given her everything she could have wanted—and yet, in the weeks after my proposition, she chewed her nails down to the studs. As the heat of summer deepened, she seemed on the verge of another meltdown. First, she took it out on Harley: when it came out that her daughter had been caught in bed with a pair of roommates from the Blue Building, she called her a ho right in front of the therapist. She made Titi Gigante almost cry with rage one day at the drop-off, when the oxtail stew that the older woman had brought for Jojo's lunch elicited not gratitude, but a downright racist rant from Rita against the cuisine of the Dominican Republic. One night on a home visit to the Purple Palace, she even insinuated, only half-jokingly, that the main reason I was helping her was because I thought that she might fuck me—and sorry baby, she said, putting ramen noodles in the microwave, but you missed your chance on that.

I hoped this was the anxiety talking. Hers had always had an acid tongue. What I couldn't rationalize so easily was that we were now only a few weeks before the trial and she still had not admitted to me that she was pregnant. Was it really so wise, I wondered, to trust somebody that I knew, for a fact, wasn't telling me the truth? Or was it just my own hurt feelings that made me doubt her now? Because at the outset of this case, I'd asked God to give me someone to believe in, but this was only half the story. What I'd really needed was for someone to believe in me.

◆

Before the day of the trial, Margarita's joint substance abuse/parenting program put on a graduation ceremony. The ceremony was in small room on the other side of the bulletproof dispensary windows at the far end of the lobby. A clinic director with a booming voice and tiger-stripes in her hair stood at the center of a circle of mostly teenaged girls sitting cross-legged on folding chairs, hands jammed into the pockets of their hoodies. This room must have doubled as a visiting room for preventative cases, or a daycare for children whose mothers got their methadone next door, because the walls were painted with an elaborate jungle safari motif. Flyers about spousal abuse, suicide hotlines, and the importance of getting tested for HIV mingled with cartoon toucans and banana-wielding monkeys swinging from green vines. A few boyfriends and children sat in chairs along the windows that looked out onto the narrow, busy street. I stood in the corner by a crooked stack of pizza boxes.

The director's speech began:

"Even though Lord knows the System ain't easy," she said, "the certificate you'll get today says that you've done your part to keep your children safe, no matter what some social-justice-ass caseworker might tell you. They don't know how strong we have to be to break the cycle. That it's more than they could ever take..." By the time she was done speaking, all of the graduates were in tears, including Margarita. A few of them sent me dirty looks. But Margarita gave a little wave.

And maybe it was the optimistic tone of the ceremony, or the flowers that I'd brought her, or maybe she'd decided weeks ago and just liked to see me squirm, but once the ceremony ended, sometime between my fourth and fifth slice of pizza, near a watering hole for the zebras and the hippos, Rita dragged two metal folding chairs toward me and asked me to sit down. She spoke in a voice so low I had to duck my ear beneath her graduation cap to hear her. I felt her breathe against my cheek. "I guess, I just wanted to be the one to save them—you know?" she said.

I told her I understood. She fiddled with her golden tassel.

"I hate it when you say you understand me, Lee. Because you don't know the half."

I rolled my eyes the way she'd taught me. "You're such a diva."

Margarita smiled. And I think this teasing must have settled something in her mind, because a moment later, she reached across my lap and grabbed me by both hands. Her palms were cold and sweaty; her golden sparkly fingernails dug lightly to my inner wrist. The brim of her graduation cap made her face look tiny. She told me she was pregnant and begged me not to take it from her. Please, Lee. Please. My friend. My Pea-Pod Todd. Please. If you care for me at all, Lee.

Of course I do, I said. I won't.

Her fingernails dug deeper into my skin. Tears fell onto my knee. She put her arms around my neck and pulled me closer to her, her cheek against my neck, her mascara running like a dirty river down my collar.

"That's alright," I said, stiffening, embarrassed by the curiosity of the other teenaged mothers. "You're OK now. You're OK."

"What the fuck is going on here?"

Over Rita's shoulder, a figure came into my view, clutching a bouquet of flowers. His hair was unkempt and tangled down his back. His face bloated and yellowish.

"Ty!" said Rita, her fingers scraping my ribcage as she pulled off from the hug. "Baby! I didn't know you were coming!"

I stood up, too quickly. I tried to give him my best Bronx handshake. Ty watched my hand pass through the air between us.

"I didn't know you two were so...close."

Rita dabbed her eyes with the back of her hand. "Oh shut up," she said playfully.

But Ty didn't laugh. The flowers hung lank by his side. His eyes were red at the edges, but like black lakes at the center. His shoulders tensed, spring-loaded. This was not the man I'd met and laughed with, my Margarita Brother. This was the myth I'd been reading about. The monster buried in the casefile, resurrected here. His energy was raw and ragged. The small room pulsated with it. The clinic director strode between the three of us. Like most parenting instructors, she had a sixth sense for impending violence.

"Honey, is this guy bothering you?" she asked.

"Who, me?" said Ty, flailing with the flowers.

"You been drinking, baby?" Rita asked him, sweetly.

"This what it is, Rita? He's in, I'm out? Lee Todd's their daddy now?"

The director went off to call the police. Rita gave me a calming look, as though to say: I got this.

"He's my caseworker, baby. Of course I invited him. He got me in the program."

"Oh yeah? What about Davey? Raul? The little stripper girl you been playing with. They your caseworkers too? Cuz what I hear, you been getting plenty of home visits lately, baby. I hear you got a lot of cases."

Rita stood from her chair so fast that it crashed onto the floor behind her. Her graduation cap flew off her head. In Ty's face now, she sent a forearm into his chest.

"You out of your fucking mind?" she shouted. "Showing up here?"

"I gotta hear about this shit from my cousin? How you think it makes *me* feel?"

"I don't give a fuck how you feel about it. Why don't you go tell Gilly how you feel?"

"Gilly? Come on. You want to talk about her? I'm talking about our *lives,* Rita."

"Our lives? Please. I haven't seen you in a month."

"So one month means our whole life didn't happen? Damn, girl. I see how it is now. Lee Todd says word one and now I'm just another bad habit?"

Under the skillful direction of the clinic director, the mothers from the program had quietly filed to the exit with their children and their boyfriends. On the sidewalk outside, they watched through the window as the show played out. We were plastic surgery addicts on TV. "Guys," I said. "This can't happen—we have to..." But neither Ty nor Rita heard.

"Please," said Rita. "You don't give a fuck about your kids. You ain't even been to see Harley since it happened. Don't talk to me about '*our whole life*'."

"I love our daughter more than anything in this world. The only thing you ever loved is Rita."

This set Rita off. She shoved him in the chest again. He didn't budge. She thought about it for a moment, then shoved him again.

"Oh, you love your daughter now? That's funny. 'Cuz lately you been acting like she's not even yours."

Ty moved toward her. Again I tried to intervene, but he shoved me into the stack of pizzas. Warm, soggy cardboard rained down upon me. By the time I'd gotten to my feet, he had her pressed against the window. I tried to grab him by the shoulders. But he was too strong. Too focused. In her husband's grip, Margarita wriggled and kicked.

"Don't worry," she said to me, spitting out the words like broken teeth over his shoulder: "This man's not going to do shit—are you, Ty? This man wouldn't hurt a fly."

"Stop! Ty! Come on guys! Stop!"

Ty clenched his hand around her throat. "You're trash, girl," he said. "Since the day I met you. All you've ever been is trash."

Rita spit in his face. "That must be why we go so fucking good together."

Ty held her up another second. Rita closed her eyes. His hands tightened on her windpipe. Her face darkened with rising blood. Finally, Ty tossed his wife behind him, directly into me. The two of us tumbled to the floor, surrounded on all sides by scattered, splayed cardboard and big-eyed, friendly jungle creatures and the shrieking of the other mothers through the window.

"I got nothing left to give you," he said, chuckling bitterly, wiping his face clean with his shirtsleeve. "I'm sorry, baby. I got nothing left for you at all."

Ty loomed over the two of us, all his violence flowing through him. Rita tried to stand but slipped on errant cardboard and fell back onto the floor, her elbow clocking me in the chin as she flailed it. Ty turned toward the exit.

"Yeah? Well, what about for Harley?" she said. "Oh, that's right I forgot. You got nothing for her too."

◆

We left before the cops arrived. I walked Rita from the clinic to the B-train, still not sure what I had seen. I tried to provide her comfort, or a shoulder to cry on, but I think between the two of us, I was the one more shaken.

"He was just drunk," Rita told me as we made our way down the hill on Fordham Road. "He gets like that sometimes— especially when we're on our on-and-off thing. I just say the meanest shit I can think of. In a week or so he'll be sobered up and he'll come around all 'Baby, I'm sorry.' I'll be like, 'Whatever.'"

"I've never seen that look in someone's eye before," I said.

"I can tell. I thought you might piss yourself. The way your voice cracked. 'Ty, no! Oh god! No!'"

"Rita, I'm serious, I just—"

"What, Lee?"

We stood together on the subway platform; I shuffled my heel across the bumps on the yellow line as she looked down the tunnel toward the coming golden light.

"Do you think you'll be safe at home alone?" I said finally.

Rita looked at me, uncertainty in her eyes. The hot breeze rushing down the tunnel made her hair go crazy. She calmed it with her hand.

"Why?" she said. "You want to...come over?"

The train was coming now, drowning us in wind and noise. The cars rattled. The brakes shrieked. Hunched abuelitas and snaggle-toothed teenagers and hyper kids with flashing light-up sneakers poured out through the doors. As they all rushed past, for a moment we were separated. She was still looking at me once they'd gone.

"Me?" I said. "What? You really think *I* could protect you? Ha. But, I mean, maybe I could get you a hotel room. Through the agency, I mean. Or—is there a friend's house you could stay at? Just with court coming up and all. Some place where he can't find you?"

"Don't be stupid, Lee."

"It's just—the way he looked at you. Right before he left. I don't know. I'm worried about you on your own..."

"I know that's hard for you sometimes."

She punched me on the shoulder, then turned and walked onto the train. It was my train too, but I didn't get on with her. Better just wait for the next one, I thought, leaning back against the tiled wall. Better leave it just like that.

The car filled. The doors closed. Through the window, she gave me a crooked Popeye smile and a painted middle finger, then was swallowed by the crowd.

# 23.

**Sometime after he had left the parenting class**—when we spoke about it later, he wasn't sure about the time—Ty found himself in Crotona Park, running the interaction over in his head. As a game of pick-up played out on the basketball court, he leaned against the chain-link fence, feeling the rust of the metal between his fingers. The strap was begging for it, barking, growling like a dog beneath the table, like Bert or Ernie smelling steak. He took a sip from the bottle in his pocket. Gordon's gin: it tastes like how it makes you feel. A teenager stood at the perimeter calling for the ball. I'm open, he said. I'm open! Yo!

Ty's pocket had been buzzing since he left us. He knew it was Rita—but she'd said all there was to say. And she was right, wasn't she? More than she even knew. What had happened to Harley hadn't happened for no reason. It was because of him. Him. Ty. Dad. The ball whipped around the three-point line. A big guy in blue shorts hit a tough fadeaway and whooped. At last, Ty looked down at his phone.

*Baby. Can we talk?*

No, she didn't want to talk. That's what women say, Lee, but they don't really mean it. If you talk, they think you're soft. The kind of guy who can't come through when you need him.

The kind of guy who likes to talk. A teenager tried to take a charge and got bowled over by a burly forward. Two teammates lifted him to his feet. Ty walked around the side, in through a chain-link gate. He thought of lying in that bed, having Rita in one arm, baby Harley in the other, their snoring rising up within him. How they fit together. Like we were puzzle pieces. He stepped onto the court. Someone missed a layup. Another got the rebound, put it up again and missed. It was like the players could feel his power coming off of him. The court tilted beneath his weight. Flowers and weeds grew out of the cracks in the concrete, straining to touch him as he passed. What had he told Margarita all those years ago in the Mount Pleasant courtyard? While the crickets moaned, and the moon looked like a keyhole into heaven and Rita's dark hair fell down at her temples and she pulled up the hood of his sweatshirt she was wearing and he decided then and there the kind of man that he would be. A father. Rita's baby's father. Every baby girl should get one. The game came to a stop. The teenager dropped the ball. It bounced softly towards him. "Yo, what the fuck?" said the teenager. When she grows up, we'll just tell her I'm her daddy.

"Jairo, right?" said Ty. And then the shouting started. And she grew up so fast.

# 24.

**The trial was at 10 AM, but I was there by 9.** The seventh floor was packed, as usual. Twenty or thirty birthparents waited amongst the pews, their children drawn around them, heads on their laps and shoulders, all huddled together, praying, dreading, crying, eating snacks and drinking soda, playing on their phones.

On the double doors to Part 13 was a piece of printer paper fixed with Scotch tape listing names, times and docket numbers. I ran my finger up and down the page, squinting at the list, unable for a moment to locate Margarita's name. *SANCHEZ, XIOMARA*...no...*SANTORELLI, ELISA*...no... For a moment, I thought the hearing might have been called off. This being summertime in Bronx Family Court, it was entirely possible that the trial had been randomly rescheduled, without notice, that one of the lawyers would saunter over around 10:15, find me and Margarita sitting together, and say: Oh, riiiiight, someone really should have caaaallled. But then I saw it, third from the top, standing at attention: *SAND, MARGARITA, 10:00 AM—11:30 AM, NN-1173-0069—TERMINATION OF PARENTAL RIGHTS.*

Good, I thought, taking my seat at the end of a long pew, fighting off the instinct to kneel and cross my chest. I told myself not to be nervous. Someday you'll look back and remember how strong you feel right now, I thought—the streaks of light on the waxy floors, the look of confidence on Rita's face when she steps off the elevator, the way it feels to know the drumbeat you've been hearing in the distance all your life wasn't all just in your head. At last, after five years wrapped in a cocoon, your transformation is complete. From dilletante musician to obsequious, drunken Nazi cuckold, to whatever you are now. Someone bold. Someone worthy. And for the rest of your life, whatever happens, whatever muffled life or salmon-colored living rooms you may return to, you'll be able to look back and know that when you were a young man, you'd had your moment. You did care, whatever Anita Flores says. You'd seen the injustice in the world and done what you could about it. You'll think about this very morning and know it was up to you.

◆

Since Rita had kicked Ty out, he'd been guilty, lovesick, feeling like a Children's Future kid again—staring at the clock in the lobby, pants soaked, waiting for his mom to show. But as Jairo's body hit the concrete, and the summer air sang with the sounds of screams and squeaking sneakers, he felt, at long last, clean. A breeze rippled through the willow trees that overlooked the court. He wasn't worried about witnesses. The ones who didn't know who he was could ask their friends about him. If anybody felt like talking, he'd be happy to explain.

There's a dazed, dreamy feeling you get after pulling the trigger—at least that's how Ty described it to me later. You've just performed an act of God—but you're still just you. While the boy's soul is on a journey to Jesus or the Devil, you just walk around the corner and get yourself a slice of pizza. He put another into Jairo's chest. Another in his balls.

On the way to Margarita's he kicked the Camaro up to 110. The headlights on the Cross-Bronx flowed together like a river set aflame.

Lately, he'd been thinking of the Poconos again—those few weeks after Rita had given birth to Harley, when the world stood still awhile. It was calm out there, so far outside of the city. Mornings, while Rita nursed Harley in bed, he'd walk onto the dock and look out across the lake. The mist rose off the water. The sunlight poured over a ream of distant hills. Birdcalls rang down from the trees. Boat engines muttered groggy good mornings as they passed. Rita came down in her American flag bikini, baby Harley in one arm, the car seat in the other. This was before the scabs on her arms, the lizard shine in her eyes, the stars she came home with one day, slurring what, baby, you don't like? No, she was something else back then. While Harley dozed off on a blanket, Rita stepped backwards down the metal ladder, whining about the cold, doggy paddling towards him in the water. Beneath the surface, she wrapped her legs around his waist, arms around his shoulders, eyes wide, laughing. No. No. I'm serious! My hair! Come on, Ty. My hair.

When he came into the Purple Palace, Rita was watching TV, wearing her SpongeBob PJs and eating a tub of mint chocolate chip. Her hair was tied up in that tight bun that he hated, her eyes puffy, skin pale and picked-at. He wasn't going to tell her what he'd done—not yet at least, so she wouldn't have to lie in case the cops came asking. Instead, he apologized for what had happened at the parenting ceremony—he hadn't been thinking straight, not for a long, long time. But baby, right now, finally, for the first time since we were kids, I feel like me again.

"Ty," Rita interrupted, "I gotta tell you something."

The nervous trill in her voice sent something in him plunging. But it wasn't bad news she gave him. Actually, it was the best thing he'd ever heard. As she told him, she placed her feet across his lap, her purple ankle socks—as though nothing at all between them had changed, would ever change, as though that's just where they went.

◆

When the 9 AM trials ended, the courtrooms emptied into the seventh floor. A birthfather wearing a red fez hat and bejeweled shoes that curled upward like elves' feet was dragged out of Part 11 by three officers, trying to dig his heels into the marble, yelling to the door that closed behind him I DO NOT CONSENT! I DO NOT CONSENT! A couple of walleyed birthparents on wheelchairs rolled out of Courtroom 4A, both of them nodding off and moaning as their daughters steered them toward the elevator. In the back corner, exiting Courtroom 6, a birthmother with braids like two snakes and a look of mischief on her face called out to one of the court officers and informed him that the judge had granted her request for an Order of Protection, of which the birthfather following her out of the courtroom was now in violation. "I'm going, I'm going," said the birthfather, speed-walking towards the elevators.

Scenes like this used to bring me down. Before Rita. Before that final leap from reason, the last flight away from fear. Back then my life was solitary confinement. Waiting for what would never come: freedom, I guess. God, in some form or another. Margarita would never be anyone but who she'd been. I'd never be anyone but this. Now, I smiled at all the birthparents gathered in the courtroom lobby. Today, my friends. Our day.

On the other end of the lobby, hordes of birthparents, lawyers, and caseworkers poured in the through the elevators. Each ping of the doors brought another wave. I calmed my nerves by memorizing the pattern of the floor tiles: a repeating grid of gray rectangles filled with multi-colored dots. I counted each dot contained in the rectangle beneath my feet. I got to thirty-two before I looked up again.

◆

Ty jumped up off the couch. Her feet went flying. "You're serious right? I mean, you're not fucking around?"

"I'm so happy you're happy, baby. Cuz I thought you might go the other way."

He put his hand to her belly. Was that a flutter he felt?

"He kicked me!" he said, breathless.

"Nah, that's just the ice cream talking."

"It's a boy in there isn't it? I can feel his strength."

Margarita took his hand.

"Actually..."

"A girl? A girl! You're saying its... An angel! A little Princess. Little Queenie. God, Rita I can't believe it! Can you? After everything. All this run-around. We got another chance."

He hugged her close, spoke into the crook of her neck. The smell of her hair. She'd used the same shampoo for 12 years. Strawberries and vanilla.

"What are we going to name her?"

"I've just been calling her 'Baby,' like a retard."

"What about after my mom?" said Ty.

Margarita laughed.

"*Debra?*"

"Fine. Fine. You know what I always liked? Jaylen. Kinda cute right? Little Jaylen?"

"Everybody's named Jaylen."

"Always gotta be original, don't you? You want to get crazy with it? Let's get crazy. Uniglow. Trayshonda. Dishwasha. Ha Ha Ha!"

Ty clapped his hands. All this heartache, all this nonsense. These ins and outs and blacks and blues and here they were: Ty and Rita. Forever. Still. "You couldn't keep us apart, Lee," he'd tell me later. "Cause even you can't stop what's bound to happen."

He thought of where he'd just come back from. The basketball bouncing slowly through his head, coming to a stop against the chain-link. Already it was just a dream. He held Rita by the hand and cried tears of joy.

"Look," he said—"We got to get you out the city, right? Before Lee figures out you're pregnant."

"Huh?"

"I mean—not tonight or anything. Tonight, we're eating fucking lobster. But soon, right? Before they realize. We'll stay in that old motel out in PA. I got cash for days. I could buy that fucking place. If you give birth in PA—our baby gets born free."

"Slow down, baby! I'm not going anywhere. I got court tomorrow!"

Jairo's blood, leaking from his skull. His mouth still open, puzzled, asking: Who are you? Am I dead?

"Court?" he said. "No, girl, you can't go to court...If the judge finds out you're pregnant, that's it. If they even think it. We got to go before they realize, right? That's the whole point."

Rita took her hair out of the bun and snapped a hair-tie around her wrist. She'd dyed blonde stripes in it last week. He thought of how it used to fall down on him—he'd look up into her eyes, into that Rita smile, and the two of them would laugh. He'd reach up and feel the smallness of her skull within it. She smelled so goddamn good.

"That's the thing, though," said Rita. "We don't have to keep it secret. Lee's got a plan so we can keep her."

Ty blinked.

"Lee knows?"

"Well, yeah."

"How?"

"Because I told him."

Rita's bare legs around his waist. The sun burning off the morning's haze. The cool black water. My hair, Ty. Come on, I'm serious. My hair. He pressed down on her shoulders, and pushed her just beneath the surface, just for a moment, just to make her laugh.

"Wait, wait wait," he said, to Rita now, holding those same shoulders with his same two hands, feeling the same knobs beneath her sweatshirt. "You told Lee—before me?"

◆

Back in the courthouse I was getting antsy. The dots in the floor tiles kicked up into a blizzard. The elevator doors pinged. Another horde burst through the gates and swarmed the lobby. Soon, I thought, her sneakers would come squeaking down the tiles. She'd be dressed in something wholly inappropriate for court. Ha. Some humongous sweatshirt and flip flops—and still have the nerve to say my suit looked stupid.

I went over my testimony in my head one last time. I had to get it perfect.

Your Honor, due to the recent progress of the birthmother, my agency is recommending that, in the best interest of the subject children, the court offer a suspended judgment of today's termination proceedings against Ms. Margarita Sand. Oh yes, of course, I ran this by my supervisor. She's in agreement. Of course.

A loud, bored call sounded through the lobby.

"CASEWORKER ON SAAAAND?"

◆

"Calm down, baby. I don't understand..."

"You know what I've done for this fucking family? And this Justin Bieber motherfucker rolls in and you think he's the one that's gonna save you? You hand him off our baby?"

"Nobody's saving me from nothing. I've been playing this dude since the first day I met him."

"What are you, sucking his dick too?"

"Oh come on..."

Ty paced around the Purple Palace. In his head, the basketball bounced off of the concrete, slowly rolling to a stop. Sneakers squeaking. Run, run, run. Ty went from the bedroom, to the bathroom, to the kitchen. It smelled like sex in here, didn't it? That sweaty, down-low stink. Here and here and here too. With Davey. With Mike T. That old-ass dude who drives the Bronco. With anyone who ever asked. Same old Rita. Used up to get used up again. No matter how much a damn certificate stuck to the refrigerator might say she's changed.

"I don't know what Lee Todd told you—but I promise you, he's not giving you our babies back. That's not how this goes. You remember how they did my mom, right? Anita Flores might as well of ate her heart raw on the witness stand."

"Your mom had a lot of problems, Ty. You know that."

"Oh and you're Mother Teresa, I guess."

"I'm a good mother."

Ty was having trouble breathing. He thought of Rita tying her shoes. Fumbling fingers. The knot that falls apart. Harley laughing. Jojo in two-day old diapers. *Plastic Surgery Addicts* on TV. Why won't you just come on time, Mom? What else is so important?

"You don't even love them, do you Rita?"

"This again?"

"You never have. Since the day we brought home Harley—I could see it your eyes."

"Are you alright, baby?"

"You couldn't even feed the turtles."

"Baby, calm down. It's me. Breathe. It's you and me here. Be here with me, OK?"

Ty knew now. He'd always known. Always would. Mom isn't coming. She's never coming. She's off with someone else.

"It's not mine is it?" he said.

Rita gave him a look he didn't recognize. Who was she, when she looked like that?

"Same old Rita, huh?" he said.

"I'm calling the cops."

"Give me your phone," he said. "I want to know his name."

He tried to snatch it from her hands, but her grip was too tight. He grabbed her by the wrist. She raked her nails across his neck. He bodied her against the refrigerator and wrenched the phone free. She charged toward him. He dropped her with an elbow to the eye. "What the fuck, Ty?" she screamed, picking herself up off of the floor gingerly, going to the freezer for an ice pack. "I got court tomorrow, dickhead!"

He put his finger to the screen and set to rifling through her phone. He felt a little better with every click. Every text to Harley. Every photo of Jojo in the Children's Future visiting room. It was in his head. It was OK. She was his. He was hers. Forever. Still. OK. Margarita touched the icepack to her eye and crouched on the floor. "How am I going to explain this to the judge? What's Lee gonna think?" Ty sat at the table, clicking, clicking, clicking, until suddenly—he went rigid.

"Oh my god," he said.

"What, baby?" said Margarita.

Ty touched his hand to his head. Was he still here? Was he dreaming?

"Oh my god," he said again.

Margarita leaned over his shoulder.

"No, no, Ty, please, baby it's not like that, I was trying to..."

In a moment, he was on her. He slammed her head onto the floor, knees pinning down her arms. He cracked her twice across the jaw, two more in the chest. How could she? How could she? Wriggling free, she bit down on his forearm, teeth piercing his flesh. He let go. Stunned and screaming, spitting blood and teeth onto the floor, she jumped to her feet. Ty walked slowly towards her. She was one of them. She was gone. She tried to run away and slipped, fell onto her back. And he could have stopped there. He knew he should, but couldn't. There's always a moment, he'd tell me later, when you know that you can still just walk away.

"What was on the phone?" I asked, not getting it yet.

It was weeks later. Maybe more. The two of us were sitting in the Anna M Kross visitors center on Rikers Island, on plastic blue connected chairs bolted to a railing. At Rikers, it's not like in the movies, where you have to sit on the other side of glass. Loved ones and caseworkers can sit right beside the inmates. Harley and Jojo had wandered off to peruse the snacks that the visitation coordinator put out for the inmates' kids.

Fun-sized bags of Doritos, Cheetos, Hi-C and Dunkaroos lay flat on a metal table.

"Huh?"

"I said, what did you find on her phone?"

Ty shook his head back to the present.

"Look, man—what happened, happened." The guard escorted Harley and Jojo back from the snack stand. Harley had two bags of Doritos—one for her, one for her father, and three more stuffed into her pockets. Jojo's lips and cheeks looked like they'd been painted orange.

"Just tell me, you piece of shit," I said.

Harley and Jojo were almost back now. Ty threw up his hands as they approached, and called to Harley: "Baby—what you doing with those? I said Fritos, baby. *Fritos*." Harley harrumphed and rolled her eyes and went back to the snack table. Ty sat back on the bolted seat and grinned at his daughter for a moment. Then his smile died. He spoke so low I could barely hear him.

"I saw the mother of my babies take off her bathrobe for her caseworker and sit her bare ass on his lap. So tell me, Mr. Nice Guy. What would you have done?"

◆

My lawyer jogged across the lobby. He was not the same lawyer as the one at the previous hearing. This one was short and merry, with thin blond hair and a rumpled suit. They were always changing them.

"You ready, Eddy?" he said.

"It's Lee," I said. Anxiety affects everybody differently. Me, it makes obtuse.

"It'll be just like you and Anita prepared. I highlight all the fuckups, and you just confirm on the record. The nodding off in the family visits, refusal of drug screens, non-compliance with mental health, the assault with the juicebox, the flagrant sexual advance, the kidnapping, the ongoing relationship with her abuser, the drug screens, the daughter's incidents at Mount Pleasant, how the little boy is in a pre-adoptive home. One by one, like that, bing bang boom. We'll be outta here by lunchtime."

"Actually," I said, "my agency wants to offer a suspended judgment on the TPR. Mom's been doing better lately."

The lawyer looked at me, unsure. Then his shoulders loosened. He took a sip from his coffee. He extended his fist for a pound.

"Fuck yeah. Makes my job easy. Standard conditions?"

I nodded.

"Sweet," said the lawyer. "I'll go tell the law guardian. You know what you're gonna say, right?"

The attorney left. It was 9:52. Another elevator unloaded. The seventh floor filled with all the birthparents in the Bronx except for one.

◆

The sunlight crept across the carpet towards Margarita's body. Blood glued her cheek onto the plush. Sunlight warmed her eyeballs through her eyelids. She saw red through the flesh.

The bones in her cheeks felt disassembled—she worried her skull might collapse into a million pieces if she tried to lift her head. The one eye that would open provided her with a view beneath the couch. There was dust and pennies and one of her teeth scattered in the darkness there.

With all her strength, she lifted herself upright, then rested the back of her head against the TV stand for what must have been an hour, breathing in and out, in and out, until she felt steady enough to try standing. Her thoughts kept breaking apart—dissolving into a thickening sludge. Ty....the baby....Harley, Jojo...court. Court! The clock on the cable box read 9:15. Thank God, she still had time. She got to her feet and stumbled toward the bathroom. From behind the mirror, she found her makeup bag. She vomited into the sink.

Her wounds swallowed up the makeup. It stung like hell. But there was no time for pain. She was alive, and that was all that mattered. She wiped the blood from her mouth and applied another layer to her jawline, feathering the brush across her throat to cover up the bluish knobs where Ty had choked her. Then she set to work on her eyes. Only one of them would open: it stared back at her from the purpled mess of her reflection, the iris flooded with a bright and striking red. Webs of yellow and purple discoloration cast outward toward the stars. She applied to these areas a clay-brown base much darker than her skin tone. When she was done, she limped to the bedroom and wrapped her head in a black scarf, put on a pair of sunglasses, and returned to the mirror.

"Your honor," she practiced—it hurt to even speak. "I can explain..."

She spat another mouthful of blood into the sink. The blood spread through the running water, thinned out in little ribbons and twisted down the drain. Through the window, she heard the 5-train hurtle through the distance—then, her phone, vibrating. Where had it ended up? It was lying somewhere in the apartment, facedown, murmuring into the carpet. She knew it was me.

She unwrapped the scarf from her head. Took off those cheap sunglasses. They only made it look worse. Like she was covering it up. What had she done wrong? Nothing. Nothing. Still, she couldn't answer. The buzzing relented.

I hung up and called again.

*Bzzzz* the phone insisted. So irritating, *bzzzbzzzzz*. It was in her head. Her soul. Her heartbeat was on vibrate. She thought of the judgment in our eyes—me, the lawyers, the judges, hell even the other birthparents in the lobby, who judged harsher than anyone. We'd know. We'd always known. *Bzzzz. Bzzzzz.* She thought of Harley—her little woman, her heart, who looked much like her that she hurt to even look at. Who needed her so bad. She saw that now. And Jojo—what about her little man? Her little tiny angry old man, who'd come out the womb looking disappointed, like he'd been misled by the brochures up in heaven. She never really knew him, did she? And he never really knew his mom at all. *Bzzzz Bzzzzzz.* She thought of the baby in her stomach—the baby! God, the baby! Little...baby? What do I even I call her? A name popped into her head then. Out of nowhere. For months it had been hiding. Waiting for the perfect time. Royal, she would call her. Royal! Little baby Royal Sand. My little Queen.

The buzzing stopped. Margarita closed her eyes. The silence breathed. It was waiting. It was hungry. She'd been avoiding the question for so long. At least since she'd found out she was pregnant, but maybe since the beginning, since the first time she'd seen me walking towards her through the lobby with my dead eyes and my smile. For a moment, she thought she might just lie back down on the carpet and go to sleep a little while. But no. That wasn't her. Had never been. Would never be. And as soon as she had pulled herself to her feet again and started moving—at least this is what I like to tell myself—she felt, at long last, peace.

◆

At 9:58, the lawyer sat back down next to me. He waggled an eyebrow. "Um," he said. "If we're going to do this deal, we kind of need Mom to be here."

"She'll show."

"Well, I admire your optimism, man. But in the event she doesn't, we have two options: we can either go ahead with the termination trial, or we can see about getting an adjournment. I need you to make the call."

The court officer came out of the double doors to the courtroom. He was old and square-headed, with a buzz cut and rosacea. He pulled a wrinkled roll of papers from his back pocket.

"Everybody here for Sand?" he asked.

"Not everybody," said my lawyer. The court officer rolled his eyes, knowing what that meant.

I leaned against the pew. She would show. Please, God. She would show.

"It's alright, man," my lawyer said to me. "You want to give her the deal, we'll just get it adjourned. No problem-o. Maybe she got sick or something. I know you caseworkers have your little favorites…"

"Hold on," I said, motioning toward my phone. "I think the mom's calling me now. What's that? Oh good. Uh-huh. Great." I hung up the phone. "I think she's in line downstairs. I'll go get her. You know how long that line gets."

And next thing I knew I was running toward the elevators. The elevator doors were opening and I was on the first floor, jogging up and down the line of birthparents outside the metal detectors. I was outside on the street, squinting through the sunlight, looking up and down 161st Street. I was shouting into my phone, being told by a kindly robot woman that the voice messaging system I had reached was full. I was back inside Part 13, my eyelid dancing a samba as the court officer called ALL RISE and I looked from Margarita's empty chair to the heavy wooden door, and my lawyer leaned over and muttered, "Well? Let's go. What do you want to do?"

I cast one last look at the door. This was it. The perfect time to make her entrance. And when I think back on this day now, this is when she bursts in, hair askew, her face swollen, bruised, her body broken and maimed, limping with a swagger: You won't believe the night I had, she says. But I'm here, right? Let's do this.

I waited for her for a lifetime. Or maybe it was just a minute. Sometimes I think I'm still staring at that wooden door, waiting for the knob to turn. I looked back at the lawyer and gave my answer, my voice barely above a whisper.

"You sure?" said the lawyer.

"Free them," I said.

# 25.

**Every time I think about turning the car around,** my foot presses the gas down harder. There's no time to really contemplate what I'm doing. Anyway, reason is overrated. Sometimes, you just need to act. For now, every mile that we drive is another reason to keep driving. Evening turns to night, which turns to a brilliant, orange dawn somewhere out in Pennsylvania. I think we're out in Amish country, judging by the busted farm windows, the bearded men in suspenders out on the fields at dawn, whipping ox to till the soil. It's like we're in another dimension—some alternate timeline of human history, with completely different rules and different logic. Maybe, I think, the consequences of what I've done won't exist in this reality. We bid them all good riddance when we drove through that wormhole back on 84. Wherever we are, pretty soon, I'll have to stop for gas again. Do they sell gas in Amish country? Maybe when Lily wakes up, we can get breakfast somewhere. I'm in the mood for pancakes.

I never saw Margarita again. Where did you go, my friend? I ask the sack of apples on the passenger seat. I read a few of your texts to Harley—your apologies, your assurances that someday she and Jo would understand the impossible choice that Lee Todd forced you into. But I had to delete

ParentInfo from my phone before the cops came to question me on Jairo's murder, so all I got were bits and pieces from your husband. And the rest is just a tale I've told myself. A fool's attempt to understand. An act of crazed, deluded devotion to try and see things through your eyes.

I probably could have pressed Harley for more information directly, but not too long after the visit to Rikers to see her father, Anita transferred her off my caseload—to LaDawn, in fact—and we never spoke again.

One time, a few weeks before I gave my notice, I thought I saw you on the 5-train, Rita, your head shaved, hood up, music blasting from your iPhone, eating a bacon-egg-and-cheese on a bagel. For a moment, my heart stopped. My fists clenched. I tried to come up with some line. What are you still doing here, I was going to ask you? You have to get out of the state! But when I looked back, it wasn't you. It was just some other light-eyed pregnant woman, a few years younger than the two of us—due any day, I'd guess.

My final chance to find out what happened would have been at at Jojo's adoption. From the look of mischief on her face, I could tell Titi knew something I didn't, but the old girl wasn't talking either. Plus, that was a happy day—there was no use talking about the past. As I testified that all the adoption paperwork was in order, I saw Harley standing in the back of Part 13, a fresh tattoo of a butterfly on her neck, scabbed and shiny, her hair dyed purple and blue. I caught her eye and smiled, but she shook her head and looked away.

"Are we all ready?" said Judge Screen.

Titi and Jojo held hands beneath the table. Titi closed her eyes.

"1...2...3...Congratulations!" Judge Screen smacked the gavel. The court officer let out a handful of balloons. Titi blew a celebratory kazoo. Jojo buried his face into the hem of her dress and cried—not sure what was happening, but feeling it, somehow. Afterward, Titi invited me to the reception in the basement of her church off Southern Boulevard. "You're part of the family too," she said, but I could tell she was relieved when I said no.

"Give him a good life, Titi," I said. "I'm moving back to New Hampshire next week."

Titi hugged me close.

"You're getting too old to have this job anyway, blanquito. You need to go make yourself some money."

So there it is, Rita. There it is, Apples. Whoever the fuck it is I'm talking to. When I look at it from this distance, I don't know why I took it all so badly. Nothing happened to me at all. Nobody died, except for Jairo, who deserved it. There wasn't any incest. Nobody killed themselves. This was just another of a million tragedies that happened every day throughout the System—that are still happening, right this very second, all around. None of them have any effect on my actual life at all. Hell, for all I know, you and Ty might have wound up back together in the end. Maybe you and Royal still visit him in jail. So what do I have to be so shaken up about? What the fuck's my problem?

Anyway, since I moved back home, my life's gone on OK. I've run my stepdad's real estate agency for years now, ever since he got sick. I even play bi-monthly sets of mostly covers at the Shaskeen down in Manchester—a little fatter maybe, a little more bleary, prone to stretches of loneliness and, about twice a year, a bout that slides into a bender. But that's how life goes, isn't it? You keep carrying on, pretending not to hear the echoes calling from the past. Well, I guess today I finally stopped to listen. The problem is, I think, as I take the car down backroads, chomping apples, tossing cores out of the window: I still can't tell what it is they're trying to tell me.

Liliana seems to have taken her new circumstance in stride. All I had to do was keep promising her that we'd be home soon, then eventually she fell asleep. When she's older, she won't remember any of this, will she? All she'll know is all she'll need to know—which is that I had her best interests in mind. That I'm the one who cared enough to go a little crazy. That I couldn't leave her life up to chance. A few hours ago, I stopped to take as much cash as I could from an ATM on the roadside, so we can live on that awhile. To think it through any further feels like bad luck.

I drive another few hours, but I'm not sure where we're headed. It occurs to me how little I've seen of America—all I know is New England, my real Dad's cabana down in Key West, and the Bronx. It might be fun to start our lives up somewhere completely different. Maybe in Ohio. Is this far enough? Could we be Ohioan? Or I could just keep on heading west. We could set up shop in San Francisco, maybe. Or in a cabin in Oregon? Or head out even further, to Japan maybe, or Vietnam. Daddy and Lily on an international adventure! Doesn't that sound fun?

Billy Joel is on the radio. I've never liked him much. It always sounds to me like he's putting on an act. Maybe I just don't get it. I threw my phone out the window a few hours ago, or else I'd be blasting Prince again. Evidently, Liliana doesn't like this song either—because suddenly she's crying. At first, I don't think much of it. But then she gets louder, more insistent. It's like, all at once, she's realized what I've done. Next thing I know she's yelling bloody murder. "Where we going?" she says. "I want to go home, Dada!" She's howling in the car seat, red-faced, desperate. I try to calm her down by singing, but it only makes it worse. Her cries are the saddest thing I've ever heard. My baby—my sweet little rock and roll angel, my gypsy princess! There's never been a person as sad as I have made this little girl. Somewhere near Sandusky, I can't take it any longer. I pull over off a dusty road and idle the car on the edges of a muddied football field with crooked goalposts. I have a solution for this problem. I sit in back with her and explain that we're going on vacation. Don't worry, honey, I say. I am your father, and I would never do anything to hurt you. You trust me, don't you, sweetie? Do you want to get some pancakes? I bet we can find some chocolate milk! For a moment, she seems to weigh this proposition. But the fix is superficial. A second later, she's inconsolable again. I want to go home, Dada, she says. I want to see Mom. She looks just like my mother when she cries: forehead scrunched, face red, lower lip trembling. Just raging against the world. Against her lot. Against me for doing this to her. Her cries jump inside me. I feel them in my chest, like little twists, my flesh wringing to a knot. I'm weeping beside her now. I can't take it anymore. How could I....I didn't mean to...

God, baby, I'm sorry, I'm so goddamn sorry baby... And as I sit in the backseat with her, her cries strike a chord within me, the same chord that's been ringing for a decade, ever since that conversation with Anita Flores all those years ago. Before I'd turned against her. Before I'd decided, for whatever crazy reason, to join up with the birthparents. I take Lily from the car seat and rock her in my arms. Snot runs down her nose onto her cheeks. Her face is purple now. She screams and screams. Her little gap-toothed howl is torture. Daddy, I want to go home. Please? OK? Please Daddy? It's OK, baby, I say, over and over: Don't worry. Shhhh. Baby. It's OK. It's OK, sweetheart. But it doesn't matter. I can't help her. I can't soothe her. How had Anita Flores put it? You can't feel someone else's pain—that's what she'd said that day in her office, and right away, I'd accepted it as fact. Some philosophical truth I didn't think to question. But as I give up trying to kiss my daughter's tears away, climb back into the driver's seat, and turn the key in the ignition, I realize this was nonsense. Just another lie I've internalized, that's brought me to where I am today. Well, from this point forward, I reject it. With everything I have—everything I ever will. All these years, what have I been thinking? Of course I feel her pain. Of course I can. I do! Every second of every day. How could I not? I love her. God. I love her.

# Acknowledgments

I first want to thank all the staff, foster children, foster parents, and birthparents I worked with at the Children's Aid Society in the Bronx from 2012-2016. Your strength, resilience, and spirit in the face of brutally difficult circumstances inspired me to write this. As it's a work of fiction, I hope you'll forgive the many embellishments I've made for the sake of telling a good story. I don't know if this disclaimer is necessary, but I should point out that none of my colleagues ever did anything like install spyware on a foster child's phone, and every supervisor I ever worked with placed the highest possible emphasis on the health, safety, and emotional well-being of the children.

This book took me almost ten years to write. Many of my friends and family helped me along the way. Ted Schroeder provided insightful and precise feedback on the tone and style. Jan Brogan told me what was working, but also, more importantly, what wasn't (even when I didn't want to hear it). My lovely wife Andrea has been unflinchingly supportive through every rejection, heartbreak, and overly dramatic mood swing. Tom Barnico, Jennifer Irving, Jake Batchelor, Barbara Shapiro, and David Kinney were also early readers who gave important feedback along the way.

I'd also like to thank Jerry Brennan at Tortoise Books, who took a chance on this book at almost the exact moment I'd begun to accept that no one would ever publish it. The version of this novel we created together is much, much more powerful than the one I originally brought to him—and that's a credit to his thoughtfulness, encouragement and guidance. I'd also like to thank my former agent Ann Collette, who believed in the book from the beginning, even when times were tough, and my undergraduate writing professor, Ernest Hebert, who, long ago, used to have me read my work aloud to him so I could see him wince and frown at every cliché or clunky sentence. I learned from him that the most important quality a writer can have is perseverance bordering on self-delusion.

# About the Author

Though *The Birthparents* is a work of fiction, Frank Santo was a foster care caseworker in the Bronx from 2012 to 2016. He now lives in suburban Boston with his wife and young children.

# About Tortoise Books

Slow and steady wins in the end, even in publishing. Tortoise Books is dedicated to finding and promoting quality authors who haven't yet found a niche in the marketplace—writers producing memorable and engaging works that will stand the test of time.

Learn more at www.tortoisebooks.com or follow us on Twitter: @TortoiseBooks.

Printed in the USA
CPSIA information can be obtained
at www.ICGtesting.com
JSHW082231210823
46947JS00002B/2